BACKCUT

Carla & Steve –
    Thanks for all you do
to preserve our precious world.
Many blessings to you and
hope you enjoy reading my book,

Cynthia S. Levesque

Praise for *Backcut*

In *Backcut*, Cynthia Levesque gives us so much: a wealth of information about the logging industry, insights into endangered species and the role they can play in developing new medicines, and even a romance—all wrapped up in a suspenseful, well-plotted environmental mystery. It's also written from a Christian point of view and relevant to the real lives of twenty-first-century people, dealing with real doubts and dilemmas. This is an impressive book.

—Linda Brinson, writer, editor, book reviewer; adjunct lecturer at
UNC Chapel Hill School of Journalism and Mass Communication, NC

Cynthia Levesque weaves a fictional tale, but one that bears truth about the greed, corruption, evil, goodness, kindness, and love found within human hearts. Her incredible story reminds us that we are caretakers of this gift called Planet Earth and shows us the Christian response to those who would harm God's gift—our home. I couldn't put this down.

—Keith Vaughn, writer, pastor, business manager, GA

BACKCUT

CYNTHIA SOULE LEVESQUE

ISBN13: 9781940269283
ISBN10: 1940269288

Library of Congress: 2014949064
Printed in the USA

Edited by Mark Weising
Cover design by Robin Black, Inspirio Design

Dedicated to the victims, patients, and families affected by the Niemann-Pick Type C disease. I hope and pray that a cure for this disease will be found soon.

Backcut *(n)*

The final cut in felling a tree, made on the opposite
side of the direction of the fall, which disconnects
the entire tree from the stump.

Prologue

Eltout Forest, central Washington State

Ed Grantham slowed his pace as he approached his log cabin. He maintained a rhythmic jog as he squinted to discern the familiar dirt path that was now camouflaged in lacy shadows cast by a brilliant full moon. A rustling noise startled him, and he glanced up to see a pair of bright yellow eyes. The creature blinked at him and then screeched and flew away, flapping its wings. Ed shivered in the coolness of the evening and wiped a sheen of sweat from his forehead.

The one-room structure was a cherished refuge for the fifty-five-year-old scientist, and Ed preferred it to any apartment he could have had in the city of Olympia. He'd built the hideaway himself by hand, the old-fashioned way, in the middle of Eltout Forest. It was just a speck among the Ponderosa pines.

Ed had never regretted moving away from the sterile buildings and cement walkways of the big city into the magnificent old-growth forest. Every evening he was serenaded by cicadas, crickets, and tree frogs as he relaxed in front of a log fire and breathed in the cool, invigorating pine air. There were no sirens, no car horns, no neighbors blasting their TVs.

Ed reached for the handle of the door, which he never locked, but stopped short. In the dim light, he saw that the thick pine door was ajar. He was certain he had closed it on his way out for his run. He cautiously pushed it inward and strained to adjust his eyes to the dark room. The flickering screen of his laptop drew his attention. That's odd, he thought. *I'm sure I shut it down before I left.*

"Is anyone there?" he said. He hesitated at the doorstep for a moment, stared into the dark room, and then entered and switched on the light. His normally tidy nest looked as though a bomb had gone off. The drawers of his antique pine desk gaped open, and his papers and books were scattered across the antique Navajo rug that partially covered the bare wood floor. Chairs were upended, and every drawer in the compact kitchen had been spilled. The mattress on his small cot had been slashed to pieces, the tufts of ticking quivering in the draft from the doorway.

Ed reached for his cell phone, but then reconsidered. Often his cell didn't work in the isolated Washington forest—and besides, he knew it would take at least an hour for the police to get there. Instead, he ran to the remains of his mattress to see if his money pouch was still there.

Just then he heard the creak of hinges behind him. He whirled around to see a massive man in a heavy black coat emerge from the closet.

"Taylor!" Ed gasped. "What are you doing here?"

"Been waitin' for you over an hour!" the goon said in a gruff voice. "It sure took you long enough to get here."

Ed slowly began to move toward the open cabin door, but the frame of the broad-shouldered man completely barred any escape. "Wait just a minute, doc," the man said. "We need to talk."

Ed had never trusted Mack Taylor, Environ-Logging's chief security officer, ever since the time he had first met him fifteen years ago. Like a sleazy bodyguard, he was always shadowing Herbert Clive Johnson, the CEO, in a creepy way that made Ed nervous.

"Sit down!" Taylor commanded.

When Ed hesitated, Taylor pulled out a small silver Smith & Wesson revolver from his coat and pointed it at him. Ed jumped at the sight of the gun.

"Did you hear me?" said Taylor. "I said sit down!" He motioned with the gun toward a nearby wicker armchair. His hawk eyes seemed to pierce right through Ed.

Ed, wide-eyed and shaking, sank slowly into the chair.

"Do you remember our little talk the other day?" asked Taylor. He perched in the chair opposite Ed and ran his palm over his dark brown hair plastered back on his thick head.

Ed tried to look calm, but inside he was panicking. "I told you and Johnson that I don't understand what you want," he blurted out. "I haven't found anything of importance. I was just doing research on the web and stumbled across some interesting information about—"

"Don't play coy, Grantham," Taylor interrupted. "I saw the books and files in your computer. We know you found something . . . something we have known about for some time. We can't afford for anyone else to find out." He gave Grantham an ugly sneer. His coarse face looked monstrous.

Right before his run, Ed had been checking for a response to an e-mail he had sent to a man named Dr. Raymond Philip Kramer. After months of research, he had finally found someone who was desperate for information about the particular species he had discovered. He had called Dr. Kramer and left a message, but the man had not yet returned his call. Ed knew he shouldn't have, but he had copied the e-mail to Stephen Hall, his Environ-Logging colleague, and Joe Anders, a consultant at the Olympia Forestry Service.

"You needn't worry that anyone knows," Ed lied, frantically scanning the room for something he could use as a weapon. "I didn't send that e-mail." Ed had documented the information in his logbook, which he kept hidden under the floorboards.

Taylor's hawk eyes narrowed as he reached for his cell phone. "We'll see what the boss says about that." He dialed a number and raised the phone to his ear.

Ed shuddered as he watched Taylor nod once and put away the phone. An icy feeling came over him and his stomach tightened when he saw the steely determination in his adversary's eyes. He said a quick prayer to draw on inner strength.

"What do you propose to do?" Ed said. "I promise not to tell anyone about it!" Just then, he spied an old walking stick that he often took with him on his hikes to ward off snakes. He grabbed it and lunged at Taylor.

Taylor gave a scoffing laugh and brought his arm up to ward off the blow. He easily jerked the stick from Ed's grasp and sent it clattering to the floor.

"That was mighty stupid of you," Taylor said as he leveled the gun. Ed slowly backed away. "But the boss says it's too late now. We gave you a chance, and you refused to cooperate. Too bad! But you're right, though—no one else will ever know. Those notes are history, and so are you."

The gun flashed, and Ed felt a jolt of heat. He slumped to the floor and suddenly felt very cold, despite a strange warmth and numbness in his shoulder. He looked and saw blood seeping into his shirt and dripping down his arm onto his treasured Navajo rug. He fought to remain conscious.

Taylor stomped outside and returned with a gallon of gasoline. In a blur, Ed saw him gather the papers on his desk, stuff them into the stove, and slosh the oily dark liquid onto the pile. The fumes began to overpower his senses, and his vision dimmed as a wave of intense pain enveloped him. He caught a glimpse of Taylor's grotesque figure lighting a match and casually tossing it onto Ed's life work, and then everything went black.

1

Offices of Environ-Logging, Olympia, Washington

Lisa Stone's new secretary, Claire, knocked softly on the door and entered the office. "Mr. Johnson is on his way down to see you, Ms. Stone," she said. "Would you like a cup of coffee or anything?" She looked not much older than a teenager, with shoulder-length blonde hair tied in a bow. She was squeezed into a short, tight dress that revealed a little too much cleavage.

"No, thank you, Claire," said Lisa. "That will be all." She would have to talk to Claire later about the appropriate dress for work, though her own attire, a light brown business suit, felt awkward. The norm at the University of Illinois, where she had graduated, had been faded blue jeans, sneakers, and casual sweaters.

She winced as she reached down to adjust the tight strap of her spiked heels, smoothed her wrinkled skirt, and pulled a small mirror from her purse to recheck her appearance. Her modest makeup enhanced her hazel eyes, ivory complexion, and thin lips. She dabbed on a little colored lip-gloss and ran a comb through her chestnut hair, releasing a strand from the simple gold cross she always wore.

It was her first day on the job, and everything felt strange. Just a few short months ago she had imagined an entirely different scenario for her life. She had been working on finishing her master's degree in environmental science when her boyfriend dropped a bombshell on her. Instead of proposing marriage, as she had hoped, he had calmly announced that he was joining the Marines.

After weeks of crying and pity parties, she had managed to pull herself together. Her sister, Linda, had reminded her of God's faithfulness and sovereignty over every area of her life. She had told her, "I know you've had a shocking blow, but God will use it for his good. Ask God to change your desires and trust Him."

Lisa had spent many hours reading her Bible and praying. She realized Linda had been right when she reminded her that this job opportunity had come at the perfect time. It had to be God opening a door—after closing a window.

Lisa bounced lightly in the plush black leather chair, ran her hand along the sleek mahogany desk, and grinned. The spacious office with its newly painted pastel walls, elegant oil paintings, and bouquet of fresh flowers was more than she had expected. She spun around to gaze out the large picture window and saw a splendid panoramic view of the State Capitol. She allowed herself a moment of gratitude for her good fortune and then checked her calendar. She had an orientation meeting scheduled for the afternoon, along with several other meetings with new co-workers.

Claire knocked softly again and entered. Lisa noticed that her face was beet red and that a portly man in a stylish suit had followed her. He was shorter than average, about five-foot-seven, and his rounded face had a small nose and steady dark brown eyes. Lisa sensed his commanding demeanor, jumped to her feet, and clumsily extended her hand. Behind her new boss—shadowing him like a vulture—stood a thuggish looking man with dark eyes that seemed to pierce right through her. He scanned Lisa's office and then stepped back into the hall.

"Welcome, Ms. Stone," the elegant man said in a deep and powerful voice. He took her hand in a hard squeeze. Lisa tried not to wince as his jeweled rings dug into her palm. "I spoke with you on the phone. I'm Herbert Clive Johnson."

"It's nice to meet you, sir," said Lisa, suddenly feeling self-conscious in her inexpensive outfit.

Johnson cleared his throat and spread his hands outward. "I hope you are comfortable here at Environ-Logging?"

Lisa smiled brightly. "Absolutely. It's a remarkable place."

"And the move? Your accommodations?" Johnson glanced out the window.

"Everything went just fine, thank you. You have been most generous."

Johnson nodded, and the two sat down. He flicked an invisible speck of lint from his trouser leg. Lisa glanced at the back of the giant who was standing like a sentinel just outside the door. She gulped.

"Mr. Johnson," she said, "do you have any specific tasks you'd like me to start doing first? And to whom do I report?"

Johnson gave a faint smile. "Call me Clive, please. You report to Stephen Hall, our senior scientist. I've discussed your work with him. We'll start out by having you look at some of the paperwork from your predecessor."

"My predecessor?" Lisa asked meekly.

"Yes, there was a scientist in your position, but he left suddenly."

She took a sip of her bottled water to hide her shock. She'd had no idea that her position had opened up in that way.

"Ed Grantham was working on the timber plan and environmental assessment of some new acreage we plan to log," Johnson said in a commanding voice. "We need you to find it and finish it for us. It's extremely important to the company." He stopped and narrowed his eyes. "As you know, we're committed to environmental protection, and you're the perfect person to keep us on track with what Grantham was doing." He rose to his feet and pointed at the door. "Please come with me."

Lisa followed Johnson to a tiny back office that was filled to capacity with two-dozen file cabinets that lined each wall. Johnson gestured toward the room. "This is where we are keeping Grantham's files," he said. Lisa noticed he was careful not to step into the narrow aisle that could barely fit a person half his size. "See what you can find here. My associate, Mack Taylor, will take you to the logging site next week." He motioned to the colossus who trailed him like a bodyguard. "Taylor is a former logger who knows the business inside out. He handles security now, but he can answer most, if not all, of your questions. Use him as a resource. Hall will meet with you soon."

Lisa looked at the file cabinets, all of which were carefully labeled and numbered, but said nothing. Johnson turned around, and she tracked him and the hulking shadow back to her office. Her head was spinning by the time they returned, and she had a dozen questions she wanted to ask. However, Johnson seemed eager to be on his way, so she decided this was not the appropriate time. Yet there was one nagging question that she couldn't let go.

"Mr. Johnson?" she said suddenly, mustering her courage as the pair turned to leave. Johnson turned and looked at her. "Can you tell me why Mr. Grantham left?" She held her breath and watched him carefully.

Johnson's face darkened. "I'm sorry, Ms. Stone," he replied, "but that's not something I can discuss with you." She felt a chill when she heard his stern tone. "If you need help with anything, please let Claire know. She's familiar with the files."

Lisa flushed and twisted a strand of hair with her forefinger as Johnson and Taylor exited the office. Suddenly, Johnson stopped and pivoted back toward her. He fixed her with an icy glare and a mask-like smile. "I'm counting on you to be a team player, Ms. Stone," he said. "You can do that, can't you?"

Lisa nodded as a tremor of anxiety gripped her stomach. Johnson looked at her once more before turning to leave. She collapsed into her fancy office chair. The happy feeling about her new job had just evaporated, replaced by a nauseating wave of doubt as to whether she had made the right job choice.

2

Offices of Environ-Logging, Olympia

Johnson sat back in his black cushioned desk chair, propped his feet on the carved teak desk, and drummed his fingers. He read his emails on the large flat-screen monitor facing him as he cradled a phone on his shoulder. "Yes, Senator, the bill has to do with salvage logging," he said in a kind voice. He could picture the young recently elected hotshot state senator Ronald Wells.

"Clive, remind me what salvage logging is," Wells said.

Johnson rolled his eyes. "This practice involves the removal of dead and dying trees caused by fire or disease." He whipped off his glasses and gazed out the window overlooking the majestic Puget Sound. He had selected the headquarters of Environ-Logging specifically for the view. The offices occupied the top three floors of the historic Longview Building in downtown Olympia and had a view of the State Capitol building in the other direction.

"I don't know, Clive," Wells said. "Isn't there some activist group that lobbied on that issue last year? 'Green Team' something or other. Anyway, I recall one of them telling me that the objective of salvage logging was to convert trees into cash . . . something about destroying the ecological integrity of the forest."

"Figures. Those tree-huggers are all the same. They don't want even one tree touched." Johnson gave a jovial laugh and shifted in his seat, wrinkling his dark blue Armani suit. He was impeccably dressed as always, with a light beige shirt and perfectly matched tie. He reached for his gourmet Italian coffee that he drank from the rare German mug he had purchased while touring Europe.

"Now, you and I both know that we can't stand in the way of progress," he said. "People need paper to write on and lumber to build houses, don't they?" He really didn't care a whit about activists or anyone else, but he knew that some ecologists were opposed to salvage logging, as they believed it destroyed the long-term sustainability of forest growth.

Wells pressed on. "But isn't it the same thing as clear-cutting, Clive?"

Johnson frowned and drew his hand through his carefully groomed silvery-grey hair. He chose his next words carefully so as not to make the senator feel stupid. "No, sir!" he said. "Clear-cutting is harvesting healthy, live trees, and it's a viable management technique. Salvage logging removes only the dead and dying trees. We practice environmentally healthy forest management. That's why we call ourselves 'Environ-Logging.' We're committed to being good stewards of the environment."

Johnson shook his head at how naïve these politicians were. He knew the term "clear-cutting" was a negative buzzword for environmentalists, and every time one of the up-and-comers came into office he would have to spend months educating the politician about his business. During the last fifteen years he had used his business acumen and way with people to almost singlehandedly build up the company to one of the largest in the state. These politicians all come around to my side eventually, he thought. Dad would be proud.

"Now, Senator, let's talk about that bill again." He loosened his belt over his slight paunch—thickened from the personalized meals he enjoyed every evening from his own private cook—and set his feet back up on the desk. After another half hour of persuasive pseudo-science, he hung up and congratulated himself for another victory.

Johnson stood up, stretched, and considered heading for the treadmill. At sixty-two, he kept himself fit through his daily visits to the gym that he'd had specially built upstairs. But instead, he sat down in his mahogany armchair, feeling very much like a king on his royal throne. He kicked off his Italian leather shoes and rested his feet on the ivory-inlaid table, almost upsetting the rare antique Chinese vase it displayed.

His secretary buzzed him. "Mr. Taylor is here, sir," she said.

The colossus stumbled into the office. His eyes were bloodshot and his face haggard. "Got any of that great coffee?" he mumbled.

Johnson gave him a dirty look. "Over there," he said, waving to the silver coffee service on a decorative table against the wall. Taylor went to the back table and poured a cup. He took a swig and sat down in the plush wingback chair facing Johnson.

"What'd you want to see me about, boss?" he asked.

"That new girl we met yesterday—Ms. Stone," said Johnson. "I want you to put a tail on her and monitor her phone . . . you know, the usual. Just in case."

"Sure, boss. You got nuttin' to worry about."

Johnson knew well what Mack Taylor was capable of. The guy was an arrogant ruffian, but he always got the job done, and Johnson had learned not to question his methods. He rose and strolled over to the window, his hands clasped behind his back.

"As I recall," he said, "Grantham had no relatives to speak of. So, our story that he quit unexpectedly and left the state should stick, should anyone ask."

"Boy, you should have seen the look on the old boy's face when I left," Taylor said, his lips curled with pride. "Everything lit up like a torch."

Johnson raised an eyebrow. "So, that means you burned the evidence that could link Grantham to our plans? Are you sure he didn't tell anyone else what he found?"

Taylor's dark eyes glowed. "Like I said, you got nuttin' to worry about, boss. Nobody will ever find anythin'."

"What about the body?" Johnson said with a scowl. "You never told me what happened to it."

"Relax, boss." Taylor held up a palm and chugged down the last of his coffee.

Johnson glared at him. This was not exactly the plan he had envisioned, but he was anxious to get the ordeal behind him.

His secretary buzzed. "Your grandson is on line three," she said.

Johnson's anger faded. He always enjoyed hearing from his only grandson. "Tell him I'll be right there."

He turned back to Taylor. "Next week, I want you to take the young lady on a tour of the logging site, but stay away from Grantham's cabin. She's young and inexperienced . . . not likely to make trouble."

Taylor set down his empty cup. "Piece a' cake, boss. She'll never know."

"Huh," Johnson grunted. "Good. And, Taylor—leave the fires to the experts."

3

Offices of Environ-Logging, Olympia

"It's awesome living here, Linda," Lisa said. She adjusted her Bluetooth and stomped hard on the pedal of her emerald-green hybrid convertible as she raced through the morning rush-hour traffic. "The weather is so much nicer than Chicago. I've got a quaint two-bedroom condo with a view to die for. And—"

"Yeah, but sis," her older sister interrupted, "you haven't told me about the job yet. How is it . . . really? You know, Dad was furious about you moving all the way to Washington State." A baby began wailing in the background.

Lisa twisted the steering wheel and scowled. Linda always knew which of her hot buttons to push. "The job is great. It's just that my boss is a little weird."

Linda gave a good-natured snicker. "What do you expect? You're an environmentalist. You were always protesting against industries like coal-fired plants. He's a big-shot executive who gets his jollies killing trees for profit. Not a good match."

Lisa winced and gripped the wheel tighter. She didn't need to hear a lecture from her sister about career choices. After all, Linda had given up her own career to raise a family. She had wound up with a successful marriage, an adoring husband, and two great kids, and at times Lisa envied her. In contrast, her perfectionist, type-A personality seemed to drive men away from her. She wondered if she would ever "have it all."

"Environ-Logging is one of the biggest logging industries in the Northwest and is well known for their environmental record," she argued. "Even their name sounds environmentally friendly! They're committed to sustainable forest management. Why else would they have hired me?" She paused and fingered her cross necklace. "And you know, I prayed about it. The Lord gave me peace that this was the right decision."

"Yes, I remember, you told me." Lisa heard screaming in the background and the sound of a spoon whacking a dish. "I need to go, dear. But I'm still waiting for an answer to my question. Don't keep me in suspense much longer. Love you." Click.

Lisa swerved into the parking lot. She was thankful that she had found a shortcut to work and that it now only took her a half hour to get there. She bounced up the steps into the spacious glass foyer and pressed the elevator button. After going through several days of orientation and meetings with the human resources department, she would finally meet her new boss, Stephen Hall.

An hour later, she was standing nervously in front of his office with notes in hand. The door was slightly ajar. "Mr. Hall?" she said as she timidly knocked.

She swung the door open. A wiry bald man with a stooped posture stood up from his chair. He looked like the quintessential librarian, with sharp eyes, horn-rimmed glasses, and an expressionless face. He wore a wrinkled blue suit, and his unmatched tie was askew.

"Nice to finally meet you, Lisa," Stephen said. He shook her hand and pointed to a chair opposite his desk. "How's everything going so far? What questions do you have for me?"

Lisa relaxed, and they began chatting about the move, her new accommodations, and her various meetings that week. She especially wanted to talk about Clive Johnson.

"Well," said Lisa, "for starters, Mr. Hall, can you give me any more details on Mr. Grantham's last project? Mr. Johnson asked me to get started on it right away, and I was hoping you could bring me up to speed."

"Please call me Stephen," he replied. His eyes crinkled as he smiled for the first time.

For the next hour, Lisa and Stephen talked about Ed Grantham, his responsibilities, and the projects he had left behind. Lisa could tell that Ed had been a good friend and co-worker to him, and the conversation helped her gain some perspective and background about her job. In Stephen she sensed a gentle and caring spirit, and she felt comfortable talking to him. But the dark circles under his eyes and his wrinkled brow made him look tired.

"I understand that Mr. Grantham left suddenly," she said. The question had been nagging her since her first day on the job.

Stephen tensed up and looked away. "Yes," he said at length. "It was unfortunate that he had to leave to care for his father-in-law. He and I came to work here about the same time—about fifteen years ago."

"I never heard the reason he left," said Lisa. "I asked Mr. Johnson about it, but it seems they don't reveal personal information about their employees."

"That would be the company line, of course." Stephen's eyes flickered to the door. She waited for him to continue, but instead an awkward silence ensued. Finally, he stammered, "Let me just say . . . that what happened to Grantham was a shame."

Her eyes widened in surprise, and she studied his face for a moment. Obviously, this was a touchy subject for him. It intrigued her to find out more . . . but she knew this was not the time.

"May I ask you another question, about Mr. Johnson?" she said. "What's it like to work for him? He seems so enigmatic, and he said something about being a 'team player.' Isn't everyone a team player?"

Stephen took off his glasses and rubbed his eyes. "What Mr. Johnson means is that he wants things done his way, and if you do what he asks, he'll treat you right. After all, he's the boss, right?"

Lisa could tell it was time to stop. "Well, I guess I better let you get back to work," she said as she stood to her feet. "Thanks for your time."

Stephen rose and extended his hand. "I look forward to working with you, Lisa. Please don't hesitate to ask for help, and remember that Claire is a good resource. She was Grantham's secretary for five years. But watch out. She's a bit of an alley cat, and there's been some talk . . ." His voice trailed off with a snicker.

Lisa's face turned pink, and she quickly backed out of his office. She brushed past Claire—avoiding any eye contact—shut her office door, leaned against it, and closed her eyes. She had lived too sheltered a life.

She settled into her fancy office chair, kicked off her stilettos, and spun around to look out the window. What other surprises are in store for me? she thought.

4

Children's Hospital, New York City, New York

Dr. Ted Dougherty hovered just beyond the door to the hospital room where Jerry Andrews lay in bed. The young boy's bony legs protruded from under the sheets, IVs snaked from his stick-thin arms, and tubes to help him breathe stuck out from his nose. As always, his mother, Doris, sat murmuring softly by his side, gently touching his jaundiced cheek.

The boy had taken a turn for the worse two weeks before, and Dr. Dougherty dreaded what was to come. For several years now, Jerry had shown the classic signs of a rare childhood disease called Niemann-Pick Type C (NPC), which was caused by a defective gene carried by both parents. Of course, no one had diagnosed it as such until the family had brought Jerry to Children's Hospital, which was known in New York for its research on children's diseases.

Dr. Dougherty had been researching the deadly disease for the past ten years, and he knew that doctors often diagnosed it as a learning disorder or just plain clumsiness, due to the fact it caused a lack of coordination in children during their preschool or early years. When NPC is present, the child lacks the ability to metabolize cholesterol and other lipids properly, which causes excessive amounts of the substances to accumulate in organs such as the liver, spleen, and brain. Always fatal, most children afflicted with the disease died before age twenty, and many died before the age of ten.

Jerry Andrews was fourteen.

Dr. Dougherty entered the room, walked over to the bed, and checked the boy's pulse. Doris looked up through her tears and acknowledged him with a weak smile. She continued stroking the boy's thin and yellowed face, gently avoiding the eye covered with a patch.

"He's still jerkin' in his sleep," said Doris, "and his eye bothers him, doc." Her face was puffy, and her eyes looked bloodshot. She could not afford a hotel room, so she had spent another long night camped out in Jerry's hospital room. Her son was all she had in the world—her husband was nowhere to be found.

"He can't swallow very well, either," she added.

Dr. Dougherty stood up, gently lifted the eye patch, and set it down.

"How are you feeling today, Jerry?" he asked as he placed his stethoscope on the boy's chest. The breathing was labored.

Jerry opened his eye, stared at the doctor as if he were a stranger, and spoke in a feeble voice. "Okay, I guess. My eye hurts a little."

"The eye looks a little red, so I'll prescribe some eye drops. We'll give you something to soothe your throat and a sedative to help you sleep. Okay?"

Jerry nodded and closed his eye again.

Dr. Dougherty turned to Doris. "Mrs. Andrews, may I speak to you outside?"

Doris stifled a sob and gently caressed her son's hair as she stood to her feet. Her light gray hair was uncombed and straggled, and Dr. Dougherty saw her glance at a pack of cigarettes on the nightstand before exiting the room. He wondered if she had sneaked a smoke in the room last night.

He led her to an empty waiting area and motioned for her to sit down. "Mrs. Andrews," he said, "I should begin by telling you that Jerry is continuing to show the classic signs of NPC." He adjusted his wire-rimmed glasses and sat down opposite her. "I realize that this may be a shock, but seizures are common at this point, along with difficulty in swallowing. His liver and spleen are enlarged, which is causing the jaundice color in his skin. We should consider placing a gastrostomy feeding tube."

Doris's eyes went wide with fright. "What's that?"

"It's a feeding tube that we would insert through a small incision in his abdomen and then into his stomach."

Doris winced, and her hand flew to her slightly open mouth. "Oh, my Lord, that sounds just awful. Will it hurt my baby?"

"We will do everything we can to make him as comfortable as possible. But we need to do it soon, because with Jerry's difficulty in swallowing, he is not getting the nutrition he needs. He is losing his strength." He wanted to add something about her smoking, but he decided against it.

"Doc, his eyes been bad for a long time." Doris shook her head. "Oh, why didn't I get him to a doc sooner?"

Dr. Dougherty looked down and sighed. "Yes, I'm sorry, but he has vertical gaze palsy, which is basically the inability to look up or down. It is one of the major symptoms linked to NPC. "

Tears began to well up in Doris's eyes. "Ain't there no cure, doc? No cure at all?"

"No, not at this time." He looked down at his scuffed white shoes instead of into her tear-streaked face. "Well, I must continue my rounds now." He got up and adjusted his white coat and the stethoscope around his neck. He hesitated, and then put his hand on her shoulder and squeezed gently. "Do you have anyone to talk to?"

Doris's eyes brightened. "I talk to God all the time," she said.

Dr. Dougherty pulled his hand away and forced a nod. He was surprised to hear this answer coming from such a pathetic figure. "I'm sure that is a great comfort to you," he stammered as he turned to walk away. This time, she reached for his arm.

"Thanks for askin', doc. I don't know why this is happenin', but I know there's a reason." She dabbed at a tear with a tissue. "God always has His reasons."

He wanted to roll his eyes but looked away instead. How many times have I heard that? he said to himself. Doris stifled a yawn and shifted in her chair.

He patted her hand. "You'd better try to sleep now. I'll check up on you and Jerry later." He walked away from the forlorn woman and made his way to the nurse's station, where he asked the head nurse to look up a cheap hotel where Doris could stay. The woman needed to get a good night's sleep, and she would get it even if he had to pay for it himself. Her son was about to die, and there was nothing he could do about it.

He walked back to his office, clicked on the computer, briefly checked his watch, and calculated the difference in time between the Eastern and Pacific zones. Once he was satisfied that his friend and colleague in Seattle would be in his office, he logged onto his Skype account and punched in the code for Dr. Raymond Philip Kramer. Might as well brief him on the latest NPC victim, he thought.

5

*Logging camp near Gray Mountain Mill,
Eltout Forest, Washington*

Lisa relaxed in the back of the black SUV and looked out the dark-tinted windows as the car twisted and turned along deep-forested winding lanes. She wore hiking boots, black designer jeans, and a loose sweatshirt. Mack Taylor and a uniformed driver sat in the front.

As they plunged into the evergreen Eltout Forest, she gaped at the towering Douglas firs, grand firs, and Ponderosa pines. "The office building is not far from the largest of the logging camps at Gray Mountain Mill," Taylor said, twisting his head in her direction. He had been quiet during most of the ride, and she was thankful for that. She had been on the job for two weeks now, and the guy still gave her the creeps.

"Where am I going to stay tonight?" she asked. She opened the window to sniff the cool, fresh air laden with pine scent.

"We put our folks up at the one motel in town, the Lazy Lodge. We'll take you there after our tour of the office, logging camp, and mill." Taylor turned back to watch the road.

They continued on to a security checkpoint, where they were asked to show their ID badges. Once they had passed through, they traveled another mile down a dark forested road until they stopped at a pinewood A-frame building. The name "Environ-Logging" was etched onto a wooden plank.

A tall, beefy, fair-haired man was waiting in front of the building. At his side on a leash was a black German Shepherd with tan

31

markings. When the car stopped, the man stepped forward, opened the passenger door, and offered his hand to Lisa.

"Hello," he said. "My name is Donny Johansen. I'm in charge here." His voice had a soft Swedish lilt. "Welcome to the Gray Mountain office. Did you have a pleasant ride down?"

Lisa stared at the dog, and her eyes widened in fear. Johansen looked at her quizzically. "Is there a problem?"

She pointed a weak forefinger at the dog. "Is the dog friendly?" she stammered.

"Oh, that's just Oso. Yes, he's friendly enough."

At that moment, Oso began barking furiously. Lisa's hand flew to her mouth and her heart stopped. She closed the door quickly. Her mind flashed back to a moment in her childhood when a German Shepherd had attacked her as she was riding her bike. She had been terrified of the breed ever since that day.

Johansen yelled at the dog, and he quieted down.

"I am so sorry, ma'am." Johansen motioned for his assistant to take the dog away. When the dog was at a safe distance, Lisa opened the door and slowly stepped out of the car. She and Johansen walked to the building, where she glimpsed elegant pine furniture, polished hardwood floors, and landscape paintings of forest scenes on the rustic wood walls. She was shown to a spacious conference room where an aerial photograph overlaid with a timber unit map was spread out on a table. Lisa noticed that Taylor had disappeared.

Johansen motioned toward a short stocky man in green coveralls and hard hat, both sporting the Environ-Logging logo. "This is David Connors, chief of operations," he said. "He'll explain what we're looking at."

Connors shook hands with everyone, took off his hard hat, and stepped in front of the table. His rugged face grew serious as he tapped the photo with a thick index finger. "This is a map of our current logging operations," he said. "The areas marked with colors, letters, and numbers correspond to the areas that are being logged. The higher the letter and number, the newer the site. For example, we are now logging in tract M-296, which has a combination of Douglas fir and Ponderosa pine. It's designated in red."

"I saw a smaller version of this in the environmental assessment," Lisa said. "Many of the forest roads were built to avoid streams and designated wetland areas."

"Yes, our consultants mapped out wetlands, fish habitat streams, and riparian regions some time ago. We built the bridges carefully to minimize damage if we have to cross one of those sensitive areas."

"Can you show me those places on the map?"

"Yes, I'd be glad to."

Lisa turned to Johansen. "And may I see the current permits on site?"

"We aim to please, ma'am," Johansen said pleasantly.

Lisa looked back at Connors. "When will we see the real operation?" she asked.

"After lunch today." He grabbed his hard hat and moved toward the door.

"We'll leave Oso in his pen," Johansen added. He looked amused.

He is certainly a congenial fellow, Lisa thought, *which is good, because I might be spending a lot of time here to get to know the operations better.*

After Connors left, she continued to pore over the logging maps. About noon, a secretary announced that lunch was ready. Johansen explained that they had hired a chef because of their isolation. She was escorted into an adjoining building, where she saw a gourmet meal of smoked salmon, saffron rice, and fresh fruit salad.

After lunch, Johansen drove Lisa along more winding and isolated roads. They stopped at a large clearing, where Connors approached them with hard hats and goggles in hand. Below them were two giant machines, each about fifty feet high, that looked like huge mechanical grasshoppers.

Lisa watched in fascination as enormous logs, momentarily suspended above the ground, were pulled by a machine hanging on steel cables three hundred feet in the air. "It's called a skyline carriage,"

Connors explained. "The mechanical pulley device has nooses of wire rope called chokers that surround the log. It picks them up and then drops them into the log-felling area down below."

Lisa drew her coat a little closer. She watched the complex machinery at work and the multitude of husky men with hard hats, gloves, chainsaws, and axes. "This seems to be a gigantic operation. How many people are employed here?"

"We have two hundred and twenty people, including all the loggers and staff at the office. It's one of our largest sites."

The group spent the next three hours touring the logging operations, including the newly reforested areas. Lisa was impressed by the efficiency. The skyline cable brought massive logs across the open area, where they were loaded onto large tractor-trailers for the trip to the mill. She learned that some of the wood was sold to retail stores as lumber, but some was also sold to manufacturers of diverse products including furniture, flooring, decks, and paper.

At the end of the long day, she welcomed the sight of the Lazy Lodge, a modest motel set in the middle of a large oak grove. The peaceful serenity was a sharp contrast to the screeching and clanking machinery she had experienced all day.

Her room was set apart in its own log cabin warmed by a cozy fire. The four-poster antique bed held a thick down comforter that looked irresistibly inviting. She kicked off her shoes, shed her thick coat, crawled into bed, and shut her eyes.

The forest noises were soothing, but she kept picturing the German Shepherd, Oso. She touched the ugly scar that ran down her leg. The vision of the dog tearing into her as she was riding her bike was still vivid after all these years. She buried her face in her pillow to stifle the tears.

6

Office of Forests, Portland, Oregon

"Can you bring me that file again?" Tom Moeller asked his secretary through the office door.

He watched the slim strawberry blonde scurry to retrieve the most recent file on Environ-Logging. He had never asked her out in the two years she had worked for him—not because he didn't find her attractive, but because he was an admitted workaholic. At least, that was what he told himself when she looked at him with those flirtatious green eyes. A few times he'd come close, but the pain of his divorce three years ago kept him from seeking romantic attachments.

His secretary sauntered into the office and handed him the file. "Anything else?" she asked, flashing her emerald eyes and sweeping her long blonde hair away from her stunning face.

Tom caught a whiff of delicate perfume and looked up from the stack of files spread across the conference table near his desk. "Yes, buzz Rob for me, please," he said, avoiding her gaze and keeping his voice neutral. "And I'll be working through lunch." She nodded and started toward the door, but then turned back.

"Can I bring you anything to eat?" she asked. "I really don't mind, since I'm going out anyway." Her beguiling tone made him glance up, and his face reddened when he saw her bat her eyelashes. She looked at him the way his wife used to, as if he were a Greek god.

"No, I'll pop downstairs and grab a bite later. Thanks anyway."

He loosened his tie and continued reviewing the documents. He had collected them a month earlier after a trip to Olympia to carry out a routine inspection of Environ-Logging. He had spent a full day in the main office pouring over the paperwork for the newest logging tracts to ensure they were compliant with forest regulations. He rubbed his eyes, took a sip of stale coffee and a bite of an old donut he had bought that morning, and grimaced.

He heard a knock at the door and looked up to see Rob O'Donnell, his longtime associate walk into the room. "What's up, Tom?" Rob asked. He looked at the stack of papers and sat down at the table beside Tom. "So, you finally got around to that Environ-Logging inspection?"

Tom shrugged. "I've been so busy, and it got buried on the desk. But something told me to look a little closer."

"Have you found anything yet?"

"No. Everything is in order, but the curious thing is that I didn't meet with Ed Grantham. They just ushered me into a big room and shoved the files at me. The CEO himself came in and informed me that Grantham was on leave and not expected back for some time."

Rob scowled. "That's really strange. Ed always wanted to participate in the inspections in the past." He began leafing through the files on the desk. "He's a stickler for accuracy. He knows more about old growth forests than any of us."

"I know . . . and that Johnson fellow sure is a pompous sort."

His co-worker nodded. "I know what you mean. I met him once, and all he could talk about was how much money his company had made the previous year."

"Well, Johnson did build Environ-Logging from the ground up in the face of a lot of competition. Fifteen years later, it's become one of the premier commercial logging companies in the area, and it's all pretty much due to that one man. I guess he deserves to boast."

Rob shrugged. "Reminds me of an old Irish saying my mother told me. 'Put silk on a goat, and it's still a goat.'"

Tom chuckled. "I plan to call Kevin at the Department of Timber Resources regional office and see what he thinks. I saw that he was the one who conducted the inspection last year. He would know if they filed the proper plans for the new tracts this year." The Department of Timber Resources (DTR) worked with the Forest Service to manage and regulate logging in Washington State. Both Tom and Rob had worked extensively with Kevin Burke in the past because his region covered Environ-Logging's operations.

Rob reached for one of the stale donuts. "Are you trying to find something unusual in the timber plans? Kevin's group should have reviewed them to determine the impact on existing fish and wildlife."

Tom scratched his head. "Not really. We both know Environ-Logging has a squeaky clean record, but it doesn't hurt to be extra cautious. They have more than five thousand acres and twenty major logging sites."

"Yes, it's an enormous operation." Rob took a bite of the donut and immediately regretted it. "I read that the company is ranked in the top ten forest management companies in the U.S."

"I wonder when Grantham is coming back. They'll be hurting without his experience."

Rob stood up and started toward the door. "Well, I think it's a good idea to investigate them further. Kevin is a good resource, and he will know what the company is up to. Is there anything I can do?"

"No. Thanks, Rob. I just wanted to get your opinion on this."

Tom reviewed the files for the next several hours. He couldn't believe the huge logging company had such an impeccable environmental record. During its fifteen years of operation, the company hadn't received one violation or fine. That wasn't normal for such a complex operation. Other logging companies that Tom had investigated normally had a few minor violations, which they corrected when brought to their attention. Something about Environ-Logging just didn't seem right. The records seemed too perfect, with everything in its proper place. It was a red flag.

Tom couldn't shake the feeling that the management was hiding something. But now that Grantham was gone, there was no one he could ask about it. He wiped his forehead and frowned as he signed the final report and closed the folders. He would keep Environ-Logging on his radar.

7

Offices of Environ-Logging, Olympia

Lisa hesitated before knocking on the slightly open door in front of Stephen Hall's office. She felt guilty. Here she was again to pick his brain like she had ever since starting her job a few weeks ago. He was an odd mousy sort of guy—quiet, reserved, and unassuming—but the wealth of knowledge he had accumulated was astounding.

Stephen didn't act like a boss. He spoke to her like a colleague and did not belittle her inexperience. However, he often seemed to be withdrawn and lost in his own little world, so she was careful not to intrude too much. She had called ahead to make sure he had no appointments.

She mustered her courage and reached up to knock on his door. Just then, she heard the phone ring inside his office. Darn, she thought. She stood outside and waited.

"Yes, I understand, sir," she heard Stephen say in a low hushed tone. "It will be done, just as you said. I promise." His voice sounded unusually anxious.

She knew she shouldn't eavesdrop, so she hurriedly knocked on the door. "Stephen, it's me, Lisa," she said, slowly pushing the door open.

He jumped up as she entered, the phone pressed to his ear. Oops, she thought. It was not good business etiquette to barge right in.

He held up an index finger, hunched over and whispered into the phone, and then hung up. "Nice to see you again, Lisa," he said. "How's everything going?" He stood up and extended his hand, always the gentleman, yet he avoided meeting her eyes. He had a look of intense concentration as he motioned for her to take a seat in front of the desk.

Lisa noticed the dark circles under his eyes behind the thick glasses that were perched on his small nose. His rumpled shirt was missing a button, and he lacked the usual unmatched tie. He seemed flustered.

"Is this a bad time to talk, Stephen?" she asked.

"No, Lisa. It's all right. What would you like to know?" His eyes seemed vacant and his shoulders sagged. Lisa sensed a tone of resignation in his voice. He spoke in a monotone, like a robot, and had a listless expression. She felt sorry for him. He was obviously overworked and stressed out.

"I'd like to talk about Grantham's work again, if you don't mind." Lisa launched into a lengthy discussion of her research and the nagging questions that had come to her mind as a result. It felt good to vent all the frustration that had been building up. During the next hour, she took copious notes as he responded with his encyclopedic memory.

The phone rang again. "One moment please," he said as he picked it up slowly. He cupped the phone with his hand and pursed his lips, as if trying to decide what to say. He looked agitated and fearful. Lisa took the cue and quickly rose from her seat.

"I see you're very busy. I'd better be going back to my office. Thanks for your help."

"No problem, Lisa. Sorry I'm a little distracted today. We'll spend more time tomorrow, okay?"

She forced a smile and walked out. By the time she got back to her office, just two doors away, she once again had a serious case of the creeps. She liked Stephen, but it still seemed as if something was wrong. She had learned from her father that a person who couldn't look you straight in the eyes had to be hiding something. She might just be imagining things, but her gut told her otherwise.

She closed her eyes and leaned against the door. She pictured Johnson's piercing eyes and chilling words about being a "team player." She walked to her desk, sat down, bowed her head, and whispered a prayer. *Lord, maybe I'm imagining this, but something doesn't seem right. Help me know what's going on around here.*

8

Headquarters of GreenForests, Kirkland, east of Seattle

Carl Ward stared wide-eyed at the email from Stephen Hall of Environ-Logging. He dropped his half-eaten tuna sandwich and reached for his cell phone.

"Betty, this is Carl. Ed Grantham is gone!"

"What? Ed Grantham, of Environ-Logging?" Betty's voice echoed softly as if she were in a tunnel.

"I can hardly hear you. Where are you?" Carl had sent her to the Legislative Building in Olympia to do research on an upcoming bill. As his assistant, she was responsible for tracking down any new logging legislation.

Betty raised her voice. "I'm in the basement, so maybe the reception is poor. But I can hear you."

"Can you believe it? Ed was a great guy—one of the best experts in old growth forests in the nation."

"I remember that he was a supporter of our work during the early years. He always kept in touch, despite working for the loggers. So, what happened?"

"I got word that he took a sudden leave of absence a few months ago. I'm going to try to find out if and when he's coming back. Betty, while you're there, see if you can dig up the records of Environ-Logging's testimony on the last few bills in Congress. I have a funny feeling about this."

"Sure, no problem. I'll see what I can do and call you later."

Carl sat down in a rickety chair at a narrow metal folding table that served as a desk in his office. The activist organization he had founded, called GreenForests, was located in a run-down office building in Kirkland, east of Seattle. Carl kept the surroundings sparse to save every dime he could.

His organization was dedicated to preserving the state's diverse forest ecosystems and watchdogging the logging industry. Ever since he was a child growing up in the Amazon basin of Brazil, he had been taught to respect God and honor His creation. His parents were Bible translators and devoted their lives to translating ethnic dialects so the native people could have God's Word in their own language.

Carl had spent months researching Environ-Logging and knew they had a squeaky clean environmental record. But now, as he again stared at the email on his computer screen, something didn't seem right. He reached for the phone again—and his tuna sandwich.

"Environ-Logging. May I help you?" said a businesslike voice on the other end of the line.

"Stephen Hall, please."

"Just a moment." Carl was placed on hold and the line went to Musak. He munched his sandwich and reached for a can of root beer. After several moments, his colleague picked up.

"Stephen, it's Carl. What's going on?"

"Nothing much," Stephen replied, his voice sounding tense. "Why do you ask?" Carl had known the older man since childhood, and he was like a second father to him.

"I got your email about Ed Grantham. What's up with that?"

An awkward pause ensued. "I was told that Grantham took a sudden leave of absence due to a relative's illness. Sorry, I don't know any more about it."

Carl noted that Stephen was guarded in his speech. Usually his friend was upbeat and a good resource for information about the day-to-day logging operations. Carl had always respected Stephen for not worrying about the appearance of their incongruous relationship. Industry workers did not usually mix with environmentalists.

In fact, his activist friends often commented on his ability to get inside information about logging legislation.

"Well, okay," he said. "I was just wondering what was going on. He really knew his stuff. "

"I know, and it's too bad." Stephen's voice contained little emotion.

"Do you know how long he'll be gone?" Another lull ensued. Carl drummed his fingers on the desk and sipped his root beer as he waited for a reply.

"Actually, it's not likely that he's coming back," Stephen said softly. "In fact, we've already got a replacement. She's been here more than a month now. Bright girl."

Carl took a deep breath. The words had struck him like a rifle blast. "You say Ed's not coming back?"

"Yeah. Hey, I'd like to talk to you more about it, but I'm very busy right now. Could we talk later?"

Carl could hear typing on a computer in the background. He gulped. It wasn't like his friend to brush him off like this, but he didn't want to press any further.

"Sure. And thanks for the heads-up about that new salvage logging bill. We're researching it right now." He started to say goodbye, but then changed his mind. "Hey, one more thing, if you don't mind."

"Sure, what's that?"

"Would you tell me the name of Ed's replacement?"

"Sure, a young gal, just out of college, named Lisa Stone. She's reporting to me."

Carl gasped. "What did you say her name was?"

"Lisa Stone. You know her?"

Carl paused and caught his breath. "Yeah . . . we're friends."

"You don't say! Well, I gotta go. Talk to you later." The phone clicked.

Carl's stomach tightened. What was his former activist partner and girlfriend doing working for an industry that was essentially his enemy? The nagging feeling in the back of his mind had just moved front and center.

9

University of Washington, Medical School, Seattle

Dr. Raymond Kramer took off his glasses, rubbed his eyes, and filled his third mug of coffee. He had slept only a few hours the previous night after reading a disturbing email from Dr. Ted Dougherty, his colleague in New York, about a young boy named Jerry. After tossing and turning in bed, he had decided to go back to the lab to work, even though it was four in the morning.

Dr. Kramer had made his life's work trying to cure the debilitating Niemann-Pick Type C disease. He had discovered Dr. Dougherty after sending out emails following the diagnosis of his best friend's daughter, Rachel. He could still see the gaunt figure of Rachel, only eight years old, as she lay dying in the hospital bed. He had vowed to find a cure for NPC, no matter the cost. He and Dr. Dougherty had since become good friends over the Internet as they swapped stories about the children they were treating. They had met once at a childhood disease conference in New York City.

The lanky doctor peered into his microscope again, carefully observing the reaction between the protein he had isolated from a frog's skin and the saliva of an NPC victim. He blinked and gripped the scope with both hands. Something was happening—the frog protein seemed to be breaking up the saliva cells. He could hardly believe what he was seeing. After years of experimentation, could it be that he had discovered the cure he was seeking?

Dr. Kramer heard a noise behind him and turned to see a tall boy and stick-thin girl, two of his senior research assistants. The boy, towering over him, was cupping his hands in an attempt to be heard over the dozen cages of small green frogs that were croaking simultaneously. Dr. Kramer rarely saw anyone in the lab before eight o'clock. He was immune to the cacophony and generally worked in the early morning hours before he started his rounds at the nearby medical center.

"Dr. Kramer, may we talk to you?" the young man said in a squeaky high-pitched voice. He was dressed in sweaty gym clothes. The girl, not much shorter than him, stood behind in the same smelly attire.

Dr. Kramer straightened and pulled on his salt-and-pepper beard. "Of course. What is it?"

"We wanted to know if we could have the day off. My sister just came into town and invited both of us to dinner at my folks' house."

Dr. Kramer looked at the pair. Just like his best students to make the extra effort to come and ask a favor in person. They were destined to be great doctors.

"Yes, absolutely." He beamed as he remembered the cocky feeling at that age.

The young lady peeked over her friend's shoulder. "May we ask what you are looking at?"

"Sure. Come over here for a closer look." He nodded toward the microscope, and the young researchers took turns peering at the glass.

Dr. Kramer stood near, cradling his coffee cup. "Do you remember me talking about searching for a cure for NPC?"

Both of them nodded. "Yes, it seems to be a worthwhile goal," said the boy. "You're looking at different species of frogs, right?"

"Yes, and this one is so rare that it's on the U.S. Fish and Wildlife Service's endangered species list. It's on the verge of extinction. No wonder it practically took a pint of blood to acquire."

Both young people looked perplexed.

"Let me put it this way. It took me six months to get through the red tape just to scrape a small sample from the frog's skin." He had spent months searching for places that had the elusive animal, ultimately finding one practically in his own back yard at the Monterey Bay Aquarium.

"Excuse me, Dr. Kramer," said the girl, "but may I ask how you came to study frogs in your research?"

Dr. Kramer suppressed a chuckle. "Of course. A couple of years ago, I read an Australian medical journal about research that had been done using proteins from the skin of frogs to treat cancer patients. The secretions from the skin, which were extracted without harming the frog, were found to kill cancer tumors."

Dr. Kramer went on to describe the paperwork he had been required to complete to not only get permission from the aquarium's board of trustees but also the U.S. Fish and Wildlife Service. He had to assure the aquarium's executive director that no harm would come to the frog. "Can you believe the director demanded a 24-hour watch to ensure the frog survived?" he added. "Well, after the frog came through unscathed, he promised I could return when I needed more samples."

"Wow," said the boy, "that's remarkable! What's the frog's species name?"

"Ganther's or Broad-leaved frog, *Litoria latolevata*."

The students glanced around the room. "You sure have gone through a lot of frogs, sir," said the girl. "But maybe it was worth all the effort."

"I hope so. We'll see." Dr. Kramer stretched and filled his mug for the fourth time, though he knew he would later regret the caffeine overdose. He was too tired to think of all the implications right now. "What time is it?"

The young man looked at his watch. "Half past seven, sir."

"I need to get ready for rounds." He paused and pulled on the tip of his beard. "May I ask you something before you leave?"

"Sure," the assistants said.

"What would you say if I told you that you could get a little extra credit in class?"

The students looked at each other, smiled broadly, and nodded their heads in unison. Dr. Kramer explained that he wanted a web search for sightings of the Ganther's frog anywhere in the world.

His previous search had shown that there had been no sightings in the U.S. in the last ten years, but he knew there were a handful of known species scattered in various zoos and aquariums.

"What does the frog look like, sir?" asked one of the students.

Dr. Kramer walked over to a laptop and pulled up a picture. "As you can see, it's about the size of your palm. It's Kelly green with a gold tint and bright yellow underbelly, and it has distinctive black markings. It also has a unique high-pitched croak that distinguishes it from all other frogs." Dr. Kramer wondered how a person could possibly discover one in the wild.

"It's gorgeous!" said the young lady. "We'll do our best, sir."

Dr. Kramer closed the laptop after the students left and grunted as he thought about the task before him. Even if he had found a cure, it seemed impossible to obtain all the skin samples that would be needed from the few frogs that were left in the world. Yet he would never give up hope of finding the miracle frog—and he had a funny feeling that maybe, after all this time, he had found the right one.

10

Offices of Environ-Logging, Olympia

Lisa opened the next set of thick three-ring binders on her desk, took a deep breath, and sipped her bottled water. Her desk was littered with permit binders, forest regulations, environmental assessments, maps of stream types, and applications.

She had realized during her first month at Environ-Logging that she knew little about logging rules and regulations. Although she had studied old growth forests in college, she had not researched the laws and regulations impacting forests that were now a necessary part of her job. At times she felt overwhelmed, but she was eager to learn. Stephen had proven to be a fascinating yet enigmatic man whom she highly respected. He reminded her of her meticulous father, but without the jovial disposition.

The phone on her desk rang, breaking her concentration. She set her bottle down in the midst of the jumbled papers.

"Hey, Lisa," said the voice on the line. "It's Carl."

Carl? It seemed odd to hear from her former boyfriend, especially since she had not told many people about her new job. She fondly remembered the times she had shared with the handsome track star majoring in law. "Hey, voice from the past!" she said, trying not to sound too surprised. "What's up?"

"I heard you are working for Environ-Logging. Is that true?" She detected a sense of smugness in the athlete-turned-activist's voice.

"Yes, Carl. I've gone over to the dark side." She looked to the window and tried not to sound defensive. "Let's just say I'm trying to get a perspective on the real world."

"Did you tear up your membership cards in Sierra Club and Greenpeace?" She heard a snicker on the line, and her face turned red.

"Of course not! I'm the same Lisa you knew before." She suppressed a giggle, knowing that Carl was right on target. "I plan to be Environ-Logging's environmental conscience," she added after a pause.

"Yeah, right. So, how much they paying you?"

"Let's just say I'll be able to pay off my college debts a lot faster than if I worked for your organization."

"That's for sure!" He chuckled.

Lisa repressed a sigh. His voice sounded the same as always. She felt a tug on her heart.

In high school, she had been head-over-heels in love with the older, blue-eyed hunk, her first serious crush. He was a committed Christian whom she had met at a church function, and his "missionary kid" roots always caused him to strive for public service. She had admired his decision to serve in the Peace Corps in Santiago, Chile, after graduating from college, even though it had caused him to break off the relationship. He had clerked at a prominent law firm in Chicago but given up the lucrative law practice to start an activist organization near his hometown.

"So . . . how is GreenForests coming along?" she asked, trying to change the subject.

"Well, it's just Betty and me now. You know, the funding dried up after the economy tanked. It seems that people have other things they need to spend money on, like food and housing."

"That's too bad, Carl."

"Yeah. I still have a few contributors who send a little each month. Nothing much to speak of, but I can afford to sit tight until the economy comes back."

Lisa snorted. Carl's grandfather was one of the richest men in Chicago, and Carl stood to inherit a considerable fortune when he died. "So," she said, stifling the urge to make a sarcastic remark, "what prompted your call, Carl?"

When Carl again spoke, his tone had changed. "Your colleague,

Stephen Hall, has been a huge source of information for me over the last several years."

Lisa grimaced. "Oh, really?"

"You really need to get to know him, Lisa. He's a good friend. I have a hunch that something strange is going on over there."

"What do you mean?" She tried to sound aloof.

"You probably know there was a fellow named Ed Grantham who worked at Environ-Logging."

"Yes, of course. I've been told that I'm his replacement."

"So I heard. Did you know anything about him?"

Lisa hesitated. She wondered how Carl knew so much about Environ-Logging. "Yes, a little. Should I?"

"I think it might help you to know what kind of person you replaced," Carl said in a businesslike tone. "He had a doctorate in forest system management. He knew everything about old growth forests and was highly respected in the field. He was so dedicated that he moved to a one-room log cabin so he could study the forest system more closely."

"I didn't know that." She frowned and wondered why Stephen had never mentioned these details in their conversations.

"He was pretty much a recluse, but it strikes me odd that he would disappear without warning. I wasn't exactly friendly with the guy, but Stephen and I go way back, and he didn't even know Grantham was leaving until afterward."

Lisa shrugged. "Maybe the family problem came up suddenly."

"Maybe, but it sounds fishy to me. I've been doing some research, and Environ-Logging's track record is just too good to be true."

"Carl, that's one of the reasons I came here—because their environmental record is so good." She was becoming exasperated with his antagonistic attitude. Then again, his organization was dedicated to scrutinizing the type of company that was now her employer.

"There's something else you should know. That CEO of yours—Johnson—spends a lot of money on campaign contributions. He gave a hundred grand last year to Senator Wells' campaign."

"Is that so unusual?"

"Not if you want to get something in return for your money."

Lisa slapped a hand on her desk. "Carl, Environ-Logging is a huge commercial company that has to deal with countless regulations and laws that go through the state legislature. If the CEO chooses to spend some money to help a couple of legislators, that is perfectly fine by me. I don't see anything wrong with that!"

Carl made no reply.

"Furthermore," she continued, "it's not unusual for a person to leave a job because of a family matter. You're being ridiculous."

There was a long pause. "Okay, okay," Carl finally said. His voice had taken on a more caring tone. "I'm sorry. I just wanted to tell you to be careful."

"You're sweet, Carl," said Lisa, softening her tone as well. "Thanks for your concern. But I can take of myself."

"Yeah, I know. All right. But call if you need anything. Hey, it's great to hear your voice."

"I will. Thanks, Carl."

Lisa hung up the phone and replayed the conversation in her mind. She knew Carl wouldn't have called unless he was really concerned. It seemed that Stephen Hall was keeping information to himself. Warning bells were going off in her mind.

She reached for an aspirin to relieve a pounding headache that had suddenly developed. She resolved to get to the bottom of this, and sooner rather than later.

11

Eagles Prairie, Olympia suburbs

Stephen Hall trudged wearily through the door of his elegant three-thousand-square-foot home in Eagles Prairie, a fashionable suburb east of downtown Olympia. On one side of the home, ceiling-to-floor windows overlooked the members-only golf course and Nisqually Reach, one of the majestic bays stemming from Puget Sound. Stephen kept a thirty-two-foot Catalina cruising sailboat there in the harbor.

He dropped his briefcase on the counter, kicked off his shoes, and went into the kitchen to retrieve an ice-cold beer.

"Hard day, honey?" asked Amanda, his wife of twenty-five years.

"Yeah, you could say that." He was bone tired and didn't feel like talking.

The lovely redhead had her hair up and was dressed simply with a bright yellow apron over her casual khakis and polo shirt. She was tending to a boiling pot of linguini noodles and a saucepan that exuded a pleasant aroma. A row of spices and a small dish of olive oil, along with a fresh loaf of French bread, sat on the ceramic-tiled table in the center of the overly large modern kitchen.

Stephen knew he should be more interested in what Amanda was doing. He cast a guilty glance out the window and looked at the well-manicured yard with its blue swimming pool and hot tub.

"How was the drive?" Amanda asked.

"The usual," Stephen answered in a monotone. "Traffic on I-5 was backed up. But no accidents."

As was his custom after work, he retreated to the den and closed the door to avoid any further chitchat. He knew Amanda would not bother him in there. She was a jewel—caring, understanding, and hard-working. She had started her own flower-arranging business after the kids had grown, but she still took the time to cook him scrumptious meals every night. He realized with another wave of shame and guilt that he had become more and more distant during the past few months.

He plopped down on the black leather recliner, put his feet up, and closed his eyes. He opened a beer he had taken from the fridge and savored the cold taste of the brew. His wife knew nothing about what was happening at the office, and he figured it was better that way. Why involve her in the mess at work? he thought. He punched a number into his cell phone.

"Roger," he said, "this is Dad. Can we talk?"

"Sure, what's up?" His son sounded cheerful, exactly what Stephen needed.

"They replaced Grantham with a new girl," Stephen said, trying not to sound depressed. "I can't believe it." He had told his oldest son much of what was going on at Environ-Logging, but not everything.

"Oh, Dad, I'm sorry to hear that," Roger said.

"Yeah. Apparently he's not coming back. I don't know what I'm going to do."

Stephen took another swig of beer and reached for the remote to the wide-screen TV. The mysterious email he had received the day before Grantham disappeared still haunted him. What was it again—to some doctor named Kramer, asking about a certain species of frog. Why didn't Grantham follow up with me? He absent-mindedly surfed through the satellite channels with the volume off in an attempt to get his mind off work.

"Dad, hang in there a little longer," said Roger. "You have to, for Mom's sake."

"I know. But she's accustomed to a rather extravagant lifestyle, and I don't want to disappoint her." Talking to Roger was good, but it brought back the bad history he was trying so desperately to escape. He had covered his tracks well.

"Son, when are we goin' fishing again?" Stephen asked, trying to change the subject. He remembered with fondness the times he had taken his two young sons fishing and sailing. They had received the same advantages during their upbringing, but his youngest son, Ben, was a drifter. He was used to the good life and could never hold down a job. Roger, on the other hand, had become a respected doctor who lived in Spokane with his wife and young daughter.

"Dad, you need to deal with the problem at hand." His son's words snapped him back to the present. "When are you going to tell Mom what's going on?"

Roger often asked this question. "I can't. It would be too much for her to take. You know she has a bad heart." He put down the remote, hoisted himself up, and wandered over to the window to see if anyone was on the fairway. He debated picking up some clubs and playing a few holes to unwind, but he knew it was too close to dinnertime. He wouldn't do that to his wife.

"I think it's time you went to the police." Roger's tone was grim.

Stephen knew his son disapproved of the way he was handling the problem. "No, I can't risk it. I really need this job. You know as well as I do that your mother and I are up to our eyeballs in debt. I was told not to involve the authorities. I have to do it their way. "

Stephen could hear a sigh on the other end of the line. "Well, Dad, you know what I think. Please be careful. This thing could get real nasty. But I support you, whatever you decide."

"Thanks, son. That means a lot."

"I love you, Dad."

The words brought a tear to Stephen's eye. "I love you too, son," he said as his voice choked up. "Thanks for taking the time to talk with me."

The phone clicked. Stephen hung his head in defeat. He knew that what he had done in the past was wrong. Even worse, the mistake he had made so long ago was causing his present life to be miserable.

"Time for dinner, dear," Amanda called.

Stephen had no appetite, but he shuffled to the door and into the kitchen.

12

Offices of Environ-Logging, Olympia

"Claire, are you sure these are the most recent files?" Lisa asked, swiping at a loose strand of hair that had fallen into her eyes.

"Yes, ma'am," Claire replied. "As far as I can tell."

Lisa frowned at Claire's revealing blouse but said nothing. The girl's attire had improved slightly since Lisa had talked to her about it, as her skirt was not as short and tight as before. Claire gently closed the door behind her, and Lisa stared at the towering pile of light green file folders. After her phone call with Carl, she had decided to investigate more thoroughly the history of the company's extensive logging operations across Washington State. For hours she had been perusing applications, environmental assessment reports, and timber plans for logging in new areas.

Based on Carl's description, Ed Grantham sounded brilliant and eccentric. What had happened to the man? Why hadn't Stephen shared more details about him? After all, he and Grantham had worked together for fifteen years. In the back of her mind, she still wanted to please Mr. Johnson by completing what Grantham had started regarding the new tracts.

She opened a file labeled "inspections" and noticed one that had recently been done. She reviewed it thoroughly and then set it aside. Hmm, she thought. *Grantham was good. If I'm going to impress the boss, I need to do better.* On impulse, she picked up the phone and dialed the number for the Office of Forests in Portland. "May I speak to Tom Moeller, please?" she asked. She munched a carrot stick while she waited on hold.

"Moeller here," said a deep voice.

"Hello, Mr. Moeller, my name is Lisa Stone. I have taken a new position with Environ-Logging as environmental project manager." She shifted in her chair.

"So I've heard. Nice to meet you, Ms. Stone."

"I noticed that you conducted an inspection a few months ago here at Environ-Logging. I was going over the records. Can we talk about it?"

"Sure . . . but everything seemed to be in order. As you are aware, Ed Grantham normally assisted me during those inspections. He really knew his stuff."

Lisa thought she heard a sigh. "Mr. Moeller, I just wanted to call to introduce myself and make sure you didn't have any other questions."

"Well, that's very nice of you, Ms. Stone."

His voice sounded intriguing, but she kept a professional tone. "I also wanted to assure you that, after reviewing the files, I am certain Environ-Logging is in strict compliance. We are maintaining our goals for reforestation, soil and water conservation, and maintenance of biodiversity and wildlife habitat."

An awkward pause followed. Had she said something wrong? Calling a government regulator out of the blue suddenly seemed foolish to her, but she decided she would be defensive and pushed the thought aside. "I also have the last three permits and applications if you need them," she continued. "They're multi-year permits, of course. As you said, Mr. Grantham knew his stuff and was very thorough."

Lisa had been boning up on the forest permit applications, which provided the DTR all the information they needed about the intended logging tract, including the reforestation plan for replanting trees taken for timber.

"I don't need those," said Tom. "I was able to get copies through the Mutual Forest Agreement."

Lisa paused. "The Mutual Forest Agreement? I'm sorry, I'm unfamiliar with that document." She felt embarrassed for not knowing what it was, but she decided to be honest with the stranger. Somehow, his voice sounded reassuring and calm.

"That's okay, Ms. Stone. Most people who are not from Washington State are unfamiliar with it. The Mutual Forest Agreement allows interested parties to look at all applications filed and comment on them." He paused. "Do you mind if I ask where you're from?"

Lisa curled a loose strand of hair around her finger and tried to picture the man on the other end of the line. "I'm from the Chicago area," she said, "but I did some summer internships in national parks. I am getting up to speed on the Washington regulations as quickly as I can."

"Ms. Stone, I didn't mean to imply that you were unfamiliar with the rules. Forgive me if I'm being too personal."

Lisa took a deep breath. "No, that's fine. Well, as I said, I just wanted to call to make sure you didn't need anything else from our files."

"Well, thank you again, Ms. Stone. I'm fine for now, but I'll let you know."

"Goodbye, Mr. Moeller."

"Goodbye, Ms. Stone. Oh, and in the future, you can just call me Tom. Bye."

Lisa reached for another carrot stick as she hung up the phone and again wondered what the man behind the voice looked like. She quickly brushed off the thought. She wasn't ready yet for another serious relationship. After all, she needed to devote all her attention to her new job. What's the point, anyway? she thought. He would probably just reject me, like the others.

She wondered if perhaps God meant for her to be single, just like the apostle Paul. She recalled reading Paul's words in 1 Corinthians about how an unmarried woman should be concerned about the Lord's affairs and "be devoted to the Lord in both body and spirit." She sighed, shook the thoughts from her head, and turned to the files with a renewed effort.

13

Office of Forests, Portland

Tom looked forward to chatting with Kevin, his college buddy, at the regional office of the DTR. Like him, Kevin was single, having recently divorced his high school sweetheart. He and Kevin got together on a regular basis to drink beer and commiserate about their failed love lives.

"Hey, Tom," Kevin answered cheerily when he picked up the phone. "How're you doing?"

"Great," said Tom. "Been on the slopes lately?" His mind flashed back to the last time he and Kevin had spent a weekend together skiing. They both loved the mountains and spent as much time as they could soaking up the breathtaking scenery and the brisk weather.

"Not yet. Not enough snow for my taste."

"I see. Well, hopefully we will get another snowfall soon." He paused for a moment and considered his next words. "Hey, I was hoping you had a minute to talk about the recent inspection at Environ-Logging."

"Sure," said Kevin. "What do you want to know?" Tom went on to fill in Kevin about the recent inspection and his misgivings about Environ-Logging.

"I don't know what to tell you, buddy," Kevin said at length. "They file their permit applications on time and have detailed timber plans. A while back, Ed Grantham told me they'd submitted a declaration of intent to abide by the latest SFI standards. That goes above and beyond any requirement for a logging company."

"Yes," said Tom, "I am aware they filed that declaration." He knew that when a company agreed to abide by the Sustainable Forestry

Initiative (SFI) standards, it meant that company promised to practice sustainable forestry techniques that would protect the forests for
future generations. "I think it's great that many logging companies
in this area make that declaration." He paused. "But, has Environ-
Logging actually conducted the required audit to determine compliance with those standards?"

"As a matter of fact, no," said Kevin. "I believe they were going
to do a third-party certification and hire a firm out of Olympia. Just
a minute—let me get the name for you." A pause ensued, and Tom
could hear papers rustling in the background. "Ah, here it is: 'Olympia Forestry Service.' You probably know that each audit team member has to have a degree in forestry and a minimum of two years of
experience."

Tom whistled. "I've heard of that consulting firm. They're very
competent. Can you send me their contact information?"

"Sure. But you know, Tom, that according to the SFI rules the
auditors won't release any information without the agreement of
the company."

"I'll contact Environ-Logging. They just hired a new girl to take
Grantham's place. In fact, she called me the other day. She sounds nice."

Kevin gave a good-natured chuckle. "Oh, I see. Finally in the
market now?"

Tom grunted. "Well, my ex just got remarried, so I might as
well be looking."

"One more thing, Tom. I visit the Environ-Logging sites each
year, and everything always seems to be in order. What's the problem, anyway?"

"There's no problem. I just want to do a more thorough review
of their operation this year." He paused. "Say, how's your newest
employee doing these days?"

Kevin laughed. "She's great. We're lucky to have her. She's very
efficient."

"I'm glad to hear that." Tom had recommended his former girl-
friend for a job at the DTR after she had graduated.

"You two ever think about getting back together?"

"No, I don't think so."

"Too bad! She'd be a great catch for some lucky guy."

Tom snickered. "Yeah, that's for sure. How about you, Kevin?"

"No, I'm happily single. I need to be more careful this time around. I've been visiting a church lately. Thought maybe I'd find a nice Christian girl." He chuckled.

Tom winced. He and his wife had attended church regularly, but his faith in God had been shattered after she left him for another man, and he had not been back to church since. "Well, be careful, Kevin. If you're going only for that reason, you'll come across as being phony."

The two chatted for another half hour about old times. When Tom hung up, he stared down at the people walking along the picturesque park in front of the Willamette River. The romantic walk was a favorite local hangout, and he noticed several couples holding hands and admiring the view. His thoughts flashed back to the first years of his marriage when he and his wife would stroll up and down that same walkway, holding hands just like the lovers he now observed. He had never imagined that he would be single again.

His gaze moved beyond to the scenic view of Mount Hood in the distance. His thoughts again returned to the Environ-Logging issue and the lovely voice of the woman named Lisa whom he had heard over the phone. He was determined to move on with his life, and perhaps meeting this mysterious woman was a step in the right direction. Besides, he was curious to see if there was anything incriminating in those audit files.

14

Offices of Environ-Logging, Olympia

Lisa was finally going to meet Tom Moeller, the man whose voice had sounded so intriguing over the phone. Tom had called and asked for a brief appointment. He had said that he was "in the area," but she wondered if there might be another reason for the visit.

She was getting her files together in anticipation of the questions that might arise when Claire informed her that Mr. Moeller had arrived. She pulled out her mirror, applied a little lipstick, and adjusted her hair. After all, first impressions are important, she thought. She heard a soft knock on the door and turned to see Claire usher in a tall and handsome man. He extended his hand and introduced himself as Tom Moeller.

Wow, what a hunk! she thought. Tom had curly raven-colored hair, a tan body, and dark brown eyes that sparkled with a mischievous light. His muscular physique indicated he frequently hit the gym. He was dressed stylishly in dark brown pants, a beige shirt, and a camel-colored blazer. She was glad she had worn one of her nicer suits today instead of her usual casual offsite garb.

"Please sit down, Mr. Moeller," Lisa said, motioning to the chair in front of her desk.

"It's Tom, remember?" He flashed a set of perfect white teeth.

"Of course," she replied, turning slightly red. His voice had a pleasant and soothing quality to it, just like it had over the phone. "And you can call me Lisa. Is there anything in particular you wanted to talk about?"

Tom shifted in his chair. "Well, I want you to know that this is certainly not an inspection of any kind."

"Thank you, Tom. I wondered about that."

"Actually, I came for a couple of reasons. First, as I mentioned, I was in the area and wanted to meet the person who took Grantham's place. Your company is large, and I spend quite a bit of time on all the paperwork that you file."

"Yes, I certainly know there's a lot of paperwork. I am happy to help you with any questions you might have." She stopped, sensing he wanted to continue.

"Also, I recently found out that Grantham had informed the DTR that Environ-Logging was going to try to get SFI certification. Do you know anything about that?"

Lisa pursed her lips. Fortunately, she had just read about this in one of the files Grantham had left. "Yes. I'm not surprised. Mr. Grantham seemed dedicated to ensuring forest sustainability and maintaining the highest level of environmental self-awareness. Do you have a question about it?"

"I'd like your permission to get a copy of the latest audit when it's available." He paused. "It's required by the SFI guidelines."

Intriguing, Lisa thought. He could have asked for that over the phone. "Of course, we have no secrets here," she said. "But I don't believe the audit has taken place yet."

"That's all right, I understand," said Tom. "I would appreciate getting a copy when it is complete." He gave her a smile that seemed to light up the room.

"Sure." Lisa felt herself turning red every time she responded. He seemed to notice her reaction, but perhaps his good looks produced that reaction in many girls. He was probably used to it.

"So," Tom said, "how do you like working at Environ-Logging so far?" He leaned forward in his chair.

"Oh, it's fine, but there's a lot to learn. I only graduated from college a few months ago."

"Really? From where?"

"I got my master's from the University of Illinois. As I mentioned to you on the phone, I grew up in Chicago." She fidgeted with her cross necklace. Why does he seem to be so interested in me?

"That sure is a long way from here."

"Yes, but I love the outdoors and nature. I—" She abruptly stopped herself. Why was she willing to reveal so much to this virtual stranger? His chocolate eyes were mesmerizing, and she found herself looking dreamily into them. She shook off any romantic thoughts and decided it was time to change the subject.

"So . . . how about you?"

"I graduated five years ago from the University of California at Berkeley with a degree in Forestry and Resource Management. I guess we have a similar passion for the outdoors."

"Yes, it sounds that way, doesn't it?" Tom made no response, and an awkward silence ensued. "So, Tom," she said at length, "is there anything else that I can do for you?"

"No, you've been very helpful." He rose, slowly extended his hand, and shook hers. He turned to leave but then halted and turned to her. "I'm here in Olympia just for the evening, and then I drive home to Portland tomorrow. I hope you don't think I'm being presumptuous, but would you like to have dinner with me tonight?"

Lisa's eyes widened and her mouth dropped open. Her heart pounded and she felt weak. "I . . . guess so," she stammered.

"Great! I'm so glad. What time is convenient for you?"

"How about . . . seven? Oh, and you need to know that I'm mostly vegetarian. But I also eat seafood. There's a fancy term for me—a pesco-vegetarian."

Tom's eyes crinkled and he flashed a grin. "Someone told me there's a great restaurant called The Italian Place. How does that sound?"

"Yes, I've heard of it. I'll meet you there at seven, okay?"

Claire escorted Tom back downstairs to the lobby. Lisa bounced on her cushy office chair, still stunned at the sudden invitation. It had only been a few months since her breakup with her previous boyfriend. Her heart still ached, and she certainly didn't feel ready for any kind of new relationship. She didn't even know what it was about her that drove men away. Still, her mind told her that she should be rational and open to new friendships—and something about this guy seemed different.

On impulse, she pulled out her cell phone and pushed the speed dial. "Linda," she said breathlessly. "Guess what? I have a date!"

15

Flowering Gardens, Queens, New York City

Dr. Ted Dougherty powered up the computer in his office before wandering into the kitchen and pulling out the leftover roast beef his wife had prepared the night before. He and his wife had moved to the exclusive planned community of Flowering Gardens about five years before. Their Tudor-style house was nestled near a large park in the quiet development built to resemble a traditional English village. It was now nine o'clock, and he had just arrived home after completing his rounds at the hospital and checking in on Doris and Jerry.

Jerry had improved slightly since he had put him on the feeding tube. Doris hadn't taken him up on his offer to stay at a place nearby, and she was looking worse for wear. He knew it was just a flophouse, but he thought she could get some sleep there instead of being wakened most of the night by nurses checking in on Jerry. However, time was growing short for the boy, and Doris knew it. It had taken a lot of courage for her to seek help, and he admired her tenacity.

The NPC disease was no respecter of social status or wealth. Just last spring, a seven-year-old boy had died at his father's luxurious estate, surrounded by loved ones. The father was the chairman of the board of a large national bank.

He wasn't feeling tired yet, so he decided to try to chat with Dr. Kramer. He knew that with the three hours' time difference, his colleague would just be nearing the end of his long workday and would probably be sitting in his office catching up on email. He was curious to find out more about the new discovery with the rare species of frog that Dr. Kramer had related a few days ago. He poured a mug of beer and fixed a sandwich before sauntering into his office.

He dialed Dr. Kramer's number on Skype, and soon the familiar face appeared on the screen. "Hi, Ray," he said. He took a bite of his beef sandwich and a swig of German lager.

"Hi, Ted," said Dr. Kramer. He had dark rings under his eyes. "How's the boy doing?"

"I don't think it will be much longer now. It's a bloody shame."

"I agree. But I might be onto something here."

"Tell me about it, Ray." He propped his feet up on the desk and settled back.

"I isolated the protein from the frog's skin, and it's reacting positively to the saliva of one of my NPC patients."

Dr. Dougherty cocked his head. "Wow! I can't believe it."

"I can hardly believe it myself. I need to run more tests, of course."

"Yes, of course. I assume you've changed dosage rates and concentrations?" Dr. Kramer nodded. "Well, sounds like you're on the right track, my man. After that, what are your next steps? Do you have enough information for a new drug application?"

Dr. Kramer's shoulders slumped and he groaned. "Sure, but I've been doing some research into it. The procedure to get a drug approved by the Food and Drug Administration is long and complicated. On top of that, there aren't enough of this species of frog available to do an adequate research study." Dr. Kramer's downcast face made him realize that many more patients would die before a cure was available.

"Cheer up, man. I can help you with the FDA application. There's a program in which you can accelerate the approval. I've done it before with another colleague. It's not that difficult."

Dr. Kramer brightened. "That sounds great! I have to submit my FDA application under the term 'investigational new drug.' Are you familiar with that?"

"Yes, of course. The application for faster approval will be separate than the one for the investigational new drug, but they can be done at the same time. We will need a drug company to sponsor us." He paused to sip his beer before continuing. "But we need a source of frogs. Where could we get them?"

"Bad news on that front. I had a couple of students do some web research on the latest sightings. A group was spotted in the wild three years ago in the Amazon rain forest, but there have been no other sightings since then. You wouldn't believe what I had to do just to get the one sample I'm using."

"Keep trying to locate a source. It's the key to getting the FDA approval." Dr. Dougherty took the last bite of his sandwich and tipped his mug toward the screen.

"Believe me, I'll try. I've certainly been praying about it a lot."

He forced a smile. "That's great, Ray. I hope your prayers are answered. I better sign off now and get ready for bed."

He ended the call and rose slowly from his chair. These religious nuts were getting to him. He couldn't understand how they could believe in something they couldn't see or feel. He felt that a true scientist should not have such silly notions. Cold, hard facts—that was all he believed in.

Still, he was curious about the strong faith he had seen in people like Doris. She certainly seemed sincere in her belief, but the poor, uneducated woman probably didn't know any better. Yet his own wife had strong faith, and so obviously did Dr. Kramer. He vaguely recalled his mother talking about "the presence of God" on the few times they attended church as a family, mainly at Christmas and Easter.

Could there really be something to it? he thought. Or is it all just foolishness? He sighed as he put away his dish and headed for bed. *Maybe I should try to find out more.*

16

Downtown Olympia, near Capitol Lake

"You look lovely," Tom said to Lisa as the host escorted them to a table upstairs by the window. The Italian Place was small but posh, with hardwood floors and antique furniture. Each table was candlelit, which made it quite romantic.

Tom and Lisa gazed out at the harbor and the boats on Capitol Lake. He was amazed by how different she looked in her simple yet elegant black dress. The slim five-foot-five beauty had swept her long, auburn hair back with a cocoa-colored pearl comb that matched her pearl necklace and earrings. He had been taken by her good looks at the office, but he was blown away by her appearance tonight.

Lisa perused the menu. "I've never eaten here before. Have you?"

"No, but I was told that all the food is fresh and homemade."

The waiter approached to take their drink order. She ordered a Perrier while he ordered a beer on tap.

"I can't decide between the vegetable lasagna or the fettuccini primavera," Lisa said with a charming frown.

"Those both sound great," said Tom. "But, you know, I think I'll have the fettuccini with grilled chicken. How about an appetizer?"

The waiter returned with their drinks, and they placed their order.

"How have you adjusted to life here in Olympia?" Tom asked. He had noticed that she wasn't wearing a wedding ring and was anxious to learn more about this attractive girl.

"I've adjusted pretty well. It's a nice place to live, so far."

Tom stared into her exotic wide-set eyes. They shone like copper, and he noticed that her tawny hair had shimmering gold highlights.

Her fair complexion was smooth, like marble. He hadn't dated such a stunning girl in quite a while. At least, since his divorce. Most of the women he went out with were smart but not exactly beauties. This one was smart and beautiful.

"Do you live far from work?" he asked, taking a sip from his mug.

"I live only about a half hour away, off Highway 101, near Grassy Park."

"Oh, I've heard of that place. It's near a college."

"Yes. I suppose the rent is cheaper there because of all the college students. What about you? How do you like Portland?"

Tom leaned back and folded his fingers in his lap. "Oh, it's fine. I have a small apartment near downtown, so I don't have far to travel either. I've been there about four years now. It's pleasant enough in the summer, but the winters are chilly. You'll discover that about Olympia as well."

"Well, Chicago wasn't exactly balmy. That breeze across Lake Michigan can pack an icy punch."

"So, tell me again what brought you out here. You said you liked nature?" He was dying to know if she had a boyfriend and hoped she might reveal something if he kept asking questions.

"Yes, I love the outdoors. I hated the congested roads and air pollution of Chicago. I worked for the National Park Service every summer I could just to escape the city." Her striking brownish-green eyes glowed as she spoke.

"Out of curiosity, which park?"

"Well, I spent one summer in Grand Teton National Park, and another at Yosemite National Park in California."

"Oh, I was in Yosemite one summer, too! Probably much earlier than you." Tom was sure he wouldn't have missed the enchanting girl if she had been there at the same time as him. "So, how did you get interested in forestry?"

"I became fascinated with the controversy surrounding the Northern Spotted Owl."

"Yes, I remember that well. It certainly had a great impact on the logging industry."

Lisa delicately folded her napkin in her lap and looked at him intently. "I did my master's thesis primarily on that owl. It is one of those rare species that relies on the old-growth forest for its habitat."

Tom munched on a piece of garlic bread and eyed her. "If you don't mind my asking, why did you choose to work for a logging company like Environ-Logging?"

She tilted her head back and laughed lightly. Her smile was captivating. "You asked the same question many of my activist friends have asked. It's true, this job seems to be a little against my nature. I actually considered working for the government. But Environ-Logging seemed to be a perfect match for my goal to serve both people and nature."

"How's that?"

"Well, I hate the indiscriminate cutting of trees. But if they have to be cut, I want to make sure it's done in accordance with environmental laws."

"I can certainly agree with that." He didn't want to ask about her knowledge of the laws, as that seemed to be a sensitive subject with her.

They chatted until the food came, and then ate quietly. Finally, he ventured to ask the question that had been preying on his mind. "Lisa, I was wondering if I could see you again—when I'm in town, that is." He was concerned she had accepted his dinner invitation out of politeness, but if she agreed to go out with him again, he would know she was interested in him for personal reasons—not just business.

She blushed. "That would be nice, Tom," she said, a noodle hanging adorably from her mouth.

He grinned sheepishly and chugged down the last of his beer. This would certainly be an interesting year.

17

Waters Park, near downtown Olympia

Stephen stamped his feet in the cold night air and shoved his hands deeper into his pockets. He had agreed to meet Mack Taylor at Waters Park at midnight to avoid discussing their clandestine plans at work. He had been pacing back and forth for more than half an hour and was eager to get back home to his nice warm bed.

He glanced around at the large, heavily forested public park. The area was not well used at night, and the remote place off the public trail where they typically met was always deserted. At last, he saw the oversized brute step out of the dark forest into the small moonlit area where he was standing.

"What's so urgent that you need to see me at this time?" he demanded, hugging his arms to stay warm.

"Now, now, Stevie," said Taylor. "Calm down. I just wanted to talk in an atmosphere of complete privacy where we wouldn't be disturbed."

Stephen grunted. He hated all the sneaking around and late-night clandestine meetings in remote parks like this one. He especially hated the condescending tone of this little worm who knew he disliked being called "Stevie."

"We need to let you know of a slight change in plans," Taylor said with a wry grin.

Stephen scowled. "What does that mean?"

"Someone's been sniffing around. We need you to do something else for us."

Stephen felt a blast of anger. What next? He had already dug a hole so deep that he would never get out of it. But he seemed to have no other choice.

"We need you to go into a file and change some wording in a document. I have it all written down here." He handed Stephen a piece of paper.

"What's this all about?"

"You know the rules, Stevie. No questions. Just do what we ask and there won't be any trouble." Taylor's face was hard and devoid of emotion.

Stephen's blood started to boil. He hated removing files and tampering with them. He hated this cold-hearted henchman and what he represented. In fact, he hated everything that was going on. He swallowed hard, pulled his shoulders back, and faced the man squarely.

"Now, look here, Mack. I think I've done enough for you already. I've already forged documents and removed critical environmental information. Now you want me to change another file?" He put his hands on his hips and raised his voice. "Get someone else to do your dirty work."

Taylor narrowed his eyes. "Stevie, Stevie. Have we forgotten our little secret? We can make life unbearable for you, and you know it."

Stephen groaned and stared at the ground. He wanted to cry, but he wouldn't give this lowlife the satisfaction of ever seeing him weak.

"Besides," said Taylor, "aren't you being well compensated? You don't want to lose that nice home now, do you? How would your wife feel?"

Stephen glowered and pointed his index finger. "Don't you dare mention my family." He opened the paper and read the contents. "Whose file is this? Grantham's again?"

"Just follow the instructions and do what you're told, and there won't be any trouble."

Taylor started to leave, but Stephen mustered his courage and blocked the way. "Just tell me one thing," he said. "How long is this going to go on?"

"Not long, Stevie, not long."

"I'm tired of the lies. And this new girl—Lisa—she's bound to find out something sooner or later." He turned away. "We're just postponing the inevitable."

Taylor curled his lip. "Don't worry about that gal. We're watchin' her. She won't cause any trouble." He waved his hand at Stephen as if dismissing him.

Stephen balled up his fists. The thought of anything happening to Lisa made his blood boil. He had grown fond of the young lady. She was so inexperienced and innocent, and she certainly didn't deserve to get involved in the mess he had created. He wanted to say something vicious, but Taylor's huge bulk moved toward him.

He stepped aside to let Taylor pass and watched until the man disappeared from view. He shivered, and not just because of the cold. He was fed up, but he saw no escape from this nightmare that seemed to grow worse every year. His suspicions about what had happened to Grantham were probably correct. He knew that Johnson and Taylor would stop at nothing to keep their dirty secrets.

The wind bit into him like piercing needles. He hung his head and slowly trudged back down the trail. He had to face the fact that he was simply a coward. He didn't have the courage to stand up to Johnson and his brute. He would call his son tomorrow and discuss his options. Could there possibly be a way out of this mess?

18

GreenForests Headquarters, Kirkland, Washington

Carl and Betty sat hunched over several boxes of files on the folding table. The six-foot-one former track star towered over the short woman as they gazed at an aerial photo of the Environ-Logging tracts. Next to the photo were stacks of binders holding Environ-Logging's testimony at the last legislative hearing.

"So, what did Johnson say again at the last hearing?" Carl asked.

Betty looked at some papers and cleared her throat. "Here is the quote: 'My company has one of the best environmental records in the nation, and we are extremely careful to protect streams and wildlife. We hire only the top firms to do research and development on the newest logging techniques that minimize impact on habitat.'"

Carl whistled. "He sure has a way with words. His lobbyists must make a mint!"

"Yes, and there are a lot of them." Betty got up to stretch and walked over to the refrigerator to get a Coke and some chocolate-chip cookies. She offered some cookies to Carl and a root beer.

"No thanks," he said, waving a hand over the table. "Just look— the photo shows that hundreds of acres of prime forest have been decimated."

Betty munched on her cookie. "That lawyer hired by Environ-Logging brought solid testimony against the last clear-cutting bill."

"How does the final language of the bill read?"

Betty again flipped through some of the binders. "Here it is: 'Trees in designated riparian areas may be cut at the direction of a certified forestry expert.'"

Carl rubbed his chin. "Riparian buffer regions are sensitive areas along streams and rivers that need protection. As you know, those areas provide shade, protection, and travel corridors for forest animals. They also stabilize stream banks and trap sediment during high water flows."

"Yes . . . I know all that. What's your point?"

"That language used to simply say, 'Trees must be planted in designated riparian areas.' I never saw any language about a certified forest expert deciding anything. Where did that come from?"

"Hmm," Betty said with a smirk. "I wonder how many 'experts' they have on their payroll. Sounds like they can do just about anything they want."

"I heard there were some last-minute changes to the bill before it was approved. Which senator added that language?" Carl stood up and started pacing in front of the window.

Betty consulted the index to the big legislative binder. "Wells. He's a new guy."

"I have a hunch that Johnson got to Wells. I know that company is up to no good. Johnson probably bought his way up the chain so he can rub elbows with senators and congressmen to get what he wants." Carl slammed his fist into his palm. "He makes a bad name for all the other logging companies that do follow the rules. We've got to find some evidence we can use against him."

During the next several hours, they pored over the testimony to try to discover anything that could implicate Environ-Logging. It quickly became obvious that the company had hired some of the best lawyers in the business. The testimony was flawless.

"It's no good," Carl said. "We can't find anything this way. They cover their tracks too well." He paused, and then slapped his forehead. "I have it! Why don't we introduce new riparian legislation?"

Betty smiled. "That sounds good. What do you want it to say?"

Carl scratched his head. "We know that the riparian buffer region is an area on either side of a stream. The buffer extends from the outer edge of the bank."

"Yes . . . and?"

"Let's introduce an amendment to the bill that increases the size of the buffer region and requires all trees to be maintained and not destroyed. And we take out the words about the 'expert.'"

Betty stared at him. "The company lobbyists would certainly attack such an amendment. It would significantly reduce the areas the company could log."

"Of course. That's why we have to be careful about the wording. We need some language that won't red-flag the amendment." Carl strode over to his desk and started typing on his laptop.

Betty looked over his shoulder as he typed. "Do you really think we can slide this under the radar of those fancy lawyers that Environ-Logging has on the payroll?"

Carl stopped typing and looked up. "We can try. Of course, we'll have to pull a few strings to get this bill introduced the proper way. We'll meet with every influential legislator that will hear us out. Someone has to do something to stop this greedy company. It may as well be us!"

19

Offices of Environ-Logging, Olympia

Lisa stared at the towering piles of paper on her desk. Each pile represented years of applications and permits, and she had spent weeks combing through them. She had carefully earmarked pages that summarized the environmental impacts of the logging operations.

She scratched her head. Each of the last fifty reports revealed that the company's operations had resulted in absolutely no environmental impact. For such a large area affected by Environ-Logging, it seemed odd that no habitat for endangered or threatened species had been discovered.

She called Claire into her office. "Have you double-checked with the IT folks?" she asked. "Are you sure all of Grantham's computer files and backup disks are gone?"

"Yes, ma'am," said Claire, looking perplexed. "I can't explain it. I'm sorry." She remained standing in the doorway. Lisa noticed her blouse was tamer than usual but that the mini-skirt was back.

Lisa waved her hand over her desk. "There's not even a trace of personal log notes or data, so I have to believe all these reports are accurate. I have no other information to go on."

She grabbed the latest report. It was bound in dark green and sported a large tree logo and the name "Olympia Forestry Service." She turned to some of the earmarked pages and read them out loud, more to herself than Claire. "The proposed action does not have a probable significant adverse impact on the environment. An Environmental Impact Statement is not required."

She paused and stared at Claire. "This is simply incredible. Every report has the same answers to the questions. Listen to this: Question #8. List any threatened or endangered species known to be on or near the site. Answer: None."

Claire's shoulders dropped. "Ma'am, I think you should be discussing this with Mr. Hall. He's been here a long time. He might have the answers you're seeking."

Lisa nodded. "Of course, Claire. Thanks for listening."

"Any time, ma'am." Clair backed out, her stilettos clicking as she closed the door.

Lisa twisted a strand of hair. Not only could she not find an explanation for the company's clean record, but the reports had missing sections to boot. To the casual observer everything seemed to be in order, but on careful reading one could see the wording was disjointed. The page numbering was odd in places, and there were tiny shreds of paper on the inside binders that indicated some of the pages might have been removed. The missing pages were always in the endangered species sections.

Claire was right, Lisa thought. It was time to talk to Stephen again. She considered him a friend now—even a mentor—and not just her boss. He treated her like a colleague of equal stature. She respected and admired him, yet even two months into the job, he seemed as puzzling and eccentric as ever. However, he had worked at Environ-Logging since day one, and if anyone knew what was going on, it would be him.

She positioned different-colored post-it notes on each of the suspicious sections and speed-dialed his number. She took a deep breath and picked up the phone. She never knew if she was bothering him too much.

"Hello," said the voice on the line.

"Stephen, this is Lisa. Do you have a few minutes to discuss something? I've been reviewing the last five years of applications and reports. Do you know why they do not show a single impact to the environment from our logging operations?"

There was a pause before Stephen answered. "Yes . . . why don't you come to my office to discuss it." He hung up the phone.

Lisa gathered the reports and marched down the hall to his office. She knocked on his door, boldly entered before Stephen could respond, and sat down on the chair in front of his desk. "Stephen, I have a problem," she said with a look of exasperation on her face. She noticed he had dark rings under his eyes and that lines creased his face.

"Yes, what is it?" he said in a weary tone, not bothering to look up.

"Well, as I said, I've been reviewing the last five years of environmental data from the forest permit applications. I just can't understand why they don't show a single impact to the environment due to our logging operations. It doesn't make sense."

Stephen looked up at her but remained silent.

"For example," Lisa continued, "I expect there are endangered or threatened species in the area." Stephen's eyes glazed over, but she continued. "But I never see anything about that in the reports." She stood and handed him the report that was opened to an earmarked page. "How do you explain that?"

Stephen scanned the pages. "Calm down, Lisa. I have a simple answer for you."

Lisa sat down and put her hand under her chin.

"We are fortunate to have excellent consultants. They tell us where any endangered species habitat might be located, and we avoid them like the plague."

"But how can they know for sure?"

"Lisa, believe me when I say that we are not impacting any endangered species. We are careful, and our consultants back us up."

Lisa looked into his tired eyes and saw resignation in them.

"But . . . shouldn't there be something in the reports if they find evidence of—"

Stephen glared at her. Obviously, it was time to go. She picked up the reports, but then hesitated. "May I ask one more thing?"

Stephen was looking down at an opened file folder and made no reply. She opened a report but didn't show it to him. "I've found strange symbols or initials in the margin of this page, like a code or something. It reads 'L.l.' What do you make of that?"

Stephen looked up. For a moment Lisa thought his eyes flickered in recognition, but immediately his expression cleared. "I don't see how it could mean anything. Why can't you trust what we've done? Contact the consultants if you want. I'll give you their information."

Lisa put her hands on her hips. "Yes, I think I will."

"I'm sorry," Stephen said in a softer tone. "I've been preoccupied with something lately and should not have been so gruff. Please don't worry about it. We know what we're doing. Now, I really need to get back to work."

Lisa returned to her office, but the nagging questions remained. Normally Stephen was helpful, but today he sounded anything but reassuring. She wondered why he was backing the consultants. It was inconceivable that they would be changing information so as not to create delays in operations, and bribery was out of the question. There was too much at stake for everyone concerned.

Her head was pounding as she tried to wrap her mind around the dilemma. Something was terribly wrong, but she couldn't put her finger on it. Suddenly, she clapped her hands as an idea came to her. The cabin where Grantham had lived probably had an electric hook up. She could find it that way.

She picked up the phone and dialed the electric company. After making her request, she heard a strange clicking noise on the line. She made a mental note to ask Claire about it in the morning.

20

Children's Hospital, New York City

Dr. Ted Dougherty heard soft sobbing coming from the hallway outside Jerry's hospital room. He entered to find Doris sitting on the empty bed. She was hunched over and weeping into a pillow. He quietly walked to the bed and sat down next to her.

Doris lifted her head. He eyes were puffy and red and her face was swollen. "I can't believe he's gone, doc," she croaked through heavy sobs.

"I am so sorry, Doris. There was nothing more we could do." He was surprised when she reached up and put her calloused hand over his.

Jerry had died the previous day of complications from NPC. Toward the end, he had contracted a pulmonary infection. Fluid had built up in his lungs, which eventually led to pneumonia. Dr. Dougherty knew that NPC was an inherited disease of the autosomal recessive kind, in which both parents had to be carriers of the mutated gene in order for the child to have the disease. A genetic counselor would have discussed all of this with Doris and Jerry's father—if he could have been found. Dr. Dougherty wanted to ask Doris if she had any other children, as there was a chance they could also carry the gene, but he didn't have the heart to do so right now.

"Doris, do you have somewhere to go?" He had already discussed with his wife the possibility of putting Doris up in their home until she could get settled.

"Doc, you've been so kind to me and Jerry. I appreciate everythin', really I do. I got kinfolk here, so don't worry. They're poor, like me, but I expect they'll take me in all right."

He nodded, feeling a bit relieved. "Would you like me to take you there?"

"That's okay, doc." Tears welled up in her eyes again.

"There's a support group for NPC families that I'd like you to contact. I think it will help." He reached for the note in his lab coat pocket that contained a hastily scribbled number and handed it to her.

"He was such a bright boy, you know. But nobody understood him like I did." Doris rubbed her eyes with a well-worn handkerchief and looked up at him. "What about the bill, doc? I ain't got no money, you know."

Dr. Dougherty took her limp hand. "We've taken care of everything, including the funeral. There's no need to worry, Doris." He had set up a special fund for victims of NPC, and over the years he had contributed substantially from his own pocket. He had also convinced a number of his wealthier patients and doctor associates to make hefty contributions.

Doris wiped her eyes and sniffled. "That sure is a blessing, doc. You know, I don't always understand God's ways, but this had to be His will."

He smiled at her, though he thought talking about God's will in this situation was absurd. His pager suddenly buzzed, and he glanced down. He had taken the opportunity to call a psychologist friend who specialized in grief counseling, and she had happened to be available that afternoon. She was now on her way up. This was his excuse to exit the awkward conversation.

"Doris, there's someone coming who would like to talk to you. Do you mind?"

She looked down at the floor and sniffled. "I guess not."

He excused himself and went outside to wait for the counselor. The elevator doors soon opened, and a dark-haired woman with fair skin and freckles shuffled toward him. He greeted her and led her inside the room.

After making the introductions, he excused himself and closed the door softly behind him. The best course of action now was to let the two talk it out. Doris desperately needed an emotional outlet, and he needed a break.

He trudged to the elevator and rode up to the rooftop parking lot. He quickly located his 1958 light blue Aston Martin, which he had given to himself on his thirtieth anniversary with the hospital. He knew it cost too much and felt a little guilty each time he revved up the six-cylinder engine to race home. But the car was worth a fortune as a collector's item, because a later model had become famous in the James Bond movies.

When he got home, his wife greeted him with a hug. As he returned the embrace, the pain of losing Jerry suddenly came rushing over him and he began to sob. He lowered his head onto her shoulder, which soon became wet from the huge torrent.

"What is it, dear?" she said as she stroked his hair to help him calm down. "Why are you so sad?"

He lifted his head and looked at her. "Why do the young ones have to be cut down in the flower of their youth? We have to find a cure for NPC—and soon." He squeezed her one more time and then pulled away to mop his face with a handkerchief.

"God has His ways, dear. They are mysterious, but we must trust Him."

His eyes flashed. "No, I can't accept that!" He slammed his hand down on the kitchen countertop. His wife jumped and stared at him.

He had seen too many children like Jerry who had been taken by this horrid affliction. For him, there was simply no possible reason why God would choose to take away these children in such a manner. He would believe in the cold, hard facts of research and not some blind faith. He had worked hard to find a cure for NPC and had even isolated the gene that caused the disease. But none of that could save Jerry.

He marched into his office and opened his laptop. He drummed his fingers as he waited for the machine to boot up, and then punched in the number for Dr. Kramer. It was time to take drastic action!

21

Tacoma, Washington

Lisa parked in a restaurant parking lot in Tacoma, about half-way between Kirkland and Olympia. A light rain had made the streets slick, and traffic was slow. A dark brown Range Rover pulled into the lot, and the driver rolled down the window. She immediately recognized the face.

"Hi, Carl, long time no see!" she said. She climbed into the front seat of the Range Rover and threw her backpack into the back seat. She noticed that Carl had his laptop open and was looking at a GPS system.

"Hi, Lisa," he said. "You look great! Want a donut?" He held up a paper bag.

"No, thanks. Still eating junk food I see." She flashed him a smile.

"You bet. Now, from the coordinates you gave me, it should take a little less than two hours to get there. It'll be dark then, just like you asked."

Lisa nodded. He was as handsome as ever—tanned and dressed in a neatly pressed light green sports shirt and khaki pants. His arms were as muscular as she remembered, and his golden-blond hair and sky-blue eyes still tantalized her. "Thanks for coming on such short notice. I didn't know who else to ask."

"I gather from the cloak-and-dagger routine that you are beginning to suspect your own company of something. Am I correct?"

Lisa frowned and remained silent. She didn't want to give him any more ammunition to harangue her about her job choice.

"How did you manage to locate Grantham's old cabin?" he asked.

"I was able to convince the electric company that I needed to obtain some important work files from his cabin. They told me the location."

"How clever! Did you ever talk to Stephen?" He glanced sideways at her.

She swallowed and turned her head toward the fogged window. "Yes, I talk to Stephen a lot, but thought I should handle this on my own. I don't want to cause trouble for him. He seems to have enough problems of his own." She feared telling Carl about her suspicions in regard to Stephen. She admired him, but at this point, she didn't trust anyone at Environ-Logging.

They chatted about old times until they approached the cutoff to Eltout Forest. Carl consulted his laptop. "According to the GPS," he said, "we make a right turn here and then go about a quarter mile and turn left."

Dark shadows appeared on the road as the sunlight faded through the mist and the forest enveloped them like a shroud. The wet road became one-lane and then little more than a path. Occasionally, they saw the flash of eyes as white-tailed deer jumped out of the way of the car.

A small log cabin emerged in the darkness. Carl stopped the car in front and reached into the back seat for his heavy-duty industrial flashlight. Lisa pulled a small LED flashlight out of her backpack.

"We should pray first," said Carl.

"Good idea." Lisa bowed her head.

"Lord," Carl's said, his voice quivering, "we don't know what we will find here, but we ask you to protect us and to show us what to do. Thanks for your help."

They stepped into the cool moist air and were greeted by the babbling of tree frogs and cicadas. Lisa pulled her jacket closer, and they shone their lights at the front door of the cabin. They approached the door and expected it to be locked, but to their surprise it swung open easily. They looked at each other.

Carl shone his light into the empty room and held his nose. "The place reeks of smoke. We'll keep the door open."

Lisa followed, trying not to cough. "There must have been quite a fire in here."

In the dim light, the place looked ransacked. Books and clothes were strewn on the floor, and a small wooden closet was half empty. A slashed mattress was in one corner and drawers upended in the tiny kitchen. They poked their flashlights into every corner and crevice of the room.

"Looks like someone was in a hurry to leave . . . or he was burglarized." Lisa noticed Carl looking into the blackened stove. "Do you see anything, Carl?"

"Yeah. The fire was in here." He reached inside and pulled out a charred notebook cover. He handed it to Lisa, who opened it carefully and shone her flashlight to examine the contents.

"It looks like the remains of a notebook—like the kind used for field notes." Lisa stifled a sneeze as she turned the brittle pages. "I can hardly breathe. Let's get out of here." She stuffed the book into her backpack and started to leave, but then saw that Carl was crouching down on the floor.

"Wait a minute," he said.

"What is it?" she asked. She shined her light on the place where Carl was kneeling.

"Come look at this," he said, motioning to her.

She looked closer and saw dark red spots on the floorboards. They appeared to be a lighter color than the surrounding wood.

"There may have been a rug here at one time," said Carl. "I think this might be blood." He rubbed the area with his hand. "Wait, I feel something odd. One of the slats is loose. See if you can find something to pry it up with."

Lisa opened a closet in the kitchen and grabbed a small pickaxe and shovel. She handed them to Carl. "Here, try one of these."

Carl pried the floorboard using the sharp end of the pickaxe. After several tries, he finally pulled one end up and shone his light underneath. "It's another notebook, but larger," he said. He reached down and pulled out a worn gray spiral notebook. He shook off the dust and handed it to Lisa.

Lisa opened it and adjusted the flashlight. "It looks like some type of journal, but many of the pages are torn. There are some entries with dates and scientific names. I wonder why it was hidden under the floor?"

"I think we'd better look at it later when we have more light." Carl replaced the floorboard and tapped it down with the blunt end of the axe.

"Yeah, let's get out of here. This place gives me the creeps." Lisa stuffed the notebook into her backpack. They walked outside into the darkness, still hearing the sound of crickets chirping and frogs croaking.

When they got into their car, they heard a low whistle that did not sound natural. "What was that?" Lisa asked, looking around nervously.

"It must have been that hoot owl." Carl's voice was calm, but his face betrayed a wary caution.

They jumped into the car and peeled down the pitch-black lane.

"That's funny," Carl said, looking into the rearview mirror. "I thought I saw something back there, where we just were."

Lisa looked back. "I don't see anything. But I'm glad to get away from that place. Something odd happened there, and we need to figure out what it was."

22

Offices of Environ-Logging, Olympia

Clive Johnson placed his German coffee mug on the desk next to the silver-framed photo of his wife. He gazed at the latest stock trends on his flat-screen monitor and clasped his hands in delight at the **sight** of his soaring stock price. He switched the screen and checked **that** all his offshore accounts were intact. He would splurge more than usual at the mountain lodge that weekend with his girlfriend.

The phone buzzed, and his secretary announced that Taylor had arrived. He turned away from the screen and looked at the door. Mack Taylor strutted in several seconds later and headed to the coffee bar. He was dressed in his usual scruffy black jeans, loud cowboy shirt, and pointed boots.

"What's going on?" Johnson demanded. He jerked his thumb at Taylor to instruct him to sit down.

"Just wanna update you on the girl," said Taylor, taking a seat. "Tailed her and her ex to Grantham's cabin."

"What?" Johnson jumped up from his chair, his eyes blazing. "How on earth did they find that cabin? And what do you mean, her 'ex'?" He glared at Taylor and then stomped to the coffee bar. He poured another cup and plopped down in a plush mahogany armchair.

"Now, listen, boss. I don't know how they found the cabin, but her ex-boyfriend is that pest Carl Ward who is giving our lawyer guys fits right now." He took a bite of the croissant he had taken and wiped his mouth with his sleeve.

"That's the fellow who went to Senator Wells last week to push through a new piece of legislation. He's trouble." Johnson slammed his coffee cup down and wagged his bejeweled index finger. "Didn't you do a background check on that girl? That piece of information should have come up."

Taylor shrugged. "It was too far back. Sorry, boss."

Johnson's lobbyists had informed him of Ward's anti-logging activist group, which was pushing a new bill in the Washington senate. In combing through the three hundred-page document, the lobbyists had discovered an obscure paragraph that would cause delays in logging by creating a burden in riparian areas. Fortunately, they had been able to find it in time and talk to the legislators. The lobbying team cost a mint, but they generally delivered what he paid for.

"So, did they find anything in the cabin?" Johnson asked. He was speaking more calmly now, but his eyes still held a warning.

"They couldn't have," said Taylor, "because we swept it clean of any trace of Grantham or his stuff. I went inside myself after they left, and it looked the way we wanted it—like he was leaving in a hurry to visit a sick relative. But—" Taylor paused and lowered his voice. "There was a loose floorboard under a rug that I removed, and—"

Johnson spit out a mouthful of coffee and cursed. "A what?"

Taylor blushed and studied the toe of his boot. "I'm not sure it meant anything, boss. There was a little space underneath the board, that's all."

Johnson leaped to his feet. "What are you talking about? You told me you cleaned up the mess!"

"I . . . I thought I did. But don't worry, boss—"

Johnson slammed his palm down on the glass coffee table. "I pay you a lot of money to clean up these things! You said you took care of everything." He paused, and then looked Taylor square in the eye. "I'm telling you right now, if they found anything of significance, there'll be hell to pay."

Taylor gulped and a muscle jerked in his cheek. But he said nothing.

"Furthermore, we must get this Carl fellow under control. Do you understand?"

"Yes, boss."

"I want you to tap his phone and start a tail on him. We need to know what he's doing at all times." Johnson clasped his hands behind his back and strutted over to the picture window to look at the vast expanse of the Capitol Building in the distance.

Taylor perked up. "Want me to get rough, boss?"

Johnson touched the screen on his computer to again call up the stock page. "Maybe. I'll try to talk to the commissioner first, and a few senators as well. That should hold off the legislation for a little while. I'll let you know if and when we need to teach that Carl fellow a lesson." He turned his attention to his screen and waved his hand, dismissing Taylor. "And find out what was under that floorboard!" Johnson yelled as Taylor headed for the door.

Johnson was good friends with the commissioner of lands, who was a key member on the Board of Resources—a powerful body that set policy and the appraisal value of lands and timber. With Johnson's encouragement, the commissioner had set aside a fund that supported timber sales, which had helped Johnson's bottom line. It didn't hurt that the commissioner had a fondness for fine wines and whiskies.

He chuckled and picked up the phone. He knew just what to say to the commissioner.

23

Lisa's apartment, near Grassy Park, Olympia

Lisa smoothed her cotton pajamas, curled up on the cold leather sofa, and covered her legs with a hand-woven afghan. Rain pelted the window, and thunder boomed in the distance. Her small but cozy apartment was located near the large forested Grassy Park. On most mornings she enjoyed jogging in the cool crisp air on a narrow tree-lined path along the lake.

She clutched an embroidered pillow in one hand and held the journal that she and Carl had found in the other. During the past three days since they had found the logbook, she had been terrified that someone would come into her office while she was reading it. So, as a precaution, she simply took it home. The logbook contained scrambled scientific research notes, some of which were barely legible. The pages were not numbered but dated, and the notes described visits to logging areas and detailed descriptions of trees and plants. Many pages were torn or soiled.

About halfway through the book, Lisa stumbled on a description of an amphibian. The notes read, "Species sighting confirmed on June 20 and June 25 by Joe Anders of OFS and myself." Lisa's eyes grew wide. She remembered that the Olympia Forestry Service had the exclusive contract for preparing forest permit applications.

She continued reading, carefully turning the torn and slightly burned pages. She stopped when she came to another sentence that said, "L.l. amphibian found in Tract M-119." She read the words again. There again was that strange symbol "L.l." that she had seen before. She grabbed her briefcase and pulled out the report on the logging areas—the one Grantham had worked on that she had questioned Stephen about. She recalled asking Stephen specifically about the strange notations in the margin and the mysterious symbols. She realized that the pages that appeared to be missing might have been the description of this amphibian.

Lisa turned back to the journal and read the next few words: "Stephen informed and told to work with OFS to determine possible critical habitat area." Her jaw dropped. She read the words again out loud: "Possible critical habitat. Stephen informed." She put the book down and clutched her head.

Her basic environmental science courses had taught her that "critical habitat" had to do with a threatened or endangered species. According to the Endangered Species Act, it was an area that contained biological and physical features essential for the conservation of a listed species. An industry was not allowed to "take" a species—which included doing any harm to the animal or its habitat—without notifying the federal agency and receiving the proper approval.

Nothing she had seen in the Environ-Logging files had identified this issue. However, according to these records, Stephen knew about the amphibian. This confirmed her suspicions that Stephen was hiding something. Yet the record did not specify the exact species or indicate if anything came of the findings.

She wondered if she should call Carl to confirm what was in the logbook. It would break his heart to know that his dear friend Stephen might be involved in a plot. She could hardly believe it herself. Her skin tingled when she remembered Carl's touch the night they had gone to the cabin, when the two had stopped for dessert at a late-night restaurant. She still cared for him as a friend, but she hadn't talked to him in years and wasn't too sure of his intentions. Maybe he was just buttering her up to get information. Besides, shouldn't she confirm her suspicions first? Or shouldn't she trust Tom with the information? He knew the operations of the company well and seemed to have taken an interest in her. But did he have a hidden motive as well?

She jumped as a thundering crack sounded, followed by a streak of lightning. The jumbled thoughts in her head—mixed with her nervousness about the weather—were starting to give her a headache. She went into the kitchen to fix a cup of green tea and find an aspirin. She was feeling sick and having trouble controlling her shaking.

I need to confide in someone right away, she thought. But who? She glanced at her watch, and then picked up the phone and speed-dialed her sister. "Linda?" she said. "I know it's late, but do you have a minute?"

"For you, dear, always," said Linda. The familiar voice was soothing, and Lisa relaxed slightly.

She told her sister about what had happened to her and Carl at the cabin, her suspicions about the company hiding information, and, finally, what she had read in the journal. "That about sums it up," she said. "What do you think I should do?"

"Lisa, this is terrible. It's obvious there is suspicious activity going on. You should probably be above-board and confront your boss with the findings."

"You don't know what he's like." She paused, unsure of whether she should reveal any additional details. "And besides, I think they're monitoring me."

"How do you know that?"

"I've heard some suspicious clicks on my office phone. I think the line might be bugged." A long pause followed. "Linda, are you still there?"

"Have you considered talking to Dad or the police about this?" Lisa knew that her father, the head of a major security firm, had the resources to find out if anyone was monitoring her phone. She paused, took a deep breath, and let it out slowly.

"No, I don't want to involve Dad. I'm fine. I just wanted to know what you thought about all this." She was glad she could not see her sister's face.

"I think you should call the police right away, sis. This is serious business. You could get hurt."

Lisa gripped the phone, still feeling weak. Her thoughts were all jumbled.

"I'm concerned about you, Lisa," Linda added gently. "Please be careful. And keep me posted."

"I'll be careful." But how do I do that? she wondered.

"Okay. Love you, sis!" Linda's voice cracked as she said these words.

"Love you, too. Bye."

Lisa fought back the tears that had started to form and went to her bedroom closet. She took down a piece of battered luggage, removed a side panel, and carefully placed the logbook inside.

24

Offices of Environ-Logging, Olympia

"Senator Wells, do you realize what this bill will mean to logging companies?" Johnson had the phone cradled in one arm and was holding a cream-cheese croissant in his hand. He had the lobbyist's report summary open on his desk.

"No, Clive," replied Wells. "Tell me."

Johnson shifted in his chair and swore under his breath. "It will create extensive delays in our operations, which will cost us hundreds of thousands of dollars."

"Why is that, Clive?"

Johnson rolled his eyes. "The larger proposed buffer region will seriously impact our logging schedules. It will force us to needlessly measure each stream width to determine each new area in which trees must not be harvested."

"Why is that so bad?"

Johnson raked his hand through his groomed hair and struggled to keep his composure. "Each stream type would have a different region. It would require us to measure hundreds of different streams on our property. The harvesting zone will change completely! Furthermore, Senator . . ." He paused, and then said in a louder voice, "This bill will not protect wildlife any more than what we are already doing."

"How's that?"

"By thinning out the canopy and leaving enough smaller shade trees to provide for wildlife habitat, we are assisting in the overall habitat protection."

There was a short pause. Then came the words Johnson was waiting to hear.

"So, what do you propose, Clive?"

Johnson grinned, propped his feet up on the desk, and leaned back in his chair. "This is what I propose, Senator."

Johnson hung up the phone half an hour later. He was pleased with himself but tired of fighting the activist scum like Carl Ward. He had already decided that if the bill went through, he would tell Stephen to alter the stream types on paper to the type that did not require any riparian buffer region. Stephen would know how to do this in a way that they would not get caught.

No one else in the company besides Stephen and that scumbag Taylor knew what Environ-Logging was secretly doing—and he intended it to stay that way. He had built this company to what it was today, and no one was going to get in his way.

His father had been a high-powered banking tycoon who demanded the best from his son and had taught him all the tricks on how to get ahead in life. He had worked hard all his life to please his father, and he was proud that his father had been able to see the success he achieved before he passed. Johnson especially prided himself on his ability to sway legislators. His way with words was a hard-earned trait he had learned from his father. It was one of the most rewarding parts of his job.

Johnson buzzed his secretary and asked her to call for Taylor. A few minutes later, the burly man entered the office and closed the door. He sauntered over to the coffee urn as usual and poured himself a large cup.

"What's up, boss?" he said.

"Please, help yourself!" Johnson said, glaring at him. Pompous little weasel.

Taylor slumped down on the plush leather sofa, spilling some coffee on the Persian rug. He blushed, eyed Johnson, and took a dirty tissue out of his pocket to wipe up the stain. Johnson frowned in disgust.

"I've been thinking about this for some time," Johnson said. "It's time we did something drastic about that Ward fellow. He's causing too much trouble. And we also need to deal with the girl. Because of your incompetence, she got that logbook from the cabin, which probably details everything we've been trying to hide."

He stopped to take a breath. He was working himself up too much over this fool, and his blood pressure would suffer as result. "You've got to get that book," he continued after a moment had passed. "I don't want her harmed, though—we can't afford to lose two scientists this soon. Besides, we'll need her to testify about those documents related to Grantham's forest permit."

Taylor carefully set down his mug and rubbed his hands together. "What do you have in mind, boss?" He cocked his head and rubbed his nose with the back of his hand. Johnson saw the gleam in his eyes.

Just then, his secretary interrupted on the buzzer. "Mr. Johnson, your daughter is on the line. It sounds important."

"Tell her to wait just a moment," he said. He turned to Taylor and held out the phone receiver. "Will you excuse me for a minute?"

Taylor took the hint and exited, slurping coffee from his cup.

Johnson pressed the line. "What's up, honey?"

"I don't want to worry you, Dad," said his daughter, "but it's about your grandson. We had to take him to the hospital last night."

Johnson gripped the phone and straightened up in his chair. "Really? Why?"

"It's nothing too serious. He fell off his bike and broke his arm. But the doctors want to do some tests."

Johnson gave a sigh of relief. "Oh, most kids do that at his age. Danny is just being a boy." They chatted for a few minutes, and then Johnson said, "Hey, honey, I'm pretty busy right now. Can we talk later?

"Sure, Dad."

"Okay, I'll call again when I get home." He put down the phone. Taylor meandered in, still clutching the coffee cup. "As I was saying," Johnson said, "deal with Ward and the girl in a way that ensures their cooperation—some kind of warning. And get that logbook."

Taylor gave Johnson an exaggerated smile. "What kind of warning?"

"Something that will scare both of them . . . a lot."

Taylor smiled, reached for the mug, and took a long sip. "I have just the thing in mind."

25

Logging camp near Gray Mountain Mill

Lisa stared in fascination at the massive machinery in front of her. It resembled a giant tractor on rubber tracks with a metal cab, except that there was a three-sectioned white mechanical claw in front of it. She visited the logging camp as often as she could get away. She loved being in the tree-laden outdoors—breathing in fresh forest air, stepping on pine needles, viewing the towering monuments that God had designed.

The behemoth maneuvered up to a Douglas fir that looked nearly one hundred feet high and set its claw vertically against the base of the tree. The cab tilted toward it, and in the middle section of the claw a hydraulic-driven chainsaw roared to life. Lisa heard an ear-grating whirring noise as the tree was cut in a matter of seconds. The top and bottom sections of the claw arms grabbed the severed tree like a toy, and then the cab rotated with the log and threw it onto a pile nearby.

"Pretty impressive, eh, Ms. Stone?" said Johansen. He and Connors were standing beside her, watching the giant cutting machine in action.

"Is that machinery new?" Lisa asked. "I haven't seen it before."

"Sorta new," replied Connors. "We got it a couple of weeks ago. It's called a 'feller buncher.' The operator in the machine 'fells' or cuts down the trees and then bunches them in stacks for another device, called a 'skidder,' to pick them up."

"I guess the rubber tracks help minimize soil disturbance," said Lisa. "But are they as efficient as the skyline cable system? It seems that you can only handle one log at a time."

"Good observation," said Johansen. "We practice both kinds of logging. This one is ground-based, while the skyline is cable-based. Cables can operate over longer distances, on soft or wet ground, and on more severe slopes, whereas this one cannot."

"Then why use this type?" Lisa asked.

"These can be used in all types of weather and are safer because the operator is protected in the cab. A human 'feller' is at risk to the danger of trees falling on him. In addition, he can't work as easily in strong wind and rain."

"I didn't think about that . . . working in the weather, I mean."

"The feller-bunchers are much faster at sawing than a human," Johansen added.

"That brings up another question I have. How much does one of these cost?"

Johansen knit his brows in thought. "Let's see. The John Deere 903-J model we bought last month listed at around $250,000." He paused to let his answer sink in. "We have twenty of those babies in this camp alone."

Lisa blinked hard, trying to wrap her mind around that tidbit of information. "What are the other types of ground-based mechanisms?" she asked.

"We have all sorts," said Connors. "Crawler tractors, wheeled skidders, tracked skidders . . . I can show you our inventory if you like."

"Yes, I would like to see it, and where you use each piece of equipment." She paused and tilted her head. "I remember reading in the environmental assessment that these crawler tractors can cause some soil disturbance."

"The disturbance is minimal," said Johansen. "Now, would you like to see the skyline operation on the north slope? That's where we took you on your first visit. "

Lisa nodded. They got into their car and rode half an hour to the north slope, where she again gaped at the immensity of the operation. Hundreds of logs were in neat stacks in a cleared area, and nearby thick cables had been strung up a steep tree-covered hill. An army of helmeted workers crawled over the logs, coupling and uncoupling cables as needed.

"The standing skyline cable system traverses about four thousand feet up that slope," said Connors. He pointed toward the top of the ridge, and Lisa's eyes followed the cables upward. He paused for her to take it all in. "As you recall, the logs are suspended by chokers, or wire loops, on the motorized carriage and then transported down to the landing. The cables minimize damage to the soil."

"I understand you can handle one thousand feet of timber per hour using the cable system," said Lisa. She had boned up on logging equipment considerably during her many trips to the logging camp.

"Very good, Ms. Stone," said Johansen. "You are correct. We have eight at this logging site."

Her eyes widened as she watched a gargantuan log being pulled up.

"That's an old-growth log," Connors said. "It's four times the size of an average log and weighs about twelve thousand pounds."

Lisa marveled at the mammoth tree. Her mind flashed back to her childhood, when she walked among the wonderland of Yosemite, awestruck at the majestic old sequoias, pines, and firs. She realized soon afterward that her true passion was studying these giants, but it troubled her that these beautiful creations of God were being logged or otherwise disturbed.

She forced her mind back to the present. "How old would that tree be?"

Connors scratched his head. "Close to one hundred years, I imagine."

She flinched as the jumbo log crashed down onto the landing, where it was picked up by a front-end loader. The mobile machine was mounted on a tracked chassis and equipped with a forklift device. Lisa watched as it dropped the log onto a semi-tractor trailer for transport to the sawmill.

"Do you mind if we go back to your office?" she asked. "I was wondering if I could look at the environmental report for tract M-230."

Johansen raised his eyebrows. "Mr. Grantham was very thorough—you should have all of the original reports at your office. We only keep the courtesy copies here, in case we have an inspection."

Lisa forced a Cheshire-cat smile and batted her eyes. "That's right. But I wanted to double-check his field notes."

Johansen nodded and guided her back to the office. She sat outside in the waiting area while he retreated to a rear storage closet. He left the door open, and she could see several gray filing cabinets. There was no file clerk or secretary in sight. He opened one cabinet and returned holding a large white notebook and expandable file folder. "Here you go," he said.

"Thanks!" said Lisa. She perused the document for about ten minutes, quietly fingering a map in the back pocket of her jeans. When she was finished, she thanked Johansen again and handed the file back to him.

She was determined to find out what had happened at tract M-119. But now is not the time, she thought. *I'll come back when no one's around.*

26

State Capitol building, Olympia

Carl dashed into the Legislative Building on the State Capitol grounds and sneaked into a seat in the upper balcony. He heard the gavel pound and the judge call the session to order. He gaped at the towering sky dome, supported by immense ornamented arches. Each time he entered the museum-like building, it reminded him of his first visit there with his father. He recalled how he would stare wide-eyed at the huge rotunda, marble walls, and Tiffany bronze lamps.

However, today he couldn't concentrate on the beauty of the building. He had visited several key senators about the bill that was now on the floor, and each visit had seemed successful. Even Senator Wells had given him a positive reaction when he explained how much the bill would protect forest resources.

Yet he couldn't get the sharp words that he had heard days earlier out of his mind. "You're dealing with the big boys now," a deep voice had barked. "Withdraw your bill or you and your girlfriend will be sorry." He did not recognize the voice, and the mention of a girlfriend confused him. The caller had abruptly hung up, leaving him feeling shattered and weak at the knees.

He had received anonymous threats before, but this one was particularly offensive. He thought briefly about reporting the conversation to the regulatory authorities, but he decided against it for Lisa's sake. In fact, he didn't even tell Lisa about it for fear of upsetting her.

His mind jolted back to the present. He looked down at the main floor and watched all the senators at their separate wooden desks, with their aides hovering around them. Each desk had a small microphone on a wire stand. His bill, number 1586, had taken weeks to move through official channels and pass through the House and the Senate. He and Betty had met with legislators night and day to convince them of the merits of the bill, and they were exhausted from their efforts. Now, everything boiled down to this one hearing—the last in the official chain, called the "third reading."

He remembered visiting the building with his eighth-grade history class and being told about the numerous symbols that commemorated Washington's addition to the Union as the forty-second state. There were even forty-two steps leading to the north entrance and a unique forty-two-star flag.

The announcement of the bill broke his reverie. "All those in favor of bill number 1586, register aye," said the Speaker of the House. "All those opposed, register nay."

Carl tapped his fingers on the desk. The minutes ticked by, and people were growing restless and murmuring softly. He hunched forward and placed his hands on the railing to steady himself. Finally, the gavel pounded again and the Speaker of the House cleared his throat.

"Roll call is complete. The nays have it. The bill is defeated and goes back to committee." Carl's jaw dropped. How could that be? He jumped to his feet and joined the crowd headed for the exit door. He whipped out his cell phone, still fuming, and dialed his assistant's number.

"Betty," he said, "the bill was defeated." He heard a groan and several swear words. He couldn't blame her. Hours of hard work were gone down the drain. The hardest part had been setting up the countless meetings with senators to try to get them to back the bill. Now they would have to go back to square one.

"I may not be back in the office for a while." He paused. "Maybe I'll go get drunk." He heard a snort.

"Boss, come on!" said Betty. "I know you, remember? You're a dyed-in-the-wool tee-totaler."

"Yeah, but people can change! Especially after what happened today!"

Betty snorted again. "Not you. You only go to dull, boring, punch-drinking, sandwich-eating church events."

Carl sighed. He opened his car door, got inside, and gripped the wheel tightly. Betty was hard to reach. Her husband had cheated on her with a much younger woman and had lied about it. When she found out, she was devastated and divorced him. After that she let herself go, gained twenty pounds, stopped wearing makeup, and grew bitter and resentful. She had tried to make her marriage work but failed. She came to the conclusion that men were not to be trusted. But Carl knew that under the tough exterior was a soft heart waiting to be loved again.

"I know, I'm not the party type," he confessed. "I'll be visiting an old college roommate who also doesn't party, so don't worry. We'll get started on a new tack next week. Take the rest of the day off."

"Thanks, boss. I can hardly wait." Betty chuckled. "And I'll do the drinking tonight for both of us!"

27

University of Washington, Seattle

Dr. Kramer pulled up the Food and Drug Administration website on his computer, opened the document he had saved, and clicked on the Skype icon for Dr. Dougherty in New York. The phone rang several times. Dr. Kramer glanced at his watch and wondered if his colleague had remembered the late appointment.

Dr. Dougherty's image soon appeared. He looked like a Chinese Santa, wearing a green silk embroidered robe, a large red sash, and a red stocking cap. He held a delicate teacup in his hand. Dr. Kramer waited while the older man adjusted his glasses and fumbled with the mouse.

They spent the next hour perusing the FDA's guidance document, which provided detailed requirements on how to obtain expedited approval of an investigational new drug. They discussed what to include in the documentation and development plan.

"It says the drug being developed must be intended to treat a serious or life-threatening condition," said Dr. Kramer. "That certainly applies."

"Yes," said Dr. Dougherty. "Unfortunately, NPC is fatal in every case."

"It also says the drug must demonstrate the potential to address 'unmet medical needs.' According to the document, that means there is either no available therapy for the condition or that the drug being developed is potentially better than the available therapy."

Dr. Dougherty sat back in his chair and took a sip from the teacup. "Ours would definitely qualify. There are a couple of therapies being tried, but there is still no known cure for NPC."

"The best news is that once we submit the application, we only have to wait 30 days before starting clinical trials." Dr. Kramer's voice was rising with his excitement. "Can you believe that? Only thirty days!"

Dr. Dougherty extended his palm. "Now, hold on a minute, Ray. Don't get too excited."

Dr. Kramer hunched over and cupped his hand under his chin. "Why? What do you mean?"

"We still need to submit the official application for the new drug. This faster process just gets us quicker FDA approval of the various phases of the drug testing. Speaking of testing, you've only completed the test tube and animal trials, correct?"

"Yes, I've tested it on rats and monkeys. The results are promising."

"We must submit those pre-clinical test results to get started. Then, as part of the FDA drug approval process, we need to submit test protocols for human clinical trials. Remember the three phases we talked about for testing an investigational new drug? Keep in mind that I'm describing textbook protocols. We can discuss everything first with the FDA."

Dr. Kramer nodded. "I understand, Ted. Go on."

"Well, in phase one, twenty to eighty healthy individuals are tested to see if the drug is toxic. We have to submit a protocol document and then wait at least thirty days for approval. Phase two is performed on groups of up to three hundred volunteers. Different doses are used to see how well the drug works. Phase three involves the largest group—up to three thousand volunteers." Dr. Dougherty adjusted his glasses and yawned. "It's the longest and most extensive phase."

Dr. Kramer folded his hands and placed them under his chin. "How 'healthy' does a person have to be in phase one? That is, can we try the drug on very sick patients with the disease?"

"Yes, in some cases. Did you have someone specific in mind?"

Dr. Kramer nodded.

"Well," Dr. Dougherty continued, "each patient and healthy volunteer who might receive a phase one dosage as part of the human clinical trials must meet certain criteria. We also need to get informed consent, because each subject must be fully informed about the nature, benefits, and risks when he or she agrees to participate."

"Can a child sign it?"

Dr. Dougherty blinked. "Are we talking about your patient?"

"Yes."

"It depends on the child's age and other factors." Dr. Dougherty covered another yawn with his hand.

Dr. Kramer looked at his watch and noted that they had been talking for more than two hours. "I see that it's late," he said. "I'm sorry."

"I appreciate that," said Dr. Dougherty. "Yes, it's late, but there is so much to do. We should think about a sponsor for the drug testing."

"You're right about that, Ted. This is going to get awfully expensive. I'll start looking right away."

"I have several contacts involved with support groups that I can send to you."

"Thank you." There was a long pause. Dr. Kramer watched as his colleague scratched his head. "What is it, Ted?" he asked.

"I was just thinking. Putting this application together is going to take a long time."

"Yes, it will."

Dr. Dougherty straightened in his chair and raised his eyebrows. "What do you say to me coming up there to help you?"

Dr. Kramer hesitated. "Are you sure you can handle the long flight?"

"Fiddlesticks, I'm not decrepit yet! But first I need to discuss it with my wife. I'm anxious to get this process started. I have many patients who could be helped by this new drug."

The two talked for a few more minutes and then hung up. After the call, Dr. Kramer stared vacantly out the window and shook his head. He was amazed at the amount of red tape that was involved in getting a new drug approved, but it would be worth it to save just one child's life. Especially the child he was thinking about.

He bowed his head and silently thanked God for the blessing of finding a colleague who felt as strongly as he did about the devastating disease.

28

Logging camp near Gray Mountain Mill

Lisa pressed hard on the gas pedal and raced down the familiar shadow-lined highway toward the logging camp. She had been rehearsing the words she would say to the security guard over and over in her mind. One way or the other, she would bluff her way into that office. After all, she had been an Environ-Logging employee for more than two months now, and she was entitled to see the files any time she wanted. She shook off the feeling that it seemed wrong—that it was somehow breaking the rules.

She knew that with the minimal staff on duty and with Johansen being out of town, she might have a few hours of uninterrupted search. Her primary goal was to find information about tract M-119 that would tie it to the strange wording in Grantham's journal. She pressed her Bluetooth and got Carl's voicemail for the umpteenth time that day. She shook her head and called Betty.

"Is Carl there?" she asked. "He's not answering his phone." She swerved to miss a squirrel that had darted across the tree-darkened narrow road.

"Tell me about it!" said Betty. "He never came back from his legislative meeting, and I haven't heard from him since the Congressional meeting. I'm starting to get a little worried."

Lisa hesitated. She didn't want to reveal her clandestine plans to Betty. "Well . . . please ask him to call me as soon as he gets in. Thanks, Betty!"

She opened the window and allowed the fresh pine air to pour in and refresh her. As she glanced up at the towering trees, she again felt both invigorated and humbled by the beauty of the forest. She said a prayer of thanks out loud to God for the natural wonder He had created and recited a song she had memorized from Sunday School. She asked God to bless her trip, even though the sneaky methods she was employing had left her feeling a little guilty.

After another hour of driving, she finally saw the gate of the camp. A heavyset man in a green Environ-Logging uniform and black cap was sitting in the guardhouse. Lisa's hands were sweaty and her insides were in knots as she steeled herself for the dialogue.

"Good morning," she said, beaming as she pulled out her Environ-Logging ID badge. The guard put down his newspaper and approached the car window. He took her badge and eyed her suspiciously.

"What brings you here on a Sunday morning, Ms. Stone?" he asked. "Don't you usually come during the week?"

She smiled sweetly. "I need to do some research right away on a new logging tract. It's important for a new bill coming up this week at the state legislature."

The guard hesitated and shook his head. "I should call Mr. Johansen. He doesn't like folks meddling around in his office. Come to think of it—" He turned his back and began walking toward the guard house. Lisa was caught off-guard and quickly realized things weren't going the way she had planned.

"Wait!" she suddenly yelled. The guard stopped mid-stride, turned around, and slowly came back to her car. "I understand completely," Lisa said, hiding her shaking hands. "I promise not to disturb anything. I'll put everything back just the way I found it. You needn't disturb Mr. Johansen on his day off."

The guard took off his cap and scratched his head. "Well, you're right that I don't like to disturb the boss. But sometimes he just shows up unannounced."

Lisa gave him her most charming smile. "It'll be okay. I won't be very long. Don't worry."

The guard rested his hand on the car and scratched the back of his head. "Hmm . . . I guess it's all right, Ms. Stone. After all, you are an employee, and you've been here before." He pressed a red button, and the metal gate slowly rose. "I'll call ahead and have a man meet you at the office to unlock the building."

Lisa breathed a sigh of relief and pulled forward. She parked in front of the office, bowed her head, and said another prayer to thank God for helping her get through the gate. Soon another uniformed guard approached carrying a large set of keys on his belt. He looked as if he had just woken up from a nap.

"Boss said you need to get into the office?" he asked.

Lisa nodded and got out of the car. The two walked to the office, where the guard pulled out the necessary key from the massive jumble, opened the door for her, and stood aside to allow her to enter.

"Anythin' else?" he said with a yawn.

"No, that will be all. Thank you very much."

She waited until he was out of sight before entering the room. She leaned against the back of the door, took a deep breath, and then went to the back storage closet. She opened file cabinet drawers and soon found the environmental assessment for tract M-119. Her hands were still shaking, and she fumbled with the pages each time she glanced over her shoulder to make sure she wasn't being watched. She soon discovered that the identical pages were missing in this copy of the assessment as were missing in her office copy, and the same pages were out of order as well. However, there was a new handwritten footnote. She took a picture of the page using her cell phone.

The barking of a dog outside caused her to race to the window, where she saw Johansen approaching the office with Oso in tow. Her heart skipped a beat. She slammed the book closed, ran back to the filing cabinet, and quickly put it back in its place. She pulled a blue file folder out of her backpack and brought it to the conference room just as Johansen came in the door.

"Ms. Stone," he said. "What are you doing here?" Oso was out of control, barking and trying to run toward her. It took everything Johansen had to hold him back with the leash. Lisa froze as the ferocious hound tried to leap at her. Her knees buckled, and she fought to control her trembling jaw.

"I . . . I was reviewing this report I found here," she stammered. "It's not at the main office, and we need it next week for important legislation." She offered the file folder to him. At least part of her statement was true.

"Let me see that," said Johansen, grabbing the folder. "You could have just called me." Oso stood next to him, his fangs showing. Her skin crawled.

"I . . . I thought you were out of town. Besides, I didn't want to bother you. I'm sorry." She hoped her sheepish look did not give her away.

Johansen handed the folder back to her and glared. "Next time, call me first." He tugged at the leash and strode away.

Lisa heaved a sigh of relief and quickly packed up her things. She slowly walked out to her car for the long ride home. Not only am I a sneak, she thought, shaking her head, but now I'm also a liar!

29

South Puget Sound

Stephen glanced at the thick forest canopy off the bow, raised the jib, and checked the mainsail. He was heading north in his thirty-two-foot Catalina sailboat, which he had named Amanda May after his wife, to an inlet in a state park located in south Puget Sound.

"Look, Dad," said Roger, pointing to the sky. "A red-tailed hawk!"

"Get ready for the port tack," said Stephen, turning the wheel. "Ready about." The boom spun around, and he trimmed the main sail as it filled. He secured the rope in the cleat, sat back in his leather captain's chair, and reached for his beer while he waited for the next tack.

The weather was perfect that day, with a light breeze and clear blue skies. He was happier than he had been in a long time, especially since his son had accompanied him on the trip. He had taken both his sons sailing since they were first able to walk. Roger had learned to sail the boat solo when he was just thirteen. But these days Roger did not get much time off from his medical practice, and he treasured every moment he could spend alone with him.

"There's an osprey right next to a hawk!" Roger shouted. "It looks like they're trying for the same fish."

Stephen laughed and tightened up the mainsail, which had started flapping. "We're not making great headway in this wind, but at least there's a lot of wildlife. I see a great blue heron near the shore on the starboard side." He pointed toward a small town on the eastern shore of the inlet. "Hey, Roger, why don't you come out on the Amanda May with me more often?"

"I just don't have the time anymore, Pop. The family stays pretty busy, especially Hannah." Stephen's granddaughter was an active twelve-year-old who was into ice-skating, ballet, and violin.

They tacked back and forth across the inlet until they reached a passage just south of a small island. The wind was steady from the starboard side, and they sailed close-hauled with the sail pulled in tight. They headed through the passage and then proceeded south until they reached the entrance to the state park.

After docking the boat, they went into the cabin to fill the ice chest with homemade chicken-salad sandwiches that Amanda had prepared and lots more beer. They grabbed their fishing poles and walked for a half-mile before finding a familiar trail.

"I remember this area," said Roger, his facing glowing as he surveyed the secluded area by the shore. "You took me fishing here several times."

The two walked through the tall pine trees that formed a picture-perfect border around the pristine sand and rock beach. Once they reached the water, they spread a red and white picnic tablecloth that Amanda had provided, laid out the food, and sat down on the pebbles.

"It doesn't seem so long ago that we came here," said Stephen. He gazed at the water and munched on his sandwich.

"Dad, can I ask you a question about your job?" said Roger.

Stephen tensed, and a muscle jerked in his cheek. He set his half-eaten sandwich down. "All right," he mumbled. His happy mood had evaporated.

"How do you do it? Who tells you what to do? I mean, what are the mechanics of—" His voice trailed off.

Stephen dropped his head as waves of shame washed over him. Roger was the only family member in whom he had ever confided. He knew Stephen's "secret" and that he had altered records at the company. But he would not reveal exactly how that was done or who was behind it. He figured the less he told his own flesh-and-blood about his criminal activity, the better.

"I'm sorry, son. I'm ashamed enough as it is, and I won't tell you the gory details. I don't want you to get mired in my problem. But I do want you to know one thing."

"What's that, Dad?"

Stephen swallowed. "I have a log in my computer of each document that I . . . changed. In that log, I explain in detail what I did to each record, and I even have a copy of the original document. So, in a way, I'm building the case against myself. At least the truth will come out eventually . . . that is, if I ever get out of this mess." He paused and sighed.

"What's it going to take, Dad? I mean, to get out of the mess?"

Stephen shook his head and averted his eyes, which had begun to tear up. "I just don't know. I'm beginning to think the nightmare will never end."

"Dad, I pray every day that God will guide you to do the right thing."

A tear sprang to Stephen's eye, and he swallowed hard. He knew that Roger was a strong Christian and went to church every week. He slumped his shoulders and looked out at the water, unable to find the words to answer his son.

"You know that God is right there beside you, right?" Roger continued. "I know you don't like to talk about religious things, but please know that He cares about what's happening to you. You can ask Him for help."

Stephen found his voice and smiled. "I appreciate that son, but can we talk about something else now?"

Roger patted him on the shoulder. "Of course, Dad. We brought the rod and reels, so why don't we go fishing?"

Stephen stared blankly at his son. He had never told anyone what he had just told his son, and he couldn't believe that he had just bared his soul that way. But he was tired of hiding the truth—he was tired of all the lies. Who else could he trust?

He thought for a long time about Roger's words. He hadn't prayed in a while, and he didn't exactly know what to say. So he kept it basic and simple. *God, please help me to do the right thing.*

30

Offices of Environ-Logging, Olympia

"Olympia Forestry Service, may I help you?" The monotone voice on the line sounded tired.

"Yes . . . may I . . . speak to Joe Anders please?" Lisa said, nervously tapping her fingers on the table.

"Just a moment, please." Lisa listened to the recorded music and waited for the voice to come back. "I'm sorry, ma'am, but Mr. Anders is no longer employed at OFS. Is there someone else who can help you?"

Lisa nearly choked. How can that be? she thought. The report was less than six months old, and the logbook entry—"

"Ma'am? Are you still there, ma'am?"

Lisa fought to regain her composure. "Yes, I'm still here. Thanks for your time." She hung up the phone and stared at it for a moment. The voicemail light was flashing. Someone had called while she was on the phone. She punched in the code and listened to the recorded message. "Hey, Lisa, this is Tom. I'm in town again. Could we get together for dinner? I know it's short notice, so if you're busy, I understand."

Her stomach quivered, and she nearly dropped the receiver. She found his number in her electronic address book and called him back.

"Hello," Tom answered cheerfully.

"Hello, Tom," she said, trying not to sound too eager. After all, it would only be their second date. "Yes, I am free this evening. I'd like to go to dinner with you."

"Great! Can I pick you up at home? Where do you live?"

"I'll . . . I'll text you my address."

"Good. I look forward to seeing you again."

Lisa hung up the phone and giggled. She couldn't believe the unexpected invitation. Tom made her heart beat in a familiar, wonderful rhythm. At least something is going right this week. But what about Carl?

Carl was still not answering his phone or returning her calls. His assistant, Betty, had not heard from him either. Lisa was still feeling shaky from the harrowing experience she had encountered at the logging camp. Now it appeared that Joe Anders, the scientist Grantham mentioned in his notebook, had vanished.

She pulled out a magnifying glass and looked at the letters in the margins of the environmental report. "L.l." had to be the name of the endangered amphibian. Stephen might have the answer, but she wasn't sure she could trust him anymore—even though it was inconceivable to her that he might be involved in a cover-up.

She buzzed Claire. "Get me all the reports for the last fifteen years from the Olympia Forestry Service. I need all the ones I don't currently have."

"Fifteen years?" replied Claire. "You mean, since our company's been in business?"

"Yes." Lisa hung up the phone.

While she waited for Claire to bring the reports, she surfed the Internet and searched for anything she could find on rare and endangered amphibians—especially those starting with the letter L. She searched the U.S. Fish and Wildlife website and called up maps of locations of endangered amphibian species in the Northwest. She discovered several species that started with the letter L, but none seemed to stand out.

Claire knocked on the door and came in wheeling a giant luggage cart with ten cardboard boxes. She had a bewildered look on her face as she started to unload them. Lisa came around her desk and helped her lift the heavy boxes.

"There's another ten boxes I need to retrieve," said Claire, gasping for breath. "I checked the electronic files and pulled all the reports from the file room, but—" She paused, turned, and went over to the door.

"What is it, Claire?"

Claire looked at Lisa and put her hands on her hips. "Well . . . I hesitate to say this, but for some reason all the reports are now out of order. I know they were in order just a few months ago, because I did the inventory myself."

"All right, thanks, Claire. Go ahead and bring in the rest of the boxes. "

A chill went up Lisa's back, and her palms grew sweaty as she started to open the reports. She searched for the names of scientists who had performed site assessments similar to the one that Anders had performed.

Claire soon returned, and together they set down the rest of the boxes. Lisa pored over the documents for hours until she glanced at her watch and realized it was time to go home and prepare for her date. At least she would be able to relax a little this evening, but she was still worried. Her thoughts swirled as she imagined what might have happened and what she should share with Tom.

She left the office and soon arrived at the door to her apartment. She went inside, threw her keys on the counter, and stepped into the living room. Her mouth flew open and she clasped her head with both hands when she saw the scene before her. The room had been ransacked. The drawers to her desk and filing cabinet had been tipped over, and papers and books were scattered everywhere. Her leather couch and matching chairs had huge rips in them, and cotton stuffing was strewn about.

The logbook! she thought. She flew to her bedroom and grabbed the suitcase from the top shelf. She tore it open and reached under the bottom panel, where she felt the familiar worn leather notebook. She took a deep breath, slid to the floor, and cradled the notebook in her arms. She was enraged that someone had broken in and violated her home, but she thanked God that the thieves had not found the book.

She reached for the phone and dialed Tom's number. "Tom," she said, trying to control her trembling voice. "I'm sorry, but I need to cancel tonight. Something's come up. Can we make it another night?"

"What's wrong, Lisa?" Tom asked.

"Nothing," she lied, trying to keep her voice calm. She didn't want to involve him in this mess. She barely knew him—and besides, she was too upset to see anyone. She didn't even know if she should call the police. "But, I would love to get together again the next time you're in town."

Tom sounded disappointed, but he agreed to reschedule for a night when he would be in town again. Lisa hung up, flung herself on the bed, and fought tears of self-pity.

What's going to happen next, Lord?

31

Seattle-Tacoma Airport, Washington

Dr. Kramer spotted a short gray-haired man in a faded brown suit walking over to retrieve his luggage. The elderly man strode with a slight stoop and had a worn expression on his face. Dr. Kramer recognized him instantly. He rushed over when he saw the man struggle to lift the heavy suitcase off the conveyor belt.

"How do you do?" he said, sticking out his hand.

Dr. Dougherty adjusted his glasses and looked at the man in front of him. His eyes grew wide. "We meet once again!" he said, shaking Dr. Kramer's hand.

"Let me help you with that, Ted." Dr. Kramer grabbed the heavy bag and touched his friend's elbow to direct him toward the exit. He asked Dr. Dougherty about the flight as they walked to his 1968 blue Oldsmobile. He patted the hood fondly when he reached the car.

"So, you're into classic cars as well," said Dr. Dougherty, running his hand along the shiny chrome trim. "Funny we never discussed this before."

"This was my father's car, and he graciously allowed me to keep it." Dr. Kramer opened the door for the older man.

"I've got a 1958 Aston Martin myself."

Dr. Kramer gave a low whistle. "Wow, that's remarkable. Wish I could see it."

Dr. Dougherty pulled out a well-worn photo of the car from his wallet. "I bought it at an auto auction some years ago. Mighty proud of it, I must say."

Dr. Kramer eyed the photo and grinned. "Well, I guess we have something else in common now."

Dr. Dougherty nodded. "So, Ray," he said, changing the subject, "I'm anxious to work on the clinical protocol and schedule our first meeting with the FDA. Fill me in on what you've done so far."

The two chatted during the drive up to Dr. Kramer's home in Bellaire, a fashionable satellite city east of Seattle. Dr. Dougherty's eyes grew wide when they pulled into the driveway. The two-story house was immaculately landscaped and boasted large picture windows, red trim and shutters, and a large covered entryway.

"My, what a lovely home, Ray!"

"Thank you." Dr. Kramer got out, opened the trunk, pulled out his colleague's bag, and headed toward the door. "It's only by the grace of God."

Dr. Dougherty eyed him closely. "I see." He shuffled up the neatly trimmed walkway after his friend. "You are so gracious to let me stay with you and your family."

"My wife and I enjoy guests. We often have church members at our house."

Dr. Kramer's wife met them in the foyer. She had been in the kitchen and was wiping her hands on a white apron. "Welcome, Doctor," she said. "Please come in."

"Let me introduce my wife," said Dr. Kramer. "I'll take your bag upstairs to your room. Dinner will be ready soon."

They moved into the spacious living room, which had a high ceiling, white paneling, and antique furniture. After their dinner together, they cleared off the dining room table, and Dr. Kramer spread out the paperwork he had been working on. During the next several hours, they discussed the procedures and timing for the FDA application and the clinical trial protocols.

"The problem I have, Ted," said Dr. Kramer, "is getting enough frogs to do my research. I've had my students looking night and day to find other sources."

"I know that Ganther's frogs are extremely rare," said Dr. Dougherty, "but we've got to find more if we want to get the drug on the market. Have you had any luck with a sponsor yet?"

"Not yet. I've got my students calling around." Dr. Kramer smiled. "You know, Ted, I was doing my Bible study the other night, and these phases of drug testing are similar to what happened to Daniel and his friends."

Dr. Dougherty looked up with surprise. "What do you mean?"

"Have you ever read the Bible, Ted?"

"No." Dr. Dougherty looked away. "My wife handles the religion for both of us."

"Well, in the book of Daniel, there was a king of Babylon named Nebuchadnezzar. When he conquered the Israelites, he selected some of the top men and ordered them to be given food from his own table—food that had been ritually offered to the Babylonian gods. Daniel and his three friends were selected, but they refused to eat the king's food. Instead, Daniel challenged the king to test them by feeding them a diet of vegetables and water while the other men ate the king's food. After ten days, Daniel and his friends were healthier and had more energy than any of the other young men."

"So what's the point?" asked Dr. Dougherty.

"You could say that this was a food or drug trial in which there was a test group and a control group. The test group proved that the vegetable diet was better."

"Yes, I suppose you're right—if you believe that sort of thing." Dr. Dougherty coughed and turned away.

"Ted, the patient of yours who died was named Jerry, right? I've got a patient named Patrick who is also critical. I want to test this drug on him."

"Why are the young ones taken, Ray? I just don't see how that can be part of God's plan."

Dr. Kramer looked down. "I don't always understand why God allows certain things to happen, Ted. But I know that He can use any situation and turn it around for good. Romans 8:28 tells us,

'And we know that in all things God works for the good of those who love Him, who have been called according to His purpose.'"

"I just don't believe that. There can be no purpose for a child suffering."

"We can't always see God's purposes now, but we will one day." Dr. Kramer paused. "I know that is hard to accept, but I have faith in God's plan."

Dr. Dougherty stood up. "I don't want to seem rude, but I would prefer that we not talk about this right now. You've been a good friend to me, and I don't want to spoil anything between us." He stretched and yawned. "Now, if you don't mind, I'm very tired and would like to go to bed."

Dr. Kramer stood. "Of course, Ted. We'll always be friends. I meant no offense. I'll show you to your room now."

After Dr. Kramer helped his colleague settle in, he returned to the living room and got down on his knees. "Please, Lord," he prayed, "help my friend Ted see you in a new way. Help him to trust and believe in you. And help us find a cure soon so Patrick can live a long, full life. Amen."

32

Near the Logging Camp, Eltout Forest Range

Lisa found herself squeezed into the back of a Bell 206 Series helicopter crammed full of sweaty loggers in orange jumpsuits. Despite her discomfort, she strained forward to peer out the windows. She had waited weeks to have this helicopter ride and was determined to forget what happened at her apartment.

The sleek black chopper, with green Environ-Logging markings on the side, had whisked her away from the roof of the company headquarters about a half hour before. They were now headed toward the Logging Camp, where she had been asked to observe a heli-logging operation.

"How many helicopters does Environ-Logging have?" Lisa yelled to the logger sitting next to her.

The burly man turned to her. "Eight!" he yelled. "We use them at various locations around the state where there's rough terrain or high slopes."

"I guess they take the place of the skyline, right?"

"That's right, ma'am. Payloads are up to 10,000 pounds per turn."

Lisa recalled that a "turn" of logs was the complete cycle in the logging operation, beginning when the timber was felled or cut, collected, and then hauled or skidded by machine to the landing area. After the logs were unhooked from the chopper, the cycle began again.

"How many logs would that be, approximately?" she asked.

The logger scratched his nose. "Let me see—depending on the size and height, it could be up to five logs. But we have to be careful. When the chopper first starts out, it's heavier because it's full of fuel, so it can't haul as many logs. Toward the end of the turn, we can put heavier loads on the towline."

She whistled. "This seems more efficient—and the site disturbance would definitely be minimized."

"Yes, we lift the logs straight up so there is little damage to the ground or any surrounding trees."

Another logger leered at her. "You're an environmentalist, right?" he asked. Lisa nodded. The logger hunched closer to her, almost touching her thigh. "The helicopters can go where no roads are possible or available. Heli-logging is the wave of the future."

Lisa tried not to gag at his bad breath, but as he spoke she remembered an issue that had been discussed a few days before about the new roads being built. She suddenly realized the wisdom of using helicopters. "But what about the cost?" she asked, adjusting her headset and scrunching toward the first logger.

"Each chopper costs about $750,000," he replied. "In addition to the cost of hiring experienced pilots, we also have to hire special crews for maintenance and repair. The choppers have to be overhauled often because they carry so much weight."

Lisa peered out the window and spied a small landing pad. They were now passing over the familiar logging camp headquarters building. As the chopper neared the site, several men jumped out, hit the ground, grabbed a long rope with a loop that looked like a noose, and attached it to the bottom of the helicopter. The 180-foot line would be used for grabbing logs and removing them from the area.

The whole operation took less than ten minutes. Lisa marveled that they were in the air again so quickly. They flew over a large forest of pines that stood straight as an arrow. She could smell the trees and hear the noise of chainsaws below. They landed in a small clearing marked with a large X that seemed to appear out of nowhere. One by one the loggers jumped out, donned hard hats and climbing gear, and attached chainsaws to their belts. The logger who had leered at her turned and licked his lips in a lewd way. She tried not to gag and vowed not to sit next to him on the return trip.

From a safe distance away, Lisa watched as the loggers scattered out in several areas and climbed up trees as tall as eight-story buildings. Soon limbs and logs were tumbling down all around. The men set the chokers or wire nooses around the logs in strategic places in order to balance the weight as the chopper lifted them.

"What are those flags for?" Lisa asked her escort. Each logger had pulled out a large orange cloth and attached it to his belt.

"To mark the logging locations so the helicopter can spot them more easily."

After an hour, Lisa jumped back into the chopper with her escorts. The chopper lifted into the air, and when she looked down she saw the towline swinging in the wind. A radio in the cockpit crackled as a logger instructed the pilot where to pick up the logs. She spied him down below, looking like a small orange speck.

"How does the pilot avoid hitting the logger?" she yelled over the din.

"He's done it a few times," said one escort. "And the logger below is experienced at grabbing the line."

The logger snatched the end of the rope and in one swift move hooked it onto several log chokers. Lisa could feel the drag on the chopper as it gradually lifted the heavy logs high into the air. In less than three minutes the logs had been transported from the site and dropped off at the landing.

Lisa was feeling dizzy and had a splitting headache after several hours of flying back and forth from the logging site to the pick-up area. However, she was glad that she had been able to accompany the loggers and get to know more about heli-logging procedures. The helicopter was enormously practical and productive—far more than what she had observed on the ground. Best of all, there was virtually no damage to the environment. She looked forward to doing more research on heli-logging technology and comparing the efficiency of the process to other types of logging.

As Lisa settled in for the ride home, she reflected on the day. I wonder if I'll get to see a helicopter in action again, she thought.

33

Near Olympia, Washington

Carl said goodbye to his friend and walked toward his car. He knew he should have called Betty to let her know where he was, but he had been so despondent about the legislative session that he had forgotten to do so. He arrived at his car, took out his cell phone, and then hesitated.

First I'll try Lisa, he thought. He knew that she was out of town on business and likely out of cell range, but he wanted to hear her voice again. He smiled when he saw that she had called several times. He speed-dialed her number, but as expected heard yet another voice-mail message.

"Tag, you're it!" he said. "Call me!" He clapped the phone shut, opened the car door, and threw his briefcase on the seat beside him. He jammed the accelerator and headed toward the I-5 Freeway north to return to his office in Kirkland.

His mind raced as he thought about the timeline for the next legislative session. Many of the senators were newly elected and needed to have the bills explained to them, so he had to try a different tack. As he considered his options, he decided to start over and introduce a brand new bill. I'll visit those new senators, one by one, to try to explain it and influence them to take my side. That's what those industry lobbyists do.

He reached for the phone to call Betty. Just then, he felt something cold and hard being pressed against the back of his neck. The phone fell out of his hand, back onto the seat. "I have a gun, so follow my directions and you won't be hurt," said a voice.

Carl's stomach tightened as his mind flashed back to the warning he had received a few days earlier after his visit to Senator Wells. He recognized it as the same deep voice he had heard that day. He swallowed hard.

"What do you want?" he croaked.

The man pressed the steel barrel even harder into his neck. "Just shut up and turn around. Go south on I-5."

Carl grimaced and nervously pulled into traffic. As he looked into his rearview mirror, he caught a glimpse of coal-black eyes and greasy brown hair on a hulking form. A pair of bushy eyebrows peeked over the edge of a green scarf that entirely covered the man's nose and mouth. A jolt of fear coursed through his body. He tried not to panic, but a sense of foreboding was welling up inside him.

Carl pressed down on the accelerator. His palms were growing sweaty, and he felt nauseous. He drove for an hour, going south on I-5 as instructed, until he was well outside the city limits of Olympia. The voice led him zigzagging down one road after another, past exclusive neighborhoods and walls of fences, and then into a deeply forested area. He felt like a rat in a maze. The man occasionally jabbed him with the gun in the back of his neck to remind him who was in charge.

Carl played numerous scenarios in his mind about what was going on and why he had been kidnapped. Why didn't I pay more attention to that warning a few days before? he wondered. The ride continued, and he became even more fearful. He glanced down at the cell phone, wondering if he would get the chance to use it. As he was about to ask a question, the voice behind him barked an order.

"Exit here, and then turn left."

Carl did as he was told and turned left at the exit onto an unfamiliar highway. He tried to observe the road signs, but he wasn't able to recognize anything. That's odd, he thought. Why would he be taking me way out here?

They passed a few isolated shopping centers. Carl quickly realized that someone could get lost here in the midst of the miles of

Douglas firs with their understory of hemlock and cedar. The high-density forest canopy blocked the daylight. A light rain began to fall, making the road slick. He turned on the wipers and continued driving. When the road turned north again, he glimpsed a tall mountain off in the distance, but he didn't recognize it.

After a solid hour of twists and turns, he heard a sharp command from the back seat to slow down. They approached a dirt road blocked by an ornate iron gate with barbed wire on top. A hand squeezed his shoulder hard, and he winced. "Turn left here, and then stop at the end of the road."

Carl looked up and saw a large wire gate with a padlock. He stopped the car as directed, and the ruffian with the green scarf got out and unlocked the gate. He was truly a colossal figure, dressed in camouflage from head to toe. He motioned for Carl to drive through the gate.

Carl briefly considered putting the car in reverse and flooring it, but the bully flashed the gun again, causing his escape plan to evaporate. He grit his teeth and slowly drove through the gate. He shuddered and tried not to think what might happen to him next. Just then, he was reminded of a few verses from the psalms that he had read. He began to recite them under his breath. "God is our refuge and strength, an ever-present help in trouble. . . .Though I walk in the midst of trouble, you preserve my life; you stretch out your hand against the anger of my foes, with your right hand you save me."

The masked figure got into the back seat and squeezed Carl's shoulder hard enough to make him wince. "No talking, just drive. Straight through."

Carl pressed down on the accelerator and again prayed. *Lord, I need your help. You promised in your Word to be with me in trouble. I don't know what is going on, but I know you can help me get through this trial. Please, give me strength.*

He felt God's presence in that moment, and a surge of hope flow through him. He clutched the wheel more tightly. No matter what, he was determined to make it with God's help.

34

Lisa's apartment, Olympia

Lisa took a last look in the mirror and powdered her nose one more time. Satisfied with her appearance, she walked over to the window and looked down. Below she saw a tall man exiting a green vehicle with tinted windows and sunroof. She patted down her skirt in nervous anticipation. Moments later, the doorbell rang.

Tom stood in the hallway with a grin on his face. He had called earlier that day to say he was in town and wanted to see her. His close-cropped black curls were slicked down, and he was dressed in tan Dockers, a beige shirt, and a dark brown corduroy jacket.

"Hello, again," he stammered. She tried not to stare. He was as handsome as she remembered him.

"Would you like to come in?" she asked.

"Sure." He walked inside a few steps and then stopped. His eyes swept over her figure, and his jaw dropped. "Wow, you sure look nice."

She felt her cheeks grow hot. She had chosen a pale blue skirt and lacy white blouse with a matching cardigan. Her long brown hair was swept back with a pink mother-of-pearl comb. "Thanks," she said, nervously fingering her cross necklace.

"Have you ever eaten at Barney's?" Tom asked.

"No, but I've heard it's a great place." She had learned of the place from friends at work, but she had never eaten there. It was a local hangout that was famous for its delicious hamburgers.

"It's not too far from here. Don't worry, I remembered that you're a vegetarian—excuse me, a pesco-vegetarian, as I recall. They have a variety of meatless dishes."

"That was nice of you!"

They left the apartment and headed for the parking lot. It was cool outside, and she was glad she wore a sweater. They approached his SUV, and he held the door open for her. "Nice car," she said. "It's a hybrid, right? I have one myself."

"I thought as much. Of course, it's good for the environment."

The restaurant was lively despite it being a weeknight. After a short wait, they asked for a table in the back, further from the sports events blaring on the big-screen TV. As they sat down and perused the menus, she tried not to let her emotions overwhelm her. She was worried about Carl, but she found it easy to be distracted by her striking escort.

"I have to try the famous Barney's burger that I read about." Tom closed the menu. "What about you?"

"I think I'll get the veggie burger."

"Good choice."

They ordered their burgers and then chatted about the weather. She dodged questions about her job but kept wondering if she should tell him about Carl. When the meal arrived, she bowed her head and prayed silently. She opened her eyes and found that Tom was watching her.

"Your faith is important to you?" he asked.

"Yes, very," she replied, trying not to sound condescending. He remained silent, and they concentrated on their juicy burgers piled high with toppings. Lisa worked up her courage to ask a question as they munched.

"Tom . . . I was wondering if I could ask you something."

He lifted his eyebrows. "Yes?"

"It's nothing personal." She chuckled. "It's about a friend."

"That's okay. What's your question?"

"My friend Carl Ward is president—well, the founder, actually— of a company called GreenForests. Ever hear of it?"

"Sure, I know about GreenForests. I've chatted with Carl, but I don't know him personally."

Lisa briefly described her friendship with Carl, leaving out the fact that he had once been her boyfriend. She explained about Carl's recent disappearance from the capitol. Tom rubbed his chin. "Do you have any reason to believe that there was foul play?"

Questions swirled in Lisa's head. *Should I tell him about the trip to Grantham's cabin? What about the logbook and my apartment being trashed?* She took a deep breath and nervously twisted a strand of hair. "Not really," she said, looking down at the table.

Tom sipped his beer. "We should report his disappearance to the police."

Lisa nodded. "I'll call Betty, his assistant, and see if she has done that."

Tom moved a little closer and put a hand on the back of Lisa's chair. "I realize we don't know each other very well, but I sense that there's something you're not telling me." His dark eyes were mesmerizing, and his voice was soothing. Lisa's heart pounded and her face went hot. Panic bubbled inside.

After a long pause, she said, "I'd rather not discuss it, if you don't mind."

Tom moved away. "That's fine," he said. "I can accept that." She saw his expression and could feel a wall building between them. "Do you want any dessert?" he asked, staring straight ahead.

"No, thank you, I'm stuffed."

They left the restaurant, and Tom was silent for most of the drive back. When they reached the door of her apartment, he gently put his hand on her shoulder. "Now, let me know what you find out from Betty about Carl. I'll be glad to make a few phone calls if you would like."

Her throat closed, and she fumbled with her keys. "Thanks, Tom. That makes me feel better." She fought back against her emotions and stared at the keyhole. "I . . . had a nice evening." She slowly turned the key in the lock.

"Me, too. Goodnight, Lisa." He abruptly turned and walked to his car—with no kiss or even a handshake. Hot tears welled up in

Lisa's eyes as she watched him drive away. She entered and promptly slammed the door shut. She swallowed back a sigh and wondered whether she had blown it for good with Tom.

There was only one thing to do now. She ran to her bed, kneeled down, and pressed her face tightly against the covers. "God," she prayed, "I don't know what to do. I'm scared. Please guide me. I need you right now."

She sat up, took out her Bible, and opened to the book of Isaiah. The verses calmed her spirit and gave her strength: "For I am the Lord, your God, who takes hold of your right hand and says to you, Do not fear; I will help you. . . . I am the Lord, your God, who teaches you what is best for you, who directs you in the way you should go."

She meditated on the verses for a moment, and then realized what she needed to do. She grabbed her bag, flew out the door, and looked around before getting into her car. She knew what she had planned had to be done in person, regardless of how late it was. She started the engine and touched her Bluetooth.

"Linda, it's Lisa. Sorry it's so late. I've decided to go to the police after all. I just thought you should know." She swallowed back a sigh. At least it's a start.

35

Restaurant in downtown Olympia

Tom looked at Stephen, who was slouched in the chrome seat across from him and Rob. The older man looked bone tired. His eyes were baggy, his face was unshaven, and his cheeks were sunken. The three had agreed to meet at a popular restaurant in downtown Olympia. They sat in a booth in the back to ensure they were away from the busy lunch crowd.

"Look, Stephen," said Tom, raising his voice to be heard over the other patrons. "As I told you, Rob and I are not here on official business. We just want to talk to you because we're concerned about what is going on at Environ-Logging." The waitress came with iced tea and took their order.

Stephen eyed Tom. "Who have you been talking to?"

"Well," said Rob, "you could say that Tom here has taken quite an interest in your company lately." He snickered.

Stephen raised his eyebrows. "Lisa? I see. So that's what this is all about." He shook his head. "How serious is it?"

Tom looked up and tried not to smile. "I don't know if it's serious yet, but I am definitely interested in the young lady."

"This gal has made quite an impression on Tom," said Rob. "Take it from me—that takes a lot for this guy!"

"Isn't that just a sneaky way to find out more about us?" asked Stephen.

"We don't generally talk about business," said Tom.

"So what are we doing right now?" asked Stephen.

"Look," said Rob, "we could come and do an official inspection, but we'd rather talk informally for the moment. Like Tom said, we're just concerned about what is going on at Environ-Logging."

Stephen remained silent and stared into his glass of iced tea.

"Stephen," said Tom, "I don't know you well, but I know that Lisa is scared for some reason. Do you have any idea why she would be so nervous? I have a feeling that something is not right."

Stephen's eyes remained fixed on the glass. "Look, your love life is not my concern. And as far as what is going on at Environ-Logging, it's not something I want to discuss with you."

Tom inhaled and tried to compose himself. "Stephen, let's get to the bottom of this. What do you know about this mysterious disappearance of Ed Grantham? We always worked with him, and then one day he's gone, just like that. What gives?"

Tom thought he saw a flicker of fear in Stephen's eyes. Stephen raised his hand. "Wait just one minute. Are you the police or something? That's none of your business. The man left unexpectedly—and that is that."

Tom frowned and exchanged glances with Rob. They had decided beforehand not to push things too far. There were other ways to investigate what was going on at Environ-Logging.

The waitress came with their order. The three of them stared at the food, not bothering to pick up the sandwiches. Stephen suddenly slapped the table, shook his head, and stood up. "Sorry, guys, but I think I'll pass on lunch."

Tom rose to his feet. "Please stay and have lunch with us. We won't mention Grantham again."

"Yes, please stay," said Rob. "The meal is on us."

Stephen shoved his hands into his pockets. "You mean the government is going to pay for my lunch? That's unethical, isn't it?"

"Not at all," said Tom. "As I told you, this is not a business call."

Stephen's tone remained cold. "I can hardly believe that, since we're not friends."

"Look," said Rob, "the food's already here. Why waste it?"

"Thanks," said Stephen, "but I'm not hungry anymore. I'm going back to work."

Tom stuck out his hand. "Well . . . if there is ever anything I can do, please don't hesitate to call."

Stephen ignored Tom's hand and stormed out the door. Rob watched him leave and then turned and looked at Tom. "Sorry about what happened. It's obvious that he's hiding something. But what?"

Tom sat down and looked at his uneaten sandwich. "Guess it's time to do our own research."

After lunch, they drove to the headquarters building of the Department of Timber Resources. Kevin Burke had said it would be a good place to start the investigation because all of Environ-Logging's correspondence was there in the master files. Tom had already reviewed the forest permit applications and timber plans, but he had not seen the more detailed environmental data.

Tom and Rob perused the files for two hours, but they couldn't find anything to implicate the company. Every report was clean, just like the files they had seen at the company office. Just then, Tom noticed a faded memo. "Look at this, Rob," he said.

Rob squinted to read the faint lettering. "Subject area is possible habitat of amphibian—something or other. No investigation warranted at this time. I can't read the name of the species, can you?"

"No. It looks like it's been blotted out. It's not on Environ-Logging letterhead either. The memo is signed 'J.A.' I wonder who that is?" Tom glanced at his watch. "They're closing soon. We need to head for home."

Rob closed the file folder he was reading. "Yeah, and the traffic will be severe right now. Let's make a copy of this memo and then leave."

During the two-hour drive back to Portland, Tom thought about the conversation he had with Stephen and how it might affect Lisa. He had been hurt when she had withdrawn from him the other night, and he realized he was acting childish toward her. He couldn't deny that his feelings for her were escalating—she was charming in every respect, and he wanted to see more of her. Grantham's disappearance and the caginess of his co-worker Stephen didn't add up, and he certainly didn't want Lisa to be in any danger.

"I'm going to get to the bottom of this, if it takes everything I've got," he said out loud, startling Rob.

36

Eltout Forest Range

Carl trembled as he felt the barrel of the gun once again press against his neck. He continued to drive as instructed down the narrow dirt road and past another iron gate. Tall pine trees cast eerie shadows on the rutted road as dusk approached. He slowly opened the car window and smelled the fresh, clean air after the rain. He was calmer now, but his mind still weighed all the possible avenues of escape from this nightmare. He had seen no other cars or people for miles.

The car came to a large open clearing surrounded by conifers of various heights. Carl winced as a hand gripped his shoulder blade in a vice-like squeeze. He assumed this was a signal to stop, so he turned off the ignition and waited for the man in the back seat to give him further instructions. In the ensuing silence, he imagined a dozen different scenarios that could enfold and nervously breathed another prayer.

"Get out," the voice ordered.

Carl grabbed his cell phone, slipped it into his pocket, and opened the car door. He hoped his assailant had not seen the swift move. Once he was out of the car, the man put a blindfold over his eyes and tied his hands behind his back with a coarse rope. He pushed Carl from behind, directing him back the way they had just driven down the road. Carl shivered in the chilly, humid air.

He stumbled forward for several minutes until he felt the sting of something sharp like a hypodermic needle going into his neck. Pain seared across his arms and down his body. As his legs buckled he tried to brace himself, but he couldn't with his hands tied. He collapsed to the ground, falling hard on the same shoulder the brute had squeezed.

When he awoke he was sitting up with his back against a tree. He was blindfolded and his hands were still tied behind his back. His shoulder ached where he had fallen, and he was groggy. He sniffed the cool forest air and heard several voices talking at once.

"What's going on?" he said, summoning the courage to speak. "Who are you people?"

There was silence for moment, and then a gruff voice said, "Welcome back. You've been asleep for a few hours."

"What did you do to me? What do you want?" Carl strained to focus and keep his emotions in check. He got to his knees and managed to pull himself to his feet. He tried to work out of the ropes around his wrists, but they cut into his flesh. He was furious that he couldn't see his captors, but he knew he needed to keep calm if he was going to survive.

"We want to ask you a couple of questions," said the voice again.

Carl stamped his foot. "How dare you do this to me!" His heart was pounding and he felt woozy, but he tried to sound calm and controlled.

"We're givin' the orders here." There was a pause, and then the man spoke in a more demanding tone. "Where's the book you found in the cabin?"

So that's what this is all about, Carl thought. He remained silent. He knew if he said anything it would only jeopardize Lisa.

A hand slapped him across the cheek and forced him back to the ground. "Why are you digging around places you don't belong? Why do you persist on fighting us with your useless legislation? Don't you know who you're dealing with?"

Carl's cheek was stinging. Rage surged through him, mixed with fear. His mind was swirling with thoughts of how he was going to survive, but the prayer he had said earlier helped him maintain his composure. He took a deep breath and smirked at his captor. "You'll never get away with this."

"Humph! Guess we'll have to teach you a lesson—and your girl-friend, too."

Carl felt strong hands pull him upright, grab both his arms, and shove him forward. The men kept the blindfold on him, and he stumbled as he walked for several minutes. He could feel his cell phone jangling in his pocket, but it was useless to him at that point. He was helpless and unable to warn Lisa.

As his captor guided him along, his mind swirled with Bible verses. At one point he began reciting aloud from the book of Psalms: "When I am afraid, I will trust in you. In God, whose word I praise, in God I trust; I will not be afraid. What can mortal man do to me?"

"Shut up!" a voice said. The man guiding him stabbed him in the side, and Carl grunted in pain. They finally stopped walking, and several men began to manhandle him up onto what seemed to be a gigantic metal apparatus. Carl prayed and steeled himself for what would happen next.

Another man prodded him in the ribs and shook his shoulders. He felt like a rag doll. The men tied a scratchy rope around his waist and stuffed a gag into his mouth. He broke out in a cold sweat.

He felt a sharp prick as a hypodermic needle entered his vein. A strange, tranquil feeling swept over him and he grew tired. His legs buckled and his body slumped forward, being held in place by the rope. He breathed a desperate prayer, and then his world went black.

37

Children's Hospital, Seattle

Dr. Kramer held the door for Dr. Dougherty as they entered the children's hospital. They had been working twelve-hour days for ten days straight and were exhausted. Everything was finally complete—including the investigational new drug applications and the clinical test protocols. Dr. Dougherty was scheduled to go back to New York City the next day, so Dr. Kramer decided to introduce him to his favorite patient. Although fatigued, they walked briskly into the foyer.

"This is one of the top children's hospitals in the country," Dr. Kramer said as he stifled a yawn.

"Yes, I've heard of it," said Dr. Dougherty. He had bags under his eyes and was trudging slowly after Dr. Kramer.

"I'd like to stop at the gift shop and buy something for the boy," said Dr. Kramer. He selected a festive turtle-shaped balloon at the large shop on the first floor, and then they proceeded to the elevator. "This hospital started out with only a few beds," he continued. "They rebuilt it, and now it takes up nearly two square blocks. They have plans to expand it by five hundred beds. The research center for cancer is top-notch."

Dr. Kramer grabbed the green balloon as they headed past the nurses' station and went to the boy's open door. He knocked and then walked inside. A young boy with red hair and freckles sat in bed reading a comic book. He had IVs stuck in both arms and looked jaundiced and stick thin. Both men smiled broadly.

"Patrick," said Dr. Kramer, "I've got a little present for you." He walked over to the boy, gently placed his hand on his arm, and handed him the balloon.

Patrick's face brightened. "Hi, doc. Gee, thanks! I love turtles."

"How are you today, son?" Dr. Kramer had refrained from picking up the chart to check the boy's progress. This was a social call.

"I'm okay today," Patrick answered in a hoarse voice. "Just a little tired."

"I'd like you to meet a friend of mine. His name is Ted." Dr. Kramer put a hand on the shoulder of the older man.

The boy pushed himself up on the bed. "Hi, Ted."

"Top of the morning to you, Patrick," said Dr. Dougherty. "That's a good Irish name, you know." His eyes sparkled as he extended his hand. "Saint Patrick is the patron saint of Ireland."

Patrick laughed and pushed himself up in bed. "Where are you from, Ted?"

"I live in New York City, but my family was originally from Northern Ireland. That's part of the United Kingdom. Do you know where that is?"

"No, not really."

Dr. Dougherty gestured grandly. "It's a long way from here—on the other side of the Atlantic Ocean. Have you ever been to New York City?"

"I haven't traveled outside Seattle. But I've seen pictures of the Statue of Liberty. I'd love to go there someday." Patrick wiggled the balloon.

"Ted is a doctor, too," said Dr. Kramer. "He traveled all the way from New York to try to find a cure for you."

"Gee, thanks, doc! Hey, do they have baseball over in Ireland?" Dr. Kramer chuckled as he looked at all the baseball posters and pennants hanging in the room.

The three chatted until the nurse came in to give Patrick a shot. At that point, Dr. Kramer checked the boy's chart and talked to the nurses. The boy's blood work looked fair, but he was still not eating much, and his liver and spleen were enlarged. Dr. Kramer kept his emotions in check as he turned to Patrick.

"We'd better go now, kiddo." He patted the boy on the head. "We'll come again soon." They said their goodbyes and left.

"That sure is a good kid," Dr. Dougherty said as they got into Dr. Kramer's Olds. Both men yawned at the same time and laughed.

"Yes, he sure is," said Dr. Kramer. "He hasn't been sick for very long. The NPC has spread faster than usual."

"I'm sorry to hear that." Dr. Dougherty rubbed his eyes.

"Yes, it was first diagnosed as a learning disability, like most NPC patients. Then he became jaundiced, and his mother brought him in. His liver and spleen were enlarged, and he exhibited vertical gaze palsy. Blood tests confirmed the disease." Dr. Kramer shook his head in disgust.

"Yes, I've had similar situations. It's quite distressing."

Both men were quiet as they drove back to the house. At one point, Dr. Kramer glanced over to see Dr. Dougherty nodding off to sleep. His friend snorted and woke up when the car came to a stop, and then reached for the car door handle.

"What about that potential sponsor you heard from yesterday?" Dr. Dougherty asked. "As—something or other?"

"Asclep Pharmaceutical Company, based out of Connecticut," replied Dr. Kramer. "It's short for Asclepius. You know—the Greek god of healing. They've agreed to consider sponsoring us."

"That's great news. But the testing will cost a lot of money."

"Let's worry about that later. We'll have dinner now and get you to bed. You have a long flight tomorrow." Dr. Kramer got out of the car, walked Dr. Dougherty to the front of the house, and opened the door for the older man. A delicious aroma drifted from the kitchen as they entered.

"Now, remember," said Dr. Kramer, "I want you available for a video-chat during our first meeting with the FDA. By the way, how long do you think it will be before we have our meeting?"

"I really don't know," said Dr. Dougherty. "I'll make a few calls to see if I can hurry it along. As I told you before, we could start the phase one clinical trials within thirty days of submitting the application, unless the FDA indicates otherwise. However, I would rather wait until we have our first meeting to make sure we are doing everything properly. Once we get expedited approval, things should go even quicker."

Dr. Kramer pursed his lips and looked up at the ceiling. "I don't know how long Patrick has. The sooner we can help him, the better."

"I have patients who are in great need as well. The important thing is to keep up the search for the frogs."

"Yes, I know. I'm doing the best I can." Dr. Kramer's eyes narrowed as he looked at his friend. "I'm confident that with God's help, we'll find that source."

38

Lisa's apartment, Olympia

Lisa hung up the phone. She was shaking, her hands were clammy, and she felt nauseous. The mysterious voice had told her to drive south on IH-5, exit after twenty miles, and stop at a gas station where she would see a black van. The last words the voice said had made her blood chill: "Come alone, and bring the logbook . . . or Carl will be hurt."

She retrieved the book from the suitcase and looked at her watch. She had only one hour to get to the destination—barely enough time if there was heavy traffic. Her thoughts raced. She picked up her cell phone and dialed Carl's assistant.

"Betty," she said, "I need to tell you something."

Lisa briefed Betty on what had happened and then waited for her to respond. When Betty spoke, her voice sounded anxious. "But . . . shouldn't you call the police?"

"No, not right now. I'm afraid Carl will be hurt. The man on the phone said not to call anyone—and to come alone. If I don't phone you by this evening, call Detective Richard Vandegeer of the Olympia Police Department and tell him everything." Lisa cradled the phone and grabbed her backpack.

"What do you mean if you don't return?"

"I have something they want. They already trashed my apartment to try to find it. Carl knew about it, so I guess that's why they took him."

"Who is this Detective Vandegeer?"

"He was the detective who took down the details the night my apartment was burglarized." Lisa had actually been on the verge of telling him her suspicions about Environ-Logging, but she had decided to wait until she knew more about what had happened to Ed Grantham. Now it seemed her worst fears were coming true. Something terrible was going on at the company after all.

"Look, I've got to go," said Lisa. "Just call him if you don't hear from me by midnight tonight. I'll be all right. Don't worry. But there is one more thing you can do."

"What's that?"

"Pray!"

Betty groaned. "Oh, you're one of those! Just like Carl!"

"Yes, I'm a Christian. I believe God will watch over me, but you can pray for my safety."

There was a long pause. "All right. I'll try."

Lisa hung up and threw the journal into her backpack. She was glad that she had taken the precaution of making a copy, which she had placed in a safety deposit box. She grabbed a jacket, flashlight, water bottle, and Swiss army knife. She slung the backpack over her shoulder, ran outside, and jumped into the convertible.

Within forty-five minutes she had located the gas station and identified the large black van parked around the side. As she watched, a large man in a denim shirt and pants stepped out of the vehicle. His face was mostly covered with a bandanna, which made him look as if he had stepped out of a Wild West movie. He walked over to her, grabbed her arm, and shoved something sharp into her back.

"Don't scream," he said. "Do you have the book?"

"Yes," she said. Lisa thought her heart would stop.

"Okay, move to the van." He pushed her toward the vehicle, forced her inside, and slammed the door shut. She flinched as the man seized her hands, tied them behind her back, and placed a cloth over her eyes.

"We won't hurt you unless you don't obey," said man behind her. She thought she recognized the voice as Taylor's, but she couldn't be sure. Her stomach was in knots as she felt the van lurch forward.

They rode in silence for the next hour. Each time Lisa tried to say something, she was told to keep quiet or she would be gagged. She felt the temperature in the van drop several degrees and caught a whiff of pine-filled air when the driver opened the window. She tried to remember how many times the car turned left and right.

The van slowed and then came to a stop. Lisa heard someone get out, followed by the sound of metal clanging. The door opened again, and the van moved forward. After another hour had passed, she had lost count of all the turns. Her arms were sore from being in such an awkward position. She tried to calm her nerves by reciting Bible verses in her head. Finally, the van slowed and stopped. The side door opened, and she felt hands grab her and pull her outside.

"Move this way," her captor grunted as he shoved her forward.

She was tired, cold, and thirsty. "Can I get my jacket and water out of my bag?"

"No. Just move forward."

Lisa walked with hesitation and stumbled blindly along. She felt the crunch of pine needles under her feet and heard hoot owls in the distance. After walking for what seemed to be an eternity, her captor jerked her to a stop and forced her to sit down. The ground was hard, and she trembled in the chilly forest air. She felt her bag land in her lap, and then her blindfold was removed. She gasped.

Directly in front of her was a feller-buncher machine, just like the ones she had seen at the logging camp. However, this time Carl had been positioned within the white mechanical claw. He was blindfolded and gagged, and his body sagged slightly against the thick rope that held him in position.

Lisa saw that several other men—all of whom were wearing scarves—were around her. The man with the bandanna stood in front with his gun pointed at her head. He was a monstrous figure. When he spoke again, she recognized the muffled voice as that of Taylor's.

"You can see we mean business," he said. He waved the gun toward Carl.

Anger surged through her. "What do you want from me, Taylor?" she gasped.

Taylor's eyes widened. "First, the book. I'm going to untie your hands now."

Lisa rubbed her arms after Taylor removed the bonds and then reached into her bag and pulled out the notebook. She threw it at him. "Get Carl down immediately!"

"Temper, temper, missy," said Taylor. "We need to get a few things straight first. Now, whatever you read in that book, you need to forget it."

Lisa glared at him and clenched her fists, but she said nothing.

"You go back to work and pretend nothing happened. No calls to the police or any of your government friends. We may need you to testify when necessary. And if you don't cooperate—" Taylor glared at the trussed-up man before him. "There won't be anything left of your boyfriend to find."

Lisa nodded. "If I do what you ask, will you leave us alone?"

Taylor smirked at her. "Of course. Oh . . . and one more thing, little lady. We know about your sister and her kids. Now, you wouldn't want anything to happen to them, would you?" Lisa felt fear mixed with rage rise within her. Taylor laughed. "Just do your job and remember to be a team player." He cocked his head in an imitation of Johnson. She recalled the blunt words she had heard on her first day.

"Okay, Taylor," she exclaimed, her eyes blazing. "I'll cooperate." She pointed at Carl. "Now let him go."

Taylor scooped up the book and gestured for the others to return to the van. The men all climbed inside, and soon the van was roaring back down the road the way they had come. Lisa raced to Carl and slowly climbed up onto the contraption. She carefully removed the blindfold and gag and cut the ropes with her knife. She lifted her bottle of water to Carl's lips.

Carl looked up at her and managed a weak smile. "My angel, Lisa, to the rescue!" Then he collapsed into her arms.

39

Offices of Environ-Logging, Olympia

Lisa stepped into the conference room and looked up at a giant flat-screen on the wall depicting an elaborate map with colored lines and symbols. She immediately recognized it from one of the consultant's reports. Stephen and Johnson were discussing something when she walked in.

Several employees were sitting around the large conference table. Taylor was standing in the back of the room, near the coffee bar. She took her place at the table, not daring to look Taylor or Johnson in the eye. She nearly choked when she remembered the look on Taylor's face just a few days ago.

"Hall," grunted Johnson, "Tell me again about the road."

"It's an unpaved road that is damaged from a landslide," Stephen replied. "It's on highly erodible soil—medium slope instability. See there." He pointed to a section of the map on the wall. "According to our RMAP, we must—"

Johnson held up a hand. "Let's not use acronyms."

"Sorry, sir. RMAP stands for Road Maintenance Assessment Program. We submitted our plan years ago. Whenever we find a road that is not meeting the standards, we assess it and either abandon it or upgrade it. By the way, we're using the latest geotextile fabric for erosion control—"

Johnson swore. "Yes, Hall, that's your job. Why did you bring me here?"

"Because of the recent drought, we had to upgrade these roads so we could get to areas where there might be fire danger. However, these new roads will traverse major salmon fish passage crossings, and we'll need to submit a new hydraulic permit. I know this is a political hotbed issue. I thought you should be aware."

Lisa was only half-listening. She fought against the urge to spill out angry words at the way she and Carl had been treated, but she knew it would do no good. Stephen seemed like a whimpering dog cowering before its master. She knew he was weak, but in front of Johnson, he seemed helpless. She turned away in disgust.

Johnson abruptly turned to her. "And what is your opinion, young lady?"

Lisa's cheeks went red, and it took everything within her to control her rage. "Sorry," she said, managing a weak smile, "but a lot has happened lately, and I'm not yet up to speed."

Johnson glared at her. "I don't pay you to be idle, Ms. Stone. I want a solution to this problem ASAP."

Stephen held up a hand. "That's my fault, sir. I haven't brought her in on this issue yet."

"Wait a minute." Lisa shook her head. Something didn't sound right. "Stephen, don't the rules state that the forest permit application includes the hydraulic permit application? If so, why are we submitting a new one?"

Stephen nodded. "That's correct, but as I said earlier, these are new roads that were not mentioned in the original application that was filed four years ago. The rules have changed, and we might need to submit a new fish passage plan in addition to building new bridges according to strict specifications."

The meeting continued for another hour. After the technical discussion, Johnson ranted about the employees' lack of efficiency and effort. His voice grew so loud at times that Lisa was sure the entire floor could hear him. Finally, he stormed out of the room with his sycophant, Taylor, at his heels. The group soon disbanded. Lisa lingered, waiting to talk to Stephen, but he scowled at her and left abruptly.

She soon found herself alone in the room. Her mind was swirling with the chaos and confusion. After the kidnapping incident with

Carl, she had decided to ask Tom for help. She couldn't trust anyone at work, and she was too afraid of the threat to her family to tell the police everything. She had informed Carl about what she had found in the logbook, so Tom had agreed to talk to Carl and see what he could do.

Still . . . in the back of her mind, she was not sure about anything or anyone. She thought about her family and shuddered to think what her father would do if she told him what had happened. Her mother would be a basket case.

She stamped her foot. What's happening isn't right, she thought. *They can't treat me like this. It's time to take drastic action. I'll confront Johnson.* She marched out the door and punched the elevator button for the top floor. Normally, she did not go to Johnson's office without an invitation, but nothing was normal these days.

Despite her resolve, her body quivered as the elevator doors opened, and she broke out in a cold sweat. She crept toward Johnson's office and noticed that his secretary was gone. It was probably her lunch break. She reached Johnson's door and started to knock, but just then she heard two voices coming from inside. The door was slightly ajar. She crouched nervously behind it, straining to hear the conversation, but she could only catch a few words.

"Tract one-nineteen . . ." she heard Johnson say. "Grantham . . . that frog . . . big problems . . . "

Her hand flew to her mouth. Could that be the endangered amphibian in the logbook? Suddenly, the conversation stopped. In a panic, she flew to the secretary's desk and crouched underneath. Her heart hammered as she heard the sound of approaching footsteps. She overheard Taylor and Johnson talking as they walked by the desk, and then their voices trailed off. She breathed deeply to try to control her shaking, and then waited another ten minutes to make sure neither was coming back. She prayed that the secretary would take a long lunch break.

When she thought it was safe, she crept out from behind the desk and quickly walked back to her office. She closed her office door and rested her head against it. She was still trembling and wanted to burst out crying. Fear and confusion overwhelmed her, like a choking, oppressive fog.

What am I going to do? she asked herself. Just then, a crazy thought entered her mind. She rushed to her desk, logged on to her computer, and spent the next several minutes searching the Internet. Her hands were still shaking when she picked up the phone.

"Hanley's Handgun Shop?" She paused. "I'd like to buy a gun."

40

GreenForests Office, Kirkland

Tom and Rob stared at Carl as they sipped lukewarm coffee out of paper cups. They were sitting in Carl's small office and listening in amazement as he related the events of his kidnapping and rescue by Lisa. Tom was glad that Lisa had finally reached out to him for help. He remembered the disappointment he had felt at the end of their last date and knew he couldn't disappoint her.

"Incredible!" said Tom, shaking his head.

"How could they do that to you!" Rob exclaimed.

"I have never been so scared in my life," said Carl. "And I grew up in the wilds of Brazil. The only thing that saved me was my faith in God."

Tom pulled out a tape recorder and laid it on the table. "Do you mind if we record this? We need to start gathering evidence against Environ-Logging."

Carl hesitated. "Yes . . . I will agree as long as your agency promises not to use it until I tell you the time is right."

Tom and Rob both nodded. For the next half hour, Tom took notes as Carl spoke about the experiences that he and Lisa had endured. "That's interesting about the amphibian," he said when Carl told him about the discovery of the possible habitat. "We found a suspicious memo about an 'amphibian' in the Environ-Logging files at DTR headquarters." He retrieved the copy and showed it to Carl.

"J.A.—those initials must stand for Joe Anders," Carl said. "At the time, he worked for the Olympia Forestry Service. He was a long-time consultant for Environ-Logging, but he's no longer with the company."

The discussion continued, with Tom and Rob interrupting Carl a number of times with questions. Finally, Rob turned off the recording.

"You need to be careful with that," said Carl, pointing to the device. "Those men meant business when they threatened us. Lisa called the police after her apartment was burglarized and spoke to a detective named Vandegeer. She was going to tell him all her suspicions, but all that's on hold now. She's afraid to tell him about the kidnapping because they threatened her family."

Tom's eyes widened and his face flushed with rage. "This is unbelievable. No wonder she's been acting so strangely."

Carl looked up. "Did Lisa tell you about me?"

"Only that you were friends when she was in high school. We've been on a couple of dates since we met about two months ago."

"That explains a lot," said Carl. "She's certainly an extraordinary girl."

Tom eyed Carl closely. "I assume you and Lisa were . . . close?"

"Yes, we were together some, when I was in college. We're good friends now."

Rob looked at Carl. "So . . . it's over between you two?"

Carl rubbed his chin. "Well, let's put it this way. It was over then, but frankly, I'd take her back in a heartbeat. That girl is one in a million."

Tom looked at Rob in surprise. He did not expect that answer. An awkward silence ensued as he and Carl eyed each other. Tom swallowed hard and finally said, "Well, I'd sure like to know how Lisa feels about that."

"So," Rob blurted out, "what's the next step?"

"We need to talk to Lisa," said Carl, "but I think her phone at the office is bugged. She told me the other day that she was still trying to gather evidence, but she was having a hard time finding anything. She was thinking about hiring an expert on amphibians to go to the new logging tract to try to locate any species in the area."

"Do you mean those guys who call up animals using a recording?" Tom asked.

"I've heard about that," said Rob, "but I've never actually seen someone do it."

Carl nodded. "Yes, these experts use sound recordings to attract certain species, like frogs, to come out into the open. When I was in Brazil, I met a scientist named Dr. Miyake who was searching for an endangered reptile in the Amazonian forest. I am thinking of recommending him to Lisa."

Tom leaned forward. "Did the logbook that you and Lisa found name the species?"

"No, all we had to go on were the symbols 'L.l.' Lisa came up with a half dozen possibilities for what species that could be." He opened his briefcase, took out several sheets, and handed them to Rob and Tom. "Fortunately, before she gave the logbook in exchange for me, she had the foresight to copy the pages. She has another copy in a safe place." Carl pointed on the page. "There, you see?"

"Yes," said Tom, "it seems to imply that the species is rare and endangered."

"The Endangered Species Act prohibits the 'take' of any listed animal," said Rob. "That basically means the company cannot cause harm or disturbance to an animal on the endangered species list. They also cannot disturb or destroy its habitat without prior approval from the government, such as through a habitat mitigation plan. The bottom line is that if this amphibian is truly on the list, and Environ-Logging is disturbing it or its habitat without authorization, they will find themselves in big trouble."

"But we don't know if there is a habitat yet," said Carl. "That's why Lisa is eager to hire an expert to see if he can find such an amphibian on their property."

"I see," said Rob. "Once the expert finds that species, the area might be declared a critical habitat, and it will be protected under the act."

Tom shook his head. "Sounds like too dangerous a plan, Carl. Don't you think we should go to the police?"

"No," said Carl. "We need to respect Lisa's wishes for now. Let's help her get onto the property to gather the evidence she needs to take down Johnson." He paused and looked down. "Lisa is planning on going next week."

"I don't like the idea of Lisa sneaking around," said Tom. "She's been through enough already. It's too dangerous."

"Believe me," said Carl, "I don't like it either. But this seems to be the only way that she can tag these guys."

"Yes," said Rob, "they do seem to cover their tracks pretty well. We couldn't find a single thing in the files to pin on them. If Lisa can pull this off, it would give us the evidence we need to stop them for good."

"I agree," said Carl. "That's why I've decided to go with her."

Tom shook his head and stood to his feet. "Carl, I really think you need to go to the police. This plan that you too are concocting is unsafe. If you really cared about Lisa, I think you would see that."

Carl recoiled as if he had taken a blow. For a moment he seemed to struggle with what he wanted to say in response, but then his face relaxed. He stood up, walked over to Tom, and put a hand on his shoulder. "Tom," he said, "do you believe in God?"

Tom look surprised. "What? I don't see how that has anything to do with this." He brushed Carl's arm aside and sat back down in his chair.

Carl returned to his chair and sat down as well. "Lisa and I are born-again Christians," he said. "We believe that God will protect us."

Tom glared at him. "Don't give me that line. If you go through with this plan, you know that you will be putting Lisa in danger."

"You need faith, Tom." He paused and reached for the well-worn Bible on his desk. "Here, let me share a few passages with you."

Tom shook his head and Rob raised his eyebrows, but neither responded.

41

Eagles Prairie, Olympia suburbs

Stephen leaned back and propped his feet up on the leather recliner in his den. He took a sip from a mug of beer and closed his eyes. The instrumental music in the background was soothing, and he tried to focus on it and close off all other noise.

He was emotionally and physically exhausted after spending so much time purging damaging information from the files and wiping out harmful data from the computers. He had to maintain his composure or he would go crazy. He still felt badly that Lisa had gotten mixed up in all of this. She was a smart kid, and the best way he could protect her at this point was not talk to her too much. He would have to keep thinking up excuses to keep her at bay.

He opened his eyes and glanced out the window at the golf course. The sun was glowing red on the horizon, and half a dozen golfers were trying to get in a few rounds before nightfall. Some people didn't have a care in the world. He slumped in his chair, took another sip of beer, and tried to relax.

He heard a soft knock and looked up. Amanda stuck her head inside. He caught a whiff of aromas coming from the kitchen.

"Didn't you hear the phone, dear?" she asked. "It's for you—someone from the office. I have a meeting tonight, so we need to eat soon." She shut the door quietly.

Stephen moaned and lifted the receiver. "Hello?" he said.

"We need a favor," said Taylor. His voice was raspy.

Stephen's eyes flashed and he swore under his breath. "I told you to never call me at home. What's the meaning of this?"

"It's urgent, or I wouldn't have called."

Stephen banged his palm on the desk. "No!" There was a long pause. "What did you say?" asked Taylor.

Stephen remained silent. The annoying sycophant always made his blood boil, but he knew this was not the time or place to argue with him. He took a deep breath and softened his tone. "What is it this time?"

"That's better," said Taylor. "I need you to take care of a small detail."

Stephen listened half-heartedly as Taylor explained the latest request. "All right," he said. "I know what to do. But I still don't understand why you had to call me at home." He forced the receiver down and turned to his computer screen.

He remembered the email he had received from Grantham just before his disappearance. He had scribbled down the name of the doctor and species of frog on a scrap of paper and shoved it into his wallet. He pulled out the scrap and began typing the name of the mysterious frog species into an Internet search.

After surfing the web for half an hour, he finally struck pay dirt. Kramer was a doctor in Seattle who had put out an appeal for anyone who had knowledge of the location of a rare species of frog called *Litoria latolevata*. Stephen wrote the contact information for the doctor on a pink sticky-note and tucked both pieces back into his wallet. He would call Dr. Kramer first thing in the morning.

He took a deep breath, shook his head, and put his head down on his desk. He lied at work, and he lied at home. He couldn't keep the truth straight if he tried. The look of apathy in his wife's eyes made him ashamed. The disappointment in his friend Carl's voice was hurtful. Clandestine meetings, sleepless nights, and hunger had all combined to make him feel completely exhausted. He tried to push out all the confusing and desperate thoughts swirling in his head.

Somehow, he knew this nightmare had to end. He started to weep—at first softly, but then uncontrollably. He felt so hopeless and desperate. What could he do? To whom could he turn? God?

He had said a prayer once before, but nothing had happened. He knew deep inside it was probably hopeless. Yet what if it wasn't? He bowed his head. *God, I know you exist. I need help right now. Please help me.*

He looked up and saw a Bible sitting on the coffee table. He picked it up and looked at the inside cover. It was Amanda's. He had never taken the time to read it. In fact, the only times he ever picked up a Bible were during his infrequent trips to church on Christmas and Easter. He held the book in his hands, unsure of what to do next. Just then he recalled his son's words on the boat: "God will guide you to do the right thing."

He flipped the book open halfway and looked at the page. It opened to Psalm 91. He stopped at verse four and repeated the words aloud: "He will cover you with his feathers, and under his wings you will find refuge. His faithfulness will be your shield and rampart."

He closed the Bible and pictured an eagle covering its chicks with its outstretched wings. Roger had said that God was with him and knew what he was going through. Could God be my refuge? Stephen thought.

He rested his head on the back of the chair, closed his eyes, and mouthed a silent prayer. *Lord, this madness has got to come to an end. I haven't asked for anything before this, but I'm desperate. I need to make a decision and act, but I don't know if I have the courage to do it. I need help. Please!*

42

Offices of Environ-Logging, Olympia

Taylor waited impatiently outside Johnson's office. His boss was no doubt on some important call with a congressman—so high and mighty. How he hated kowtowing to the pompous jerk. After years of loyal service, Johnson still treated him like a dog. Taylor knew he wasn't the smartest cookie in the world, but he also wasn't the dumbest. He knew Johnson only kept him around to do the dirty work so he could come off looking squeaky clean. He needed some leverage in case things went sour.

He looked over to see the secretary get a buzz on her phone. She turned to him and smiled. "You may go in now, Mr. Taylor."

Johnson was sitting in his usual manner—his brown Armani suit open to reveal his appalling gut and his feet propped on the desk. He had his eyes glued to the flat screen in front of him and didn't bother to look up. Taylor, as usual, headed for the coffee bar. He loved that Italian coffee and couldn't possibly afford it himself.

"You called for me, boss?" he said as he sat down on the plush sofa.

"Yes," said Johnson. "I'm very busy today, so we need to make this quick. I have several congressmen waiting for me on an important call. I called you here to get the update you should have given me as soon as you returned from your last 'mission.'"

Taylor eyed him but said nothing. He was tired of being abused. Didn't loyalty count for anything?

"Did you hear me?" said Johnson, his voice beginning to rise in anger. "I want a report on that Carl fellow. How did he react to your latest 'persuasion'?"

Taylor took a sip of coffee. "I haven't heard a peep from him, or from the girl. Guess we scared 'em enough. The look on that kid's face when he realized—"

"Save the theatrics," Johnson interrupted. "Just keep an eye on both of them. We might need to take more drastic action later."

Taylor forced a grin. "Sure, boss. You know me. I'll do whatever it takes."

"And another thing. One of my sources at the courthouse informed me that someone was snooping around in our files the other day."

Taylor looked up. He usually heard about these things well before Johnson did. "When was that?"

"About a week ago. I thought that's what I paid you to do—to keep up with these things. Find out who it was and put a tail on him."

Taylor's face went red, and he gripped his coffee mug. "You betcha, boss," he said, gritting his teeth. "Don't worry, I got it covered." He was infuriated but knew he should keep his temper in check.

"You know I'm good friends with the police commissioner," Johnson continued, "so you don't need to worry about getting in trouble."

Taylor remained silent. There went the arrogant jerk throwing his weight around again.

Just then, the phone buzzed. "Mr. Johnson," said the voice on the intercom, "your daughter is on line three."

"I want to take this call, Taylor. Wait a moment." Johnson picked up the phone and listened for several minutes.

Taylor got up, poured another cup of coffee, and reached for a couple of gourmet cookies. His cheeks were still hot. He was so fed up with the sleaze ball. The guy was dishonest, egotistical, and pompous. But, he was still the boss. He needed to maintain his composure, or he would break the guy's neck.

"I'll be right over," said Johnson. His face looked grim as he put the phone down. "Taylor, something has come up, and I need to leave for the hospital right now. We'll continue this discussion later."

Taylor nodded his head. He sauntered back to his office, his thoughts mulling over the conversation and similar ones in the past. *He thinks*

I'm so stupid. I'm nobody but a slave to him. Well, I've got one up on you, boss. I know all about your secret trysts with that seductress Claire. Your wife will be very happy to have an excuse to take you to the cleaners, if I decide to tell her.

He thought about the phone call Johnson had received and realized it was probably about his precious grandson. He picked up the phone and called Johnson's secretary to find out which hospital her boss was headed to. He rubbed his hands together. It would be useful to get some more information about the boy to go along with what he already knew about the affair. Not so stupid after all, eh, boss? he thought.

43

Camden, New Jersey

Dr. Dougherty sat in a pink plastic chair at a rickety kitchen table and looked at Doris's tired expression. She poured tea into two chipped cups and set down a plate of plain biscuits. She wiped her hands on a stained apron before sitting down.

"I'm so glad you decided to visit, doc," she said. "It was good of ya to come. Sorry about the looks o' this place." She waved a frail hand around the shabby room.

Dr. Dougherty looked around the tiny apartment and noticed holes in the walls, a cracked ceiling, and ragged carpet. The kitchen had a musty odor, and a cockroach was crawling across the floor. On the wall above the threadbare sofa in the living room was a shiny cross next to a faded picture of Jesus. Next to a well-worn armchair was a table with a small glass vase of plastic flowers and a framed photo of Jerry.

In spite of the poor conditions, somehow there was an atmosphere of peace about the place. It had been a month since Jerry's death, but Doris seemed calm. He felt comfortable in her home.

"It's all right, Doris," said Dr. Dougherty. "I just wanted to see how you were doing." He took a sip of the weak tea and a bite of the biscuit. It was stale.

"You're very kind, sir. I know you did all you could for my poor boy." She looked away with a pained expression.

Dr. Dougherty mustered his courage. "I wanted to ask you something . . . something I never got around to asking at the hospital."

"What's that?" Doris asked, looking up at him.

He hesitated. He didn't want to open up old wounds, but it was necessary. "Do you remember what I told you in the hospital—that NPC is a disease that requires both parents to be carriers of the gene?"

"Yes."

"So . . . what I want to ask—" He looked away.

"Doc, what is it?"

He swallowed hard and met her gaze. "Doris, do you have any other children? What about your husband? I need to know if the gene has been passed on."

"No, Jerry was my only child," she answered wistfully. "I ain't seen his dad in a month of Sundays. He split as soon as he heard I was pregnant."

"Has he ever tried to contact you?"

"No, but I wish he had. We coulda used some money over the years. We barely scraped by."

"I don't mean to pry into your personal affairs," said Dr. Dougherty, pressing gently, "but how are you set up for money? Do you have enough to live on?"

Doris reached for his hand and squeezed it. "Doc, you're one of the kindest men I ever did meet. As I told ya before, I trust in the Lord. I don't know why this happened to me, but it happened for a reason. The Lord'll get me through this." She looked up at the picture of Jesus on the cracked wall.

Dr. Dougherty forced a smile. "Your faith must give you great comfort."

"That is sorely true. My Jesus has helped me whenever I had me problems." She wiped her eyes with a torn cotton rag. "Do you have faith, doctor?"

He squirmed in his chair. "I believe in God, if that's what you mean. My wife and I attend church, but she's the religious one in the family."

"Doc, I mean no disrespect . . . but what I mean is, do you have faith in the Lord Jesus as your Savior? It means a lot more than just goin' to church on Sundays."

Dr. Dougherty couldn't help but blush. He made no reply. Just as when he had talked to Dr. Kramer, the conversation was uncomfortable for him. Suddenly, he desperately wanted to leave.

Doris saw his body language and put her hand to her mouth. "I'm so sorry, doc. I'm far too bold for my own good. Please forgive me."

"Don't worry about it. I just don't like talking too much about religion." He turned away.

"It's all right, doc. I been doin' enough prayin' for the both of us. And if you don't mind my sayin', I been praying a lot for you lately."

Dr. Dougherty's eyes widened. "You've been praying for me?"

"Yes, doc. I could tell in the hospital you didn't believe me when I said God had a reason for takin' my Jerry. You see, I don't blame God for his death."

"You don't? Why not?"

"Don't get me wrong. There's not a day goes by I don't cry my eyes out. But God didn't cause my boy to die. That was just pure evil showin' itself in the world. It's been here ever since God created man and he chose to sin. There wasn't nothin' that could be done about it."

"But don't you think God could have cured Jerry?" Dr. Dougherty knew he was opening up raw wounds. He hated to ask the question, but he wanted to know how the woman before him could have so much faith.

"Doc, my favorite verse in the Bible is Romans 8:28. It says, 'And we know that in all things, God works for the good of those who love Him, who have been called according to His purpose.' You see, God's makin' me a better, stronger person than before."

Doris's words struck him like a lightning bolt. It was the same verse that Dr. Kramer had quoted. He couldn't believe it. What was going on here?

"You look like a ghost, doc," Doris said with a smile.

"It's just . . . that someone else quoted that same verse to me, only a month ago."

"I see. Sounds like the Spirit is workin' on you. That's what prayer does, you know."

Dr. Dougherty gave her a vacant stare. "Maybe you're right." He paused and shook his head. "I would like to talk to you more about your faith, Doris. If you have time, that is."

Doris got up and poured him another cup of tea. "It would be my pleasure."

44

GreenForests Office, Kirkland

"If we take this road, there is a trail that leads here." Lisa tapped on the dog-eared logging map on the table in Carl's office. "You know, Carl, Tract M-119 is close to Grantham's old cabin."

"That makes sense," said Carl. "So, you think on Sundays there are fewer employees at the camp?"

"Yes, it seemed that way last time. I don't think we'll see any activity at the tract." Lisa tried to sound sure, but her insides were churning.

Tom hunched over to take a look at the map. "Are you sure you can bluff your way out if you get caught?"

"Of course," said Lisa. "I'll just turn on the charm, like last time." As long as she didn't run into Oso, she would be just fine. "Carl, I'm really glad you could convince Dr. Miyake to come."

"Yes," said Carl, "he's truly amazing. When he heard we might be looking for an endangered species of frog, he dropped everything for the chance to check it out." He paused and raised an eyebrow. "But remember, we need to keep him in the dark about being on Environ-Logging property. We need to keep him focused on the task at hand—locating that frog."

Dr. Gary Miyake of the Miyake Wildlife Consulting Company had agreed to go with the pair to search for the endangered frog. The sixty-five-year-old had a long list of credentials, including a bachelor's degree in forestry and a master's and doctorate in wildlife management, with a specialty in reptiles and amphibians. He had twenty-five years' worth of experience in forests all over the world, and his expertise in identifying rare and endangered species was unmatched.

Lisa and Carl had hired Dr. Miyake under the aegis of Carl's company so as not to arouse suspicion at Environ-Logging. They both knew the danger he could face.

"Okay," said Tom, "while you're off gallivanting in the wilderness, I'll be searching for the elusive Mr. Joe Anders—aka 'J.A.'"

Carl looked at his watch. "It's time."

Lisa nodded and folded up the map. They gathered their belongings and headed for Carl's Range Rover. Lisa had dressed casually in beige khakis and a white polo shirt. She had put on a dark green pullover sweatshirt to ward off the morning chill.

Dr. Miyake had flown up from Los Angeles the day before, and they were to pick him up at his motel. When they arrived, they found the older man waiting for them. He was dressed simply in a tan shirt, dark blue Dockers, and scuffed black tennis shoes. He got inside the car, and they continued south.

"Do you have any idea what type of amphibian we are looking for?" Dr. Miyake asked. He grabbed a thick book from his bag. "I brought my textbook *Amphibians of the Pacific Northwest* just in case. You said the name started with an L and might be rare?"

"That's right," said Lisa. "I've got a list of the ones we believe it might be. We're hoping you will find the right one." She reached for her backpack and handed him a piece of paper.

Dr. Miyake hunched forward to retrieve it, his brown eyes sparkling behind thick wire-rimmed glasses. "Where is this place we're going? Why do you suspect there might be one on your property?"

Carl took his eyes off the road for a second and looked at Lisa. She took the cue and turned to look Dr. Miyake straight in the eye. "Dr. Miyake, it's difficult for us to explain any more at this time. Can you just trust us about the location and accept the fact that we believe one is there?"

Dr. Miyake wrinkled his brows, scratched his beard, and settled back in his seat. An awkward pause followed. At length he said, "Of course. Whatever you wish. I was just curious." He folded his arms, turned toward the window, and remained silent for the rest of the trip.

Lisa sighed. She was glad that Dr. Miyake had stopped asking questions. They were on dangerous ground, and the less he knew, the better.

An hour later, Tom motioned to Lisa and tapped the GPS. The turnoff to Tract M-119 was coming up soon. She looked at the map and searched for the road.

"There it is," she said, pointing toward a narrow dirt road that led off the main highway. Carl turned onto it and slowed down. They were jarred back and forth, often hitting potholes as they crept along the rough road. Tall pine trees, straight and majestic, cast shadows along the route. They swerved and jostled for an hour as they went deeper into the Eltout forest.

"Lisa, look," said Carl. He slowed to a crawl and pointed at a padlocked gate just ahead. The name "Environ-Logging" was firmly etched on a wooden plank alongside a sign that said "No Trespassing." Lisa stepped out of the SUV and took out a set of keys. She tried several before finding the one that opened the gate. She knew that Dr. Miyake had seen the plank, and she hoped he would not ask if they were trespassing.

Carl moved the vehicle forward. When Lisa returned, his eyes flitted down to the keys. She put her fingers to her lips and cast a glance backward. She would explain later that she had "borrowed" the keys from security under false pretenses. They proceeded along a slightly smoother road before coming to a large cleared area.

"I think this is as far as we can go by car," said Carl. "The rest is on foot." He parked the car inside a grove of trees away from the road, got out, and stretched. Lisa and Dr. Miyake followed him.

"According to the map," said Lisa, "Tract 119 is on the right, about five hundred yards ahead of us." She pointed toward a thick-forested hill. "It might be a little rough going to get there."

Lisa consulted the map one last time before leading the way. The air became crisper and cooler as they entered the forest. The familiar sounds of crickets and screech owls greeted them as they stepped gingerly through the maze of ponderosa pines and Douglas fir. They could hear a woodpecker chipping away in the distance and caught glimpses of white-tailed deer through the thicket. Finally, they came to a small clearing.

Lisa pointed at the map. "Stop. It's here."

Unlike a typical logging tract, felled logs lay on the ground in bunches, and they were interspersed with live trees. Organic debris had been mixed with scattered wood chips and half-sawn timber.

"It looks like they started logging here but stopped," said Carl. He turned to Dr. Miyake and rested his hands on his hips. "What do you think?"

Dr. Miyake looked around. "The habitat is certainly disturbed, so we won't find anything here. Let's go on a little further."

They walked outside the cleared area toward a thicket of trees. As they went along, the air became cooler and damp. "I think we're approaching the edge of some wetlands," said Dr. Miyake.

Carl glanced around the area. "Why don't we set up here?"

"Yes, this looks like it could be habitat," said Dr. Miyake. He retrieved a black box and set it in the middle of the cleared area. He opened it and switched on a battery-powered tape recorder. He adjusted the volume, and sounds of frogs and toads croaking in various tones emanated from the speakers. "Now we hide a short distance away and wait."

An hour later, they were still waiting to observe any animals moving in the area. Lisa was cold and her body ached, and she was just about to suggest that they move locations. Just then, she heard a sound she was not expecting—a dog barking in the distance. Lisa's heart leapt to her throat as she recognized the distinctive bark.

45

FDA Headquarters, Maryland

"Safety, Dr. Kramer, safety," said Dr. Katherine Chan. She faced the assembled group in the large conference room at the Food and Drug Administration center. "That's the emphasis of phase one studies. Our expedited approval process does not mean we compromise our standards for safety."

Dr. Kramer flushed and shifted in his chair. He sat at one end of the conference table next to a man with red hair who was the representative from Asclep Pharmaceutical. No fewer than eight white-lab-coated doctors at the other end stared at them as if they were aliens. Dr. Kramer was exhausted and wearing wrinkled clothing, having just arrived in Maryland the night before at midnight. This first meeting with the FDA was crucial to the success of the project.

Dr. Chan, a dark-haired, petite woman wearing a light gray business suit, frowned at him. "We agree that your work with lab animals looks promising," she said. "But we need to know the side effects and how the drug will metabolize in the human body." She paused and looked over her thin wire reading glasses at a male colleague with thick black eyebrows. He returned the stare and nodded. Dr. Chan narrowed her eyes and said in a stiff tone, "We are sorry to say that your clinical test protocol for human testing lacks adequate documentation."

The words were a stunning blow to Dr. Kramer. His face turned red and he glanced at his colleague, who cleared his throat and looked away.

"We see your schedule of tests, procedures, and amount of dosage," one of the white lab coats chimed in. "But you lack detailed information about how you will monitor each patient. For example, there is no reference to how you will track a patient's vital signs and blood chemistry."

"We can provide that information," mumbled Dr. Kramer. "We only have about twenty volunteers so far, but we're still looking."

"We'd prefer at least forty volunteers in phase one if possible," a voice across the room said. "And what about voluntary consent forms? Have they all signed?"

Before either man could respond, they were bombarded by questions coming from all directions.

"What about dosages and the length of each trial?"

"What is your surrogate endpoint—the marker that represents a clinically meaningful outcome?"

"How will you deal with side effects?"

"Wait just a minute!" said a booming voice from the middle of the table, interrupting the cacophony. Dr. Ted Dougherty had joined the conference by speakerphone. "We fully intend to follow all the required protocols. Don't worry—you will get all the information you request. This isn't the first go-round for me, and I know what to do. Remember that we have lives at stake here." He paused to allow these last words to sink in. "As you know, there is no cure for NPC, and hundreds of children and young adults have the disease. We need to start trials immediately."

There was an awkward silence before Dr. Chan replied. "Hello, Ted," she said. "It's Kathy."

Dr. Dougherty's booming laugh reverberated across the room. "Greetings, Kathy. You didn't expect to ever hear from me again, did you?"

Dr. Chan stared at the phone and waved her hand as if Dr. Dougherty could see it. "We understand the situation, Ted. We'll work with you on all these aspects. But . . ."

Dr. Kramer leaned forward. Here it comes, he thought.

"Our biggest concern is the lack of supply. You say in your application that you cannot find a good source of the amphibian called *Litoria latolevata*. What have you done to locate this rare species?"

Dr. Kramer cleared his throat. "Ted, I'd like to answer that. We've sent requests to hundreds of zoos across the world. There are only about a dozen that have this particular frog in captivity, but we are hopeful that one will respond soon."

"You say there have been none found in the U.S. in the wild?"

"That's correct." Dr. Kramer tried to keep his tone optimistic. "Our best chance is to find them in captivity."

"Is there any way to manufacture the frog's skin chemically or artificially?" asked the man with the thick eyebrows.

"Not yet," said the Asclep representative. "Of course, that is the ultimate goal, but right now we are only at the preliminary stages. We need to study the real frog species before we can begin to duplicate it in the laboratory."

There was an awkward lull as the white coats shuffled papers and cleared their throats. Dr. Kramer had never felt so out of place. After several more minutes, Dr. Chan looked across the table at her colleagues. "Any more questions or concerns?" she asked.

A few of the white coats turned to each other and mumbled. Some shook their heads while others nodded to Dr. Chan. No one spoke.

"Very well then." Dr. Chan looked at Dr. Kramer and waved her hand at the folders on the table. "You present a good case for your first round, and we are confident that you'll provide the necessary details we require. We agree that the drug is truly needed, because as you stated, there is no cure for NPC. On the basis of that, we are inclined to grant you faster approval. You may proceed with the phase one testing. However—"

Dr. Kramer glanced sideways at his colleague and steeled himself.

"This approval is contingent on finding a good, solid source for the amphibian."

Dr. Kramer's eyes widened. That was exactly what he was afraid she would say.

46

Near Tract 119, Eltout Forest, Washington

Carl, Lisa, and Dr. Miyake froze at the sound of the dog. Lisa could not believe her ears. She looked at Carl. "I know that sound. It's Oso, Mr. Johansen's German Shepherd." Her eyes darted toward the noise.

"Who is Mr. Johansen?" asked Carl.

"He's in charge of the logging camp. That dog is always with him. It can only mean one thing, but I don't see how—"

She grabbed the Smith & Wesson from her backpack. She had waited the mandatory five-day period, but she did not yet have a concealed weapon permit and felt nervous just holding it. She had never used a gun in her life.

Carl looked down at the weapon in Lisa's hand. "What in the world are you doing with that?"

Lisa remembered when she and Carl had taken part in an anti-gun protest march. "Just taking precautions. You know what happened last time."

Carl placed his palm on her hand. "What's got into you? Put that away."

Lisa shoved the gun back into her backpack. Luckily, Dr. Miyake hadn't seen it. She strained her ears. "It sounds like Johansen's coming from the road. I think we should head in the other direction." She cast a glance over at the scientist, who looked perplexed but kept silent.

Carl pointed toward a hill in the opposite direction of the road. It was thick with tall pines and underbrush. "Up there. Let's see if we can find a place to wait until they pass. Hopefully they won't see the car." He dashed over to the wooden box in the clearing and turned off the recording.

Lisa turned to Dr. Miyake. "I know we have a lot of explaining to do, and I'm sorry. But please trust us when we say that we need to leave this area, now."

Dr. Miyake furrowed his brows. "I had an idea something wrong was going on. I should never have come without more information." He grabbed the box from Carl and tucked it under his arm.

"Sir," said Lisa, grabbing his arm, "I actually work for Environ-Logging, and we are on their property. However, I have reason to believe they are hiding evidence of an endangered species. But we've had some trouble and—"

Carl brought a hand up to cut her off. "No time for explanations now. Let's get going." He began moving away from the noise, and Lisa and Dr. Miyake followed. They trudged up a steep hillside through thick stands of pine and heavy undergrowth that scratched their arms and legs. Lisa slipped a few times and barely caught herself from falling. She pulled off her sweatshirt and wrapped it around her waist. Gradually the sound of the barking dog decreased.

"Look, over there," said Carl. He pointed at a rock opening near the top of the hill. "It looks like a small cave." Lisa noticed that he was barely sweating, while she was panting from the climb. Dr. Miyake was winded as well.

The three approached the top of the hill, where there was a rocky outcropping with a small cave opening. Carl bent down and entered. A few minutes later, he reemerged. "There's enough room for all of us in there. But I warn you—there is an awful smell inside." Lisa and Dr. Miyake crouched and followed him inside.

The area opened up into a small cavern that was tall enough for them to stand. A smell of smoke, mold, and feces lingered in the air. Lisa saw a torn Indian rug lying on the ground. Charred ashes lay in a heap.

"This places really stinks," she said. "It's so bizarre. Someone was here for a while." She held her nose and lifted the dirty rug.

"Yeah, it looks that way," said Carl. "Maybe some vagabond was living in here." He poked around using his small flashlight. A broken chair lay sideways on the floor next to a battered wooden table, and other debris littered the floor. Dr. Miyake looked around and frowned. He took up a position near the cave entrance and looked out.

"Hey, Carl, look at this," said Lisa. She shone her flashlight at red blotches on the rug. "What do you make of it?"

Carl turned the rug over in his hands. "I don't know, but those blotches are strange. Some sort of red ink or dye, perhaps."

"Could it be—blood?"

"I can't imagine why it would be blood." He looked up, and something caught his attention. "What do we have here?" He dropped the rug, walked over to a place on the wall, and shined his light on what appeared to be a crude drawing in black charcoal.

Lisa walked over, squinted, and pulled out her cell phone to take a picture. "It looks like a frog, doesn't it, Carl?"

"Sure does." He shone the flashlight to the back of the cave. "Listen, do you hear something?"

"Yeah, it sounds almost like water dripping." Carl starting walking to the back of the cave, and Lisa followed after him. Both stopped abruptly when they heard a shout.

Dr. Miyake was waving his hands frantically. "Hey, guys! I think I see smoke!"

Lisa and Carl rushed to the cave opening. They looked down and saw flames coming from the direction they had just traveled.

"I think the clearing is on fire!" Lisa shrieked.

47

Klamath Falls, Oregon

Tom slouched in his SUV and stared at the dilapidated house trailer in front of him. He had spent hours driving through run-down neighborhoods to find the house of Joe Anders. Street signs were either defaced or missing. He observed an abandoned lot on one side of the street and a junkyard with high weeds on the other.

He swallowed hard, got out of the car, walked up the cracked walkway, and knocked on the rusty metal door. After several minutes, a husky voice responded from inside. "Who is it?"

"Tom Moeller. We spoke on the phone."

The door opened a crack, and an unkempt face with scraggly beard appeared. "Show me some ID." The voice was gruff, and Tom thought he spied a gun in the stranger's hand.

Tom pulled his ID out of his wallet and held it up. The man grabbed it and closed the door again. A few seconds later, the door opened, and he was ushered inside. Tom walked into the dilapidated room. The walls were chipped and cracked, and the ceiling was full of black patches and peeled paint. Cheap vinyl tiles covered the floor in places, and a stench of cigarette smoke lingered in the air. The man gestured with his beer can to the only furniture in the room—a worn fake-leather sofa.

"Mr. Anders, you're a hard man to find," said Tom. "By the looks of it, you don't like strangers, either." Tom was finding it hard not to hold his nose. Anders looked and smelled like he hadn't showered in days. He had on a dirty T-shirt and faded blue jeans with holes in the knees.

"You got that right," said Anders. "That's the way I want it." He dragged a fold-up chair from the kitchen and planted himself in it. "You can call me Joe. Wanna beer?"

"No, thanks. I appreciate you seeing me. You know why I'm here, right?"

Anders burped and threw the can toward the kitchen. "I figured someone would catch up to me. I was hoping it'd be the law and not them."

"You mean Environ-Logging?"

"Yep." Anders grabbed a pack of cigarettes off the floor and pointed it toward Tom, who shook his head. Anders shrugged, pulled out a cigarette, lit up, and blew the smoke toward the ceiling.

"First of all, can you tell me what happened to Ed Grantham?"

Anders narrowed his eyes. "Why do you want to know?"

Tom leaned forward and explained who he was and why he was there. "You'll be helping us greatly if you cooperate."

"You don't know Environ-Logging very well, do you?" Anders flicked his cigarette ash on the floor. "Then again, it's about time the truth came out."

Anders had worked as a wildlife management specialist for the Olympia Forestry Service for the past seven years. He had been assigned exclusively to Environ-Logging and knew Ed Grantham well. The two had discovered a rare amphibian during a wildlife survey they had performed to complete the forest permit application.

"At first we heard a distinctive, high-pitched croak that almost sounded like a whistle," he said. "Then, after several hours, we finally spotted it. We were able to take a few pictures, and we even made a crude drawing of the gorgeous little creature in charcoal on the wall of a nearby cave. When we got back, Grantham discovered it was an extremely rare type of frog. Apparently it has not been seen in the U.S. for more than ten years."

"Who did you notify about this finding?" asked Tom. "And what happened to those photos?"

"When we returned to the office, we called a special meeting, because we knew how important this finding was. As you know, this could have shut down Environ-Logging operations for some time. The meeting was just with Environ-Logging's president, Clive Johnson." Anders paused. "We were excited, even though we knew it was bad news for them. We brought the photos with us."

"What happened then, Joe?"

"All hell broke loose. That slimy CEO called my boss and told him that if I didn't stay quiet about what we'd found, he would make sure we were both fired. They grabbed the photos and tore them up right in front of us. I told that stuffed shirt where he could go and stormed out. But that's not the worst part. The next day, I got the axe, just like he said. I couldn't believe it."

Joe stopped and lowered his head. "I was escorted out the door that very day by security. I only had time to scribble down a few notes before I had to leave. Then, to top it off, a few days later this thug followed me home, busted into my apartment, and said that if I ever said anything to anyone, he'd hunt me down and kill me." Joe lifted his head, balled up his fist, and swore several times. He coughed from his cigarette and went to retrieve a beer from the refrigerator.

Tom waited several awkward minutes for Anders to return and slouch back down into his chair. "Considering what I've learned about Environ-Logging," Tom said, "I'm not surprised about what happened to you. But I am sorry." He looked at Anders with sympathy. During the next half hour, he described what he, Carl, and Lisa had discovered. "We're building up substantial evidence against them. So, the bottom line is this: how would you like to get back at them?"

Joe's eyes grew wide. "I've lost everything because of those guys— my career, my house, my reputation. But before I go out on a limb, I need to know if you really have enough evidence to take them down."

Tom paused. "If you agree to testify, it will certainly bolster the case we're building. As you know, the company is powerful. I can't guarantee your safety."

"I don't have any proof," said Anders. "I left that place literally with the shirt off my back. It will be their word against mine."

Tom nodded. "That's okay. Your sworn statements will confirm what we have gathered so far."

Joe stood up and put his hands on his hips. "Okay. It's time I did the right thing. They need to pay for what they've done—and not just to me, but to Ed."

"What do you mean?"

Joe shrugged and shook his head. "Nothin'."

Tom was sure Joe was hiding something, but he decided this wasn't the time to press the issue. The man was clearly hurt and venting his anger. Tom got up and gently put his hand on Anders's shoulder.

"Listen, Joe. I'm sorry about what happened to you and Mr. Grantham. But we'll make them pay, one way or another. I've got to go, but we'll be in touch."

Anders looked out the blinds and watched Tom get into his car. When Tom had driven away, he closed the door, sat down, and thought about the last time he had seen Grantham. The man had not checked in with him at their usual contact time, so he had gone to Grantham's cabin in search of him. There he had found some charred remains and a trail of blood that led up the hill to the cave where he and the doctor had often gone to relax during their investigations. He was still haunted by the vision he saw there of Grantham lying on the Navajo rug in a pool of his own blood.

Anders buried his head in his hands. He was still petrified of Johnson and his goon Taylor. And who knew whether or not Johnson was setting up this whole thing to trap him? No, he said to himself, I won't tell anyone what I found in that cave. At least, not until I absolutely have to.

48

University of Washington, Seattle

Dr. Kramer clapped his cell phone shut, reared his head back, and laughed so loud that one of his students dashed into the office.

"Sir, are you all right?" the boy asked.

"Yes, son, I'm fine. Just very happy." He bounced on his chair.

"I'm glad. Good news about the frog?"

"You betcha. Thanks for asking." Dr. Kramer flipped over his laptop, glanced at his watch, and called Dr. Dougherty on Skype. Soon, the old man's haggard face appeared. His friend was wearing a colorful Japanese-type kimono and cradling a cup.

"What is it, old chap?" said Dr. Dougherty. His eyes looked tired.

"Sorry to disturb you, Ted. Just wanted to tell you the good news. We have the approval! We can begin phase one testing."

Dr. Dougherty's eyes crinkled, and he broke into a huge smile. "How on earth did that happen?"

"Director Briggs at the aquarium in Monterey agreed to let me use the few frogs they have as long as I don't harm them." He paused. "It's a temporary solution. We still need to find a long-term source."

"That's incredible, Ray. Congratulations." Dr. Dougherty set down the cup and clasped his hands above his head in a victory gesture.

"I'm sorry to tell you that I need you right away to help carry out the testing protocols. You know how to do it a lot better than I do." Dr. Dougherty's smile faded. "I realize I'm imposing on your schedule. I shouldn't ask you to come, because it may take several weeks, or even a month to finish testing. But you realize how important this is."

Dr. Dougherty nodded. "Hmm. I guess you're right, Ray. Not to be immodest, but I would be of immense benefit to you. I'll check my schedule . . . but I suppose I can break away for a few more weeks to help you get started."

"I was hoping you would say that. I'm very grateful."

The two chatted for the next half hour about the phase one protocol and the schedule for informing the FDA. When Dr. Kramer noticed his colleague yawning one too many times, he decided to terminate the conversation. "So, you'll let me know as soon as you have flight arrangements? You know you are welcome to stay with us again."

Dr. Dougherty assured him that he would, and the two said goodbye. Dr. Kramer bowed his head after the conversation ended and thanked God that his colleague would come back to assist him. The older man had a wealth of experience that would be advantageous during the process.

He knew the next person he needed to call. He grabbed his cell phone and dialed the number. "Hello, Patrick," he said. "I have great news." The hospital had just released the boy a few days earlier because his condition had become stable.

"Dr. Kramer!" said Patrick. His voice sounded weak but cheerful. "It's great to hear from you."

"Son, I'm going to be able to give you that medicine we talked about very soon. Have you talked it over with your mother?" Dr. Kramer had given him the consent form a few weeks ago.

"Yes, sir. She's still not sure about it. But I want to give it a try."

"Your mother has to agree, Patrick, because you're too young to make that decision. You know we talked about the risks involved."

"I know. But since there's no cure for what I have, this seems like my only hope."

Dr. Kramer knew that for the boy's sake he should remain silent for the moment about the details of the possible side effects or whether the drug would actually work. Neither he nor Dr. Dougherty knew the dosages for adults, much less for children. It would be a huge risk for the boy. "Son," he said, forcing an optimistic tone, "you know we'll do our best to help you."

"Okay, I'll talk to mom about it more and get her to sign. Do I have to go back to the hospital for the treatment?"

"I'm afraid so. We need to see what happens after we give you the drug."

Patrick grunted. "I hate hospital food."

Dr. Kramer chuckled. "I know. I hate it too."

He continued to chat with the boy for a few minutes and was glad to hear Patrick's voice so full of energy and life. He agreed to visit him the following week and then hung up the phone with a sigh. How many more kids like Patrick would have to face an uncertain future?

49

Regional Office, Department of Timber Resources

Tom leaned over and eyed the spindly fellow in a T-shirt and blue jeans sitting in the back seat. His bookish face contrasted with his long, wavy brown hair, which he had drawn back in a ponytail. A single earring adorned his ear and a tattoo of a dragon was prominent on his upper left arm. Boy, the Fish Division must be pretty relaxed in their dress code policy, Tom thought.

"So," he said aloud, "how long have you been with the division?"

"About five years," the field biologist replied, adjusting his wire-rim glasses. "It's a great place to work."

Tom and Rob had driven north of Portland to the regional office of the Washington Fish Division to pick up the young biologist. Rob had then driven the bulky company SUV to meet Tom's friend Kevin, who was with the Department of Timber Resources. Their joint mission was to review a new Environ-Logging hydraulic permit application that could require stream-crossing structures be built to allow for fish passage.

"Guys, don't you just love it up here?" said Tom, gazing in admiration at the magnificent evergreens overshadowing the highway. "The drive is breathtaking."

"Yeah," the tattooed biologist replied. "It's great getting out of the office. That's what I love about the job the most."

"It's certainly spectacular," Rob said. "We did have a serious volcanic eruption here, though."

Tom took a deep breath of the pine air and peered out the window. "You're right there—the forests were decimated when Mount

Saint Helens erupted. It's hard to believe that they once looked like the ones around Mount Rainer." He stopped and waved a hand. "Aren't these trees awesome? I'd love to have my office here. It's so peaceful and refreshing. I don't know about you guys, but my cramped office space gives me claustrophobia. I'll take the forest over the city any time."

An old-fashioned log building came into view. It was situated in a remote area and overlooked a large pond surrounded by pines. Rob pulled up to the structure, and Kevin came out of the building to greet them. He escorted them inside, where they sat down around a roughhewn table fashioned from a downed log and carved pine-wood chairs. The windows were open, and the room smelled like fresh pine needles.

The group introduced each other and chatted for several minutes, and then Kevin pointed to a report and map spread out on the table. "As you know," he said, "the Road Maintenance Assessment Program was approved when Environ-Logging submitted their forest permit application. However, there are new roads they want to build that are not included in the original project, which has triggered a new fish passage plan."

"This permit includes several bridges built over salmon passage areas," said the field biologist. "The bridges need to meet certain design criteria, and there are restrictions on when they can be built based on expected salmon spawning."

Ever since Tom had met with Stephen, he had been on high alert when it came to Environ-Logging. He had asked Kevin to look for new actions involving the company, and Kevin had called him when the fish passage plan appeared. The Fish Division worked closely with the DTR whenever fish habitat was involved and a permit had to be approved. Anything having to do with a logging company affecting salmon habitat was a red flag. The permit would have to be handled with kid gloves.

The biologist fingered the ring in his earlobe. "We'll need to go out and take a look at each stream crossing. If we see evidence of salmon spawning, we have to delay the construction. Of course, the company won't be happy about that. Do you want to go along with me, Tom?"

"Yes, that would be great," said Tom. "We would like to know more about what they're doing." Just then, his cell phone buzzed. He picked it up and heard a faint voice that he instantly recognized. "I can hardly hear you, Lisa. What's going on?"

"I have a problem," Lisa said. She was coughing and her breathing was labored. "I need to ask you for another favor."

"What's wrong? Do you need help right now?"

"No, I'm okay. I just need you to do something for me. "

"Just a minute." Tom excused himself from the group and walked into an adjoining office. "Now, what's going on, Lisa?"

"I'm sorry to have to ask you, but could you meet me? As you know, my office phone has been bugged." In between coughs, she rambled something about a cave and a fire. "We managed to get the fire under control after we left the cave. It was really weird, that cave. Someone spent time there." She coughed again.

Tom was glad that she had reached out to him once again and was looking to reestablish the connection between them. He agreed to meet her the next day at a location halfway between Olympia and Portland. He clapped the phone shut at the end of the call and walked back to the meeting room.

"Rob, may I speak with you in private?" he said when he had returned. Rob nodded and followed him a short distance away out of earshot of the others. "Can you go somewhere with me tomorrow? It's urgent."

Rob noticed his colleague's frenzied expression. "Sure . . . what's going on?"

"Something to do with Environ-Logging. My suspicions about that company have just been confirmed. I'll explain later."

The two soon rejoined the others, who were discussing details of the permit. Rob turned to the field biologist. "So, when can we do the inspection?"

"We're snowed under right now," he replied, "but we can prob-ably find time in a couple of weeks."

"The sooner we can do that inspection, the better," said Tom. "There's more at stake here than meets the eye."

50

Olympia Firing Range

Lisa cradled the handle of the Smith & Wesson. The black handgun did not yet feel comfortable in her hand. She nervously lifted it and pointed.

"Now, see if you can hit that target over there," said the instructor. He put a hand on Lisa's shoulder and helped her aim. She pulled the trigger, but her aim was high and she missed the target. The kickback was stronger than she expected.

"That's okay," said the instructor, patting her shoulder. "Try again." This time, she managed to hit inside the outer circle. She kept practicing until she was able to hit the inner circles. It helped when she imagined the faces of her bosses at Environ-Logging in the target area.

Ever since the kidnapping, she had been barely able to restrain her resentment and rage. She was embarrassed and ashamed about what had happened to her and Carl. She also hated having to get Tom involved—he must think she was completely helpless. She had always been so self-sufficient, but now she felt like a total failure. She needed to get back in control.

After an hour of practice at the range, she clicked on the safety and placed the gun into her backpack. She didn't know if she would have the courage to actually use the weapon against someone, but it made her feel more in charge to have it . . . or at least a little safer. But would she ever feel completely safe again?

When she reached home, she fell facedown on her bed. Despair filled her, and she heaved great sobs into her pillow. Her head exploded in a miasma of confusion. Nothing seemed to make sense anymore.

Why is this happening to me? she thought.

She cried for so long that her pillow became drenched. At one point she considered calling her father, but she ultimately decided against it. There was no reason for him to become implicated in this awful scheme.

In three short months, her picture-perfect existence had been turned on end. All her life, she had been told do the right thing, to tell the truth. She had been happy, carefree, and blissfully naïve about the bad side of life. Now, it seemed as if everything she believed in was a lie.

Clearly, her boss was hiding something—something important enough for him to have her kidnapped and threaten to kill. But why? Just for money? Did no one care anymore about the environment? And what was that fire in the clearing all about? This strange new world had made her a thief, a liar, and a pistol-packer, and she felt ashamed. Did the end justify the means?

She sat up, blinked away the tears, and slammed her fist down on the bed. How could anybody do this to her? Wasn't she just trying to do what was right? "God," she said, bowing her head in prayer, "please help me. I don't know where to turn. I'm lost."

She reached for her Bible and turned to Psalm 40, her favorite. "I waited patiently for the Lord; he turned to me and heard my cry. He lifted me out of the slimy pit, out of the mud and mire; he set my feet on a rock, and gave me a firm place to stand."

She sniffled and thanked God for confirming that He knew what was going on in her life. She had faith that He would lift her up and provide a firm place for her to stand. *I need to be more rational and have faith that God will see me through this.*

Faces appeared in her thoughts as she prayed. Carl was sweet, and they had experienced a lot together. But Tom was attractive and kind, and he really seemed to care for her. Then another face came to mind: Stephen. He seemed so gentle and compassionate, yet so desperate and sad. There was no doubt that something was deeply troubling him—a secret that he was trying to hide.

Suddenly, she had a thought. She got up, looked into the mirror, wiped her eyes with a tissue, and dabbed on some face powder. She grabbed her car keys and jacket and dashed out the door. Lord, she silently prayed as she drove, *I believe you want me to find out the truth; I'm not sure this is the way, but please help me now.*

Lisa arrived at the offices of Environ-Logging, parked in her usual space, and strolled toward the building. She tried to remain calm so as not to arouse suspicion from the security guard inside. When she reached the heavy glass doors, she gathered her courage and pushed them open.

"Ms. Stone," said the guard. "What brings you here so late in the evening?"

Lisa batted her eyes and reached for her ID badge. "I forgot something in my office for an important meeting tomorrow." *God, forgive me for lying.*

"No problem." The guard took her ID and swiped it into the computer. She winced when she realized there would be a record of her visit—but she had no choice at this point. She retrieved her badge and entered the elevator, but she had no intention of going to her office.

The hallways were dark on her floor, and she could hear someone vacuuming down at the other end. She walked toward Stephen's office, turned the knob, and was relieved to find it unlocked. She went inside quickly, walked to the window, closed the blinds, and turned on her flashlight. She figured she had about half an hour before the cleaning people reached the office.

She shined the light over Stephen's desk, though she had no idea what she was looking for. She began opening file drawers and poking around, all the while trying not to disturb things. One desk drawer was locked. *That must be the one,* she thought. She took out her Swiss army knife. Within a few minutes, she had shimmied the lock and opened the drawer.

She found a checkbook inside along with some scraps of paper. She opened the checkbook—though she felt nervous about violating her boss's personal property—and reviewed the register. The balance in Stephen's checking account was more than $100,000! She returned the checkbook and picked up the scraps of paper. Each had a date and time with the words "meet Taylor." She saw a pink sticky note with the name "Dr. Raymond Kramer" written on it and a phone number. She jotted down the information, shoved the papers back into the drawer, and locked it again.

Just then she heard the sound of the vacuum cleaner coming closer. She cast one more glance at the desk and carefully peeked out the office door. The hallway was empty. She crept to the elevator and took it to the ground floor. She faked a smile to the security guard, waved, and signed out. She sprinted back to her car.

Once safely inside, she leaned her head against the seat back and heaved a sigh of relief. Add "spy" to that list, she thought.

51

Offices of Environ-Logging, Olympia

Stephen swallowed hard and cast a glance at the framed photo on his desk of his wife and sons. He opened the desk drawer and pulled out his wife's Bible. He didn't have the nerve to open it, so he just stared at it. Now was the time to make a change, to turn the tables. He was tired of being the patsy for a bunch of crooks.

What's the first step? He looked up and saw a message from Lisa on his computer. *That's it. I'll talk to Lisa and tell her everything. Then I'll confess to Amanda.* He stood up, squared his shoulders, and marched down the hallway toward Lisa's office.

At that moment, Taylor came around the corner. "Where you goin'?" he said. He grabbed Stephen by the lapels and spun him around.

Stephen straightened up and looked the brute in the eye. "Leave me alone."

"What did you say?" Taylor glared at him and strengthened his grip.

Stephen yanked Taylor's hands off and gave him a shove. "I said leave me alone." He turned his back and walked away. He was proud of himself for standing up to Taylor, even though his stomach was churning. But with Taylor's eyes boring into his back, he lost his courage to see Lisa and took a roundabout way back to his office.

When he arrived back, as he anticipated, there was a knock on the door. Taylor barged in, settled down in the chair opposite the desk, and looked him square in the eye. "You seem different. What's goin' on?"

"Nothing. Just leave me alone." Stephen didn't want to start an argument right then, but Taylor wouldn't take no for an answer. He leaned across the desk and pulled Stephen forward by the tie. He kept pulling until Stephen's face was only inches away.

"Now, you listen to me," he said. "If you don't do what we say, your secret is out. Everyone will know what you did, and your career will be history." Taylor was practically frothing at the mouth, and Stephen almost gagged at his bad breath. "You'd better learn that we play hardball, old buddy."

Stephen's face turned red, and he started to choke. Taylor let go and pushed him back into his seat.

Stephen straightened his shirt and tried to catch his breath. His eyes were burning as he glared at the ogre. He wanted to punch Taylor in the face, but he swallowed hard and kept silent. He didn't want to give the goon the satisfaction of a response. The guy was scum, and there was no reason to talk to him further.

Taylor flashed a grin and left the room snickering. Stephen buried his face in his arms and pounded his fists on the desk. The nightmare would never end. His shoulders shook as sobs engulfed him. After several moments, he raised tear-soaked eyes to look at the picture on his desk. He shook his head. For the sake of my family, I can't let this continue. There is only one thing left to do.

Stephen started typing furiously. An hour later, he saved the document to a thumb drive and deleted all traces of the document from his computer. He had typed out a complete confession, combined with a list of all the files he had altered over the years. He trembled as he removed the thumb drive and put it into his pocket. This evidence would be enough to take Johnson down—and the company as well—but it would also put him in prison for years.

He drove to the yacht club, got on board his Catalina cruiser, and cast off the lines. He motored out from the dock, raised the mainsail, and cut the engine. After placing the steering wheel on auto, he went downstairs to fix a drink. There he found the Beretta 92 nine-millimeter pistol that he had purchased years before to protect himself while sailing.

He went back up on deck, sat in the captain's chair, and set the gun in his lap. He slowly sipped his Canadian Club scotch whiskey and watched his surroundings as the boat moved forward. The setting sun displayed a magnificent array of crimson and gold lines accentuated by the dark blue of the ocean. The sea was still and smooth as glass. Fish were dancing back and forth under the bow. The lights of the port faded away along the horizon, and soon he was alone out in the open water.

Under any other circumstances, it would have been an ideal time to relax and take it easy. But Stephen had other things on his mind tonight. He reflected on the past fifteen years and how much he had drifted away from his wife and family. His whole world had been dedicated to his work. How had he allowed things to get so out of control? He had lied, cheated, and schemed to get where he was, and what good had it done him? Now it seemed as though he was in a bigger mess than ever before.

He ran his fingers over the pistol in his hand. He had invested wisely, and his wife would be well taken care of. His sons had their own prosperous businesses. But deep down he knew that Amanda would be devastated, and he would miss seeing his sons—especially Roger. A tear came to his eye as he pictured his granddaughter.

Just then, his mind flashed back to the psalm he had read in his wife's Bible. "He will cover you with his feathers and under his wings you will find refuge." He looked down at the gun. "Lord," he said, "I need that refuge you talk about! Please help me!"

Suddenly, the deck tilted and the sails began to flap wildly. The boat lurched forward, causing the gun to fall from his lap. Stephen struggled to straighten the wheel and put the sail down to half-mast. Soon the boat had righted and was rocking normally. Stephen was shaking as he sat down in the captain's chair, closed his eyes, and bowed his head. He listened to the familiar swishing of the waves.

"Was that a sign, Lord?" he said. He pulled his cell phone out of his pocket and speed-dialed Roger's number.

52

GreenForests Office, Kirkland

Carl grinned as he hung up the phone. Lisa had agreed to go on a date with him. He had debated for a long time about whether to ask her, since he knew she was dating Tom. However, after she had risked her life to save him, he realized she was still the courageous, amazing woman he had loved years ago.

"Betty, enlarge that area," Carl said, pointing to a fuzzy green spot on the small projector screen. He stood up and walked over to it. Betty zoomed in on the computerized wetlands map that he had overlaid with logging tracts.

"This mapping tool is powerful," she said as she expanded and contracted the logging tracts on the screen.

"Yes, it's a sophisticated mapping tool based on the latest GIS data. It's part of the DTR forest system."

Carl studied the screen while Betty slurped the last of her Coke. "Where did you get these logging area maps, anyway?"

"It's all public information, Betty. I got them by going to the DTR offices." He didn't want her to know that Lisa had smuggled them out of the offices of Environ-Logging. He didn't like lying to Betty, but needed to protect Lisa. "By overlaying these maps, you can see that logging might have taken place on designated wetlands areas. Here, look at this spot." He pointed to an area on the screen.

Betty looked closely. "Sure looks like it, boss. Maybe we've hit pay dirt."

Carl was glad that Betty restrained her curiosity, and they continued to observe the tracts. He pursed his lips, sat down, and took a sip of his iced tea. He was tired of being humiliated and intimidated by Environ-Logging's heavy-handed methods. The company was not only hurting innocent people but possibly also destroying critical habitats for important species. Even so, he still didn't like the idea of stealing maps from their offices to prove a point.

Betty broke into his thoughts. "What's bothering you, Carl?"

He turned his head. "Do you think it's possible the company noted those wetland areas in their applications but moved them somewhere else? I can especially see them doing that if the company was building a road or landing." He paused. "By doing so, they could create a mitigation plan that would be approved by the agency beforehand."

"Yeah, like that happened." Betty rolled her eyes. "I think it's much more likely that they doctored the maps."

"Well, we didn't see any evidence of mitigation plans in our research."

Betty slapped her hand on the table. "I hate to beat a dead horse, but even if we could prove the company logged on wetlands, there's no evidence that any endangered species are there. They cover their tracks too well."

Carl rose, raked his hands through his hair, and walked over to the window. She was right. There was still no hard evidence that there were any endangered species on the logging property. But why else would the company go to such extremes to intimidate him and Lisa? He had thought long and hard about all the possible ways to implicate the company, but none of them would work if Lisa were harmed. There had to be another way—a more indirect way—to take the company down.

Suddenly, an idea came into his thoughts. He turned back to Betty. "I think I know the way to stop these people."

Betty looked up. "What's that, Carl?"

Carl pointed to the maps on the screen. "We fight them one more time on the political front—we introduce new wetlands legislation."

"They're too well connected. Remember what happened last time?"

Carl shook his head. "We'll play their game and beat down the doors of the legislators. We'll make them listen to us this time." Betty looked skeptical but said nothing. "Last time we tried changing the riparian wording, so we'll take a different tack this time. We will change the wording more subtly so that ultimately the buffer region for the wetland area will be increased."

"Right!" said Betty. "The logging companies have to determine their wetland types and provide buffers, just like with the riparian regions."

"Yes, and if the wetland overlaps the riparian region, the company has to leave whichever buffer provides the most protection."

"So we can use these maps to indicate which wetlands are not being adequately protected by the existing regulations."

"No, I won't use these maps. But I will convince them another way."

Betty raised her eyebrows. "You won't use the maps? Why not?"

Carl ignored the question. They worked for the rest of the day on the delicate language change and finally completed the necessary paperwork to submit a bill to the legislature.

Carl turned to Betty as they prepared to leave. "See if you can get me an appointment with Senator Wells."

"You aren't going to tell him—"

"Don't worry. I'll be my sensitive, sweet self. But I will get his attention."

Betty frowned. "Environ-Logging's not going to like that."

"No . . . but we'll backcut them."

"Backcut? What does that mean?"

"It's a logging term. It refers to the very last cut needed to fell a tree. The cut disconnects almost the entire tree from the stump just before it falls."

"Timber, Environ-Logging!" said Betty, mimicking a tree falling. "Kaboom!"

53

Near the University of Washington, Seattle

Lisa parked her car in a deserted parking lot and breathed a sigh. Her nerves were shot, and she was tired. She had driven for an hour, crisscrossing streets all over the city. Every five minutes she had looked in the rearview mirror to make sure she was not being followed. She had decided on this remote place, well away from the prying eyes watching her apartment and monitoring her phone calls.

She looked around before exiting the car and then approached an isolated phone booth. She took a deep breath, pulled the piece of paper out of her jean pocket, and looked at the phone number she had taken from the sticky note in Stephen's desk. She glanced around at the streets one more time before dialing.

"Hello?" she said when the line picked up. "Is this Dr. Raymond Kramer?"

"Yes, this is Dr. Kramer," said a deep voice. "What do you want?"

"Dr. Kramer, my name is Lisa Stone. I work for Environ-Logging. I'm sorry about the short notice, but can I meet with you right away? It's terribly urgent." Lisa knew she was being rash, but she was desperate. "I need to explain what is going on with my company. I got your name from my supervisor, though he doesn't know I'm calling you."

"What is this all about?"

"That's what I'm hoping you can tell me. All I know is that Environ-Logging is covering up something, and I think you can help me figure out what."

"I don't know—I don't think I want to be involved in this."

"I'm afraid you are already involved. Please, Dr. Kramer, I just need a few minutes of your time."

Dr. Kramer sighed. "Very well. My office is at the medical school at the University. Do you know where—"

"I don't want to meet at your office. Is there another place near the campus where we can go?"

"Yes . . . there's a little Thai restaurant near here. I often go there for lunch. It's about three blocks from the campus."

"It will take me about half an hour to get there."

"Okay, I will see you then."

Lisa followed Dr. Kramer's instructions and quickly found the restaurant. She parked in the back of the building and looked around before entering the front door. The host seated her at a private table near the back of the half-empty restaurant. She sat down and perused the menu.

Soon, a tall man with a rounded nose and distinguished beard entered. He looked professional in his dark blue sports jacket and tan pants. His eyes searched the patrons until he saw Lisa beckoning him to the table. She rose when he arrived and extended her hand.

"Thank you so much for meeting me, Dr. Kramer."

Dr. Kramer nodded and extended his hand. They sat down, and a waitress came to take their order. After she left, Dr. Kramer looked at her and shook his head. "Well, now that we are here, can you tell me what this is about? Why the cryptic invitation and clandestine behavior?"

Lisa explained what had happened since she began working at Environ-Logging. Dr. Kramer's eyes widened when he heard about the kidnapping and near-murder attempt. "This is unthinkable," he said. "Why don't you go to the police?"

"We can't take that chance until we have more evidence. I have some colleagues working on that right now."

The waitress arrived and delivered their food. Dr. Kramer nibbled at his curry chicken while Lisa just picked at her food. She wasn't hungry, even though she had not eaten all morning.

"I still don't see how this involves me," said Dr. Kramer.

"Well, as I said, I found your name and phone number on my boss's desk." Lisa paused and looked at him. "What is your connection to my company? Why would my boss have your name and phone number in his desk?"

Dr. Kramer paused, put down his fork, and rubbed his beard. "The only contact I have had with your company was with a man named Ed Grantham. About six months ago, he sent me an email and then left a voicemail message. He said something about doing some type of research and finding my name online. But I never got a chance to call him back."

Lisa leaned forward and placed her elbows on the table. "What kind of research, doctor?"

"Please, call me Ray. I'm researching a cure for NPC—that's Niemann-Pick Type C disease. It's a fatal childhood disease that affects hundreds of children each year, and there is no cure. At least, not yet."

"Not yet?"

"No, but a colleague and I are working on one. Some time ago, I discovered a species of frog that may provide the cure. That's why Grantham contacted me."

"What is the name of the species?"

"Well, it's commonly called the Ganther's or Broad-leaved frog, but its species name is *Litoria latolevata.*

Lisa's eyes grew wide. So that's what "L.l." stands for, she thought. "What exactly did Grantham tell you? How do you use the frog? Where are you finding it?"

Dr. Kramer held up a hand. "Hold on a minute. I'll answer all your questions." For the next half hour, Dr. Kramer explained in detail about his research and his new drug application with the FDA. Lisa sat mesmerized as she realized the implications of finding the species.

"Lisa," said Dr. Kramer, "I must tell you that we still need to find a solid source for the species. We have a temporary supply at the moment, but it won't even last through the phase one testing." He stopped and looked away. "There are lives at stake. In particular, the life of a nine-year old boy whom I happen to care about."

Lisa swallowed hard and stared into his eyes. "This explains a lot, Ray. I can't promise you anything for sure right now, but I believe I might be able to help you."

Dr. Kramer gave her a quizzical look. "If you can help me, I'd be eternally grateful."

"Believe me, Ray. I'll do everything in my power to locate that source of frogs."

54

University of Washington, Seattle

Dr. Kramer and Dr. Dougherty sat down in the tall lab chairs. They had spent another long day examining patients, drawing blood, and questioning the first set of ten healthy volunteers.

"I can't believe we're two weeks into the phase one testing and have no results so far."

Dr. Dougherty looked at his colleague's expression. "Cheer up, man," he said. "We've only just begun. I didn't expect to see anything yet."

"Yes, but I was hoping something would happen. I know Patrick only received two small doses, but gee—"

"Remember we have many more subjects to test. Each group will get a little higher dosage."

Dr. Kramer nodded. "So . . . what are we looking for besides adverse side effects?"

Dr. Dougherty adjusted his glasses and scowled as he sipped his tea. "Why can't I find a good cup of tea this side of the Rockies?"

"Sorry about that, Ted. Guess we go more for coffee in these parts. You've heard of Starbucks and Seattle's Best Coffee?"

"Hmm. Guess I'll manage. But about your question—the blood work will tell us how the drug is affecting the test subjects' bodies. As you know, we increase the dosages for each new group. We're looking for the maximum tolerated dosage—the point at which intolerable side effects show up."

"When do we move to phase two?"

"Not until we've gone through all the subjects and received the FDA approval."

Dr. Kramer clucked and shook his head. "Patrick doesn't have that long."

"Well, it won't do any good if we test our subjects and they die or fall seriously ill from the side effects."

"I guess you're right." Dr. Kramer sighed. "Plus we still have the source problem. It's becoming increasingly difficult to get frog samples from—"

"We just have to find more frogs somehow. The last thing Kathy . . . er, I mean, Dr. Chan . . . said was that we needed a long-term source of *Litoria latolevata*. That's the key to the entire research program."

"I know." Dr. Kramer paused. "I've been praying about it night and day. I know God wants us to find it, and if it's His will, He will make a way for it to happen. Jesus said in the book of Matthew, 'If you believe, you will receive whatever you ask for in prayer.'" He paused and stared into space. "But sometimes I lack faith."

Dr. Dougherty shook his head. "Do you really believe—?"

"With all my heart, Ted. I wish you would, too. Perhaps you will change your mind and accompany my family to church next Sunday?"

Dr. Dougherty scratched his head and made no reply.

"I mean," continued Dr. Kramer, "you've said that you need to have more faith. Let me help you explore that idea by exposing you to the preaching of the Word of God and some fellow Christians."

Dr. Dougherty paused a moment and considered his friend's words. "You know . . . I think I will."

"Splendid! I look forward to it. Now let's go visit Patrick, shall we?"

The two jumped into Dr. Kramer's Oldsmobile and drove the few short minutes to the nearby children's hospital. When they arrived, they found Patrick in bed, hunched over a laptop playing a computer game. He had been readmitted to the hospital for the experimental treatments, and the doctors were observing him for any possible side effects. A young boy was curled up in a bed next to Patrick's.

Patrick looked up when the two came into the room. He looked tired, and his face had a gray pallor. "Dr. Kramer, it's great to see you!"

"What's up, my little man?" Dr. Kramer was concerned by the boy's appearance, but he grinned and put his hand on Patrick's shoulder.

"Look what I got—a new laptop." Patrick proudly held out the shiny black notebook computer. "My mom bought it for me yesterday."

"That's great, son."

"Oh, and I've got a roommate now! His name is Danny." Patrick turned toward the young boy, who was now sitting up. He looked about the same age as Patrick, but with brown spiked hair and fair skin. His face was wan, and he looked thin as a rail. His eyes exhibited vertical gaze palsy, a classic sign of NPC.

"How do you do, Danny? My name is Dr. Kramer, and this is Dr. Dougherty. He came all the way from New York City." Dr. Kramer extended his hand.

Danny stuck out his bony arm and shook hands. "Are you Patrick's doctor?" he asked.

"Yes, we help with his care."

"Danny has the same thing I do," said Patrick. "Can he have that new medicine you're giving me?"

Dr. Kramer looked at Dr. Dougherty and winked. "Sure, we'll see what can be arranged. We need to get Danny's mom and dad to sign the papers."

"My mom will be here soon," said Danny, "and maybe my grandpa. He's a really important man."

"Oh, really?" asked Dr. Dougherty. "What does he do?"

"He's the head of a big company that cuts down trees to make wood for paper. We all need paper, you know."

Dr. Kramer looked at Dr. Dougherty. "We certainly look forward to meeting him," he said.

55

Restaurant in Olympia

Lisa parked in front of the restaurant and ran a comb through her tangled hair. She looked at her faded blue jeans and brushed some lint off her modest pink oversized sweater. She slipped out of the car and entered the restaurant, where she spied Carl in a back corner. He was sipping a frosty mug of root beer at a small round table with a checkered tablecloth and a candle. The quaint Italian restaurant brought back memories of their first date during her freshman year.

She had met Carl when she was a senior in high school. He was four years her senior, and she was very naïve. At the time he represented everything she had been looking for in a man—tall, athletic, and drop-dead handsome. They both loved the environment and crusaded together for saving wildlife and promoting clean air and water. Best of all, he was a devoted Christian.

She had thought it was the perfect match, but things began to fall apart after she entered college and he graduated. He joined the Peace Corps and stopped contacting her, and finally they lost touch altogether. He had broken her heart, but she had since moved on with her life. Now, as she slipped into the chair opposite him, she wondered about his intentions. After all these years, did he just want to be friends, or did he want more?

"How's it going, Carl?" she asked.

"Great!" he said. "Thanks for meeting me here. I wish you had let me pick you up."

"That's okay. I should thank you for driving all the way down from Kirkland."

"Only took about an hour. The traffic was light." She noticed his gold hair and baby-blue eyes sparkling in the candlelight. It sent a shiver down her spine.

Lisa ordered her favorite dish—fettuccine alfredo—and Carl his favorite—beef lasagna. She remembered how she had turned vegetarian shortly before she had begun dating Carl, after she had viewed a video on how cows were slaughtered. He always gave her a hard time about it in a good-natured way.

After several minutes of small talk, Lisa asked a question that had been on her mind. "I know you told me business could be better, but how is it, really?" She couldn't believe he would worry that much about money given his rich grandfather. Yet she also knew that the subject of his inheritance was a sore one.

Carl swallowed and looked her in the eye. "I'm not too worried, but with fewer funds coming in, we can't be as effective. We have a few volunteers, but not nearly enough." He looked into the candlelight.

"So . . . what do you think happened to Stephen to make him change so much?" she asked, changing the subject. "I mean, he doesn't sound like the guy you knew growing up." She remembered Carl talking about how he had hung out at the Hall residence after primary school, before his parents had been called to Brazil. He had said that he felt the Halls were like his own family. He was still good friends with Roger, Stephen's oldest son.

"I don't know, but it must have been something terrible. Stephen won't talk about it."

"I'll be honest with you, Carl. I can barely look Stephen in the eye. I trusted him once, and now I'm so disappointed in him. I know he must be involved somehow." Lisa winced and took a swig of bottled water.

"I don't blame you for thinking that. I can hardly believe it myself."

"There's no one there I can trust. That company has made me a different person." Her head fell, and her hands slipped to her side. It felt good to unload the feelings that had been building up for weeks.

"I've been so worried about you working there. It's incredible that you still want to stay. It's got to be tough." He reached for her hand and held it in his palm. "I still care, you know."

She looked up into his eyes. "I know, Carl."

"I guess you've talked to Tom and know what Joe Anders of the Olympia Forestry Service told him?"

"Yes, I did. What was strange was that Joe implied that something bad had happened to Grantham, but he didn't go into any details."

Carl paused and stared intently at her. "I hope you don't mind me asking . . . but, are you and Tom serious?"

She blinked and looked at her plate. "Well, I don't know yet. We haven't talked much about our Christian beliefs, and that's pretty important to me."

"But you have feelings for him?" Carl's voice rose, and he squeezed her hand.

Lisa swallowed and pulled her hand away. She cared for Carl, but she wasn't ready to make any kind of commitment. Yet she had to admit that the longer she sat with him, the more the old feelings were coming back.

"Carl, it's been a long time since we were together—and you left me, remember? I don't exactly know what you're asking, but, yes, I'm fond of Tom."

Carl looked away. "I'm sorry, Lisa. I know I shouldn't have expected anything after all this time. But when I saw you again, I started hoping and praying that you would still have feelings for me."

She cupped his chin and turned his face toward hers. "Well, I didn't say I was going steady with him."

He turned to her and flashed that captivating smile that had always melted her heart. After everything that had happened to her, she couldn't believe this man still cared so deeply for her. She sighed. What else could be in store for her?

56

Environ-Logging Offices, Olympia

"Yes, Senator Wells, I understand," said Johnson. He shifted in his chair and propped his stocking feet on the desk. "But that wetlands bill is not productive. As I explained to you before, when it comes to riparian regions, a larger buffer zone is not necessary." He stifled a burp due to an extra-large lunch at the country club.

"Listen, Clive," said Wells. "Last week I talked at length with Carl Ward, the fellow who wrote the bill. He was mighty convincing about how much the bill is needed to protect wildlife. I'm pretty sure I'm going to support it."

Johnson cursed under his breath but said nothing in response until he had collected his thoughts. "At least give me the chance to meet with you one more time. My lobbyists have studied that bill extensively and found many problems with it. I would like a chance to change some of the language."

"Of course. But I'm not likely to change my mind this time. I must go to a meeting now. Can we talk later?"

Johnson hung up and swore at the top of his lungs. He grabbed a crystal paperweight and hurled it against the wall, shattering it into pieces. His secretary knocked on his door and poked her head into the office. "Excuse me, sir, but is there something wrong?"

Johnson quickly composed himself, though his face remained bright red. "No, everything's just fine. Please get me Taylor." The secretary nodded and shut the door.

Johnson hobbled to the wall-to-wall bookshelf, grabbed several books, and threw them on the floor. He clicked a latch, opened a hidden compartment, and pulled out a fifty-year-old bottle of Chivas Regal Royal Salute. He had purchased the bottle of Scotch, valued at $10,000, at an auction in Edinburgh. He poured a small glass and downed it in one gulp.

Five minutes later, Taylor knocked and entered. "You wanted me, boss?"

The man's haggard face and bloodshot eyes made Johnson nauseous. He gestured to him and muttered, "Come in and sit down." His breathing was steadier now. He chugged another shot of Scotch. Taylor eyed the Scotch bottle and began walking toward Johnson.

"Stop right there," Johnson said, putting his hand out. "You're crazy if you think you're getting any of this."

Taylor's face reddened. He shuffled to the coffee bar instead and kept his back to Johnson. "So, what did you want to see me about?"

"That Carl fellow is becoming too much of a pest. He went to Senator Wells behind my back. This will create huge problems for us." Johnson paused and took another swig of the Scotch. His voice dropped. "I want you to get rid of him."

Taylor swung around and spilled some of his coffee on the rug. "Really?"

"And that Lisa girl, too. She's become too much trouble. I want them both gone."

Taylor shrugged and turned back to the coffee bar. "Whatever you say, boss."

"You need to be careful. There can be no trace of the incident back to us. It must be an accident that no one has reason to question."

Taylor made no reply and kept his back to his boss. Johnson set his glass down hard on the table and glared at him. He was fed up with this sniveling cur, but he knew Taylor was the only one he could trust to carry out the grisly business. "Is there a problem with what I've asked you to do?"

Just then, his secretary knocked and poked her head in the door. "Sorry to disturb you, but your daughter is on line three. It sounds quite urgent."

Johnson lurched to the desk and lifted the phone.

"Dad," said his daughter, "it's about Danny. Um, I'll just get right to the point. It's bad news."

Johnson stumbled to the other side of the desk, sat down in his chair, and gripped the phone. His stomach dropped and he went cold inside. Taylor turned and stared at him. "Go on," Johnson said.

His daughter paused and heaved a sob. "Dad, brace yourself. He has a terminal disease."

Johnson's mouth dropped, and his eyes became fixed and vacant. "How long does he have?"

"The doctor doesn't know, but he thinks only a few years. He's already showing the classic symptoms."

Johnson could feel the blood draining from his face. A tear sprang to his eye and his throat closed. "What kind of disease? Who's treating Danny? I want to meet him."

The two talked for several minutes. Johnson hung up, wiped his eyes, and gazed at Taylor as if he had forgotten he was there. He gulped, and then his eyes grew stern. "I regret that you heard that exchange, but it's too late." He pointed his finger at Taylor. "I expect you to keep this between us, Mack." He rarely called Taylor by his first name and hoped the familiarity would create the necessary impact.

Taylor nodded and gave just the slightest hint of a sneer. "Of course, boss."

Johnson shook his head and dismissed him with a wave of his hand. How stupid of me to let him hear that phone call, he thought. *The sniveling cretin better keep his mouth shut, or else. I'll find a cure for my grandson if it's the last thing I do.*

57

Environ-Logging Offices, Olympia

Lisa closed her eyes and rested her forehead on top of the mound of reports spread out over her desk. Her head was pounding and her eyes were bleary. Every day at work was a nightmare. She walked zombie-like, in a perpetual state of shock, unable to focus and fearful of everyone. She hated every minute at Environ-Logging, but she knew that it would be best to stay on the job to covertly gather evidence.

Carl had been incredibly supportive and caring during their date a few nights before. When they had kissed goodnight, intense feelings that she thought had long been buried had come flooding back. He was so easy to talk with, and their Christian commitment and lifestyles meshed. But she was still attracted to Tom, even though she had known him only a few months, and he seemed to care deeply for her. The rollercoaster of conflicting emotions had only compounded her current level of frustration about her job.

She still could not find one shred of information that would implicate Environ-Logging or Johnson. There seemed to be absolutely no concrete evidence to show that the company had discovered and destroyed the habitat of an endangered species in violation of the Endangered Species Act. Then there was the promise she had made to Dr. Kramer about finding another source for the elusive frog.

Yet there was a ray of hope. Tom had discovered from Joe Anders that the frog had been seen in a location other than Tract 119. The tract number had never been written down, but Joe had described the location. Perhaps if she went back to the logging camp office she could secretly look through the records again. Or maybe the cave held some hope.

The cave. Her head popped up off the desk. How could she have forgotten it? She pulled out her phone and took a better look at the picture she had taken of the frog drawing. Just then, she heard a knock on the door.

"It's me," said Stephen, entering her office. Before closing her door, he glanced up and down the hallway. "May I talk to you for a minute?"

Lisa gestured for him to sit down.

"I sense you've been avoiding me lately," he said. "I think I know why."

Lisa stared at him vacantly and remained silent.

"I need to get something off my chest. It has taken me a long time to say what I am about to tell you. My wife doesn't even know the full truth." His eyes were red and his voice was barely above a whisper.

"Go ahead," said Lisa. "I'm listening." She had to fight the urge to throw him out of her office.

"I think perhaps you have come to realize that this company is not as ethical as you might have assumed. I am to blame for much of that. I've been altering records for years in order to hide a truth that was discovered about me."

Lisa's eyes grew wide. "What truth is that, Stephen?"

Stephen turned away and stared at the floor. "I'm not prepared to tell you yet. I haven't even told my family. But suffice it to say, Johnson has been holding it against me ever since he found out. I foolishly went along with whatever he asked in order to keep my job and my good salary."

Lisa wanted to say "and kickbacks, too," but this wasn't the right time. The man in front of her was almost in tears. His hands were shaking and his lip quivered.

"For fifteen years I've been living a lie," he continued. "As the years went by, money became more important to me than integrity.

Gradually, I became numb to everything. I simply followed orders and never questioned why. The only thing that mattered was maintaining the lifestyle that my family had come to enjoy." He stopped and bowed his head.

Lisa didn't know what to say or even whether she could believe him. Was he telling the truth, or was this some elaborate scheme set up by Johnson to trick her? She took a deep breath and watched his face, which became contorted as if in great pain.

"You see," he said, choking out the words, "when Grantham disappeared, I should have realized how low the company would stoop to keep their evil secrets. But, being the coward I am, I did nothing. Until the other day . . . " He stopped and looked up. "If not for the grace of God, Lisa, I wouldn't be here today."

Lisa suddenly realized that she had never considered what he was going through. She felt a surge of compassion. She quickly understood that instead of being angry with him, she should have been praying for him.

"What now, Stephen?" she asked.

"I'm here to tell you that it's over. I'm coming clean." He looked at her and set his mouth in a thin, firm line.

"I'm sorry for what you've gone through, Stephen, but frankly I can hardly believe what you are saying. Nevertheless, if it's true, I could really use your help."

"I mean it this time. God got hold of me, thanks to my wife's prayers and His persistence. I want to bring these guys down no matter what it takes." He clenched his fists. "In addition to what I already know, I've learned some new information that will be of use to both of us."

Lisa's mind flashed back to the register she found in his desk. She still wasn't sure she could trust him. Yet there was a hard determination and sincerity in his eyes.

"Are you sure no one followed you into my office?" Lisa was certain now that her phone was tapped and that her every movement was being monitored.

He nodded and looked her in the eye. "I think you'll believe me when you hear what I have to tell you." She leaned forward to catch his words. "Johnson's son has a rare disease called NPC."

Lisa blinked. "You're kidding me. How did you find that out? Did you know—"

"Yes, I knew about Dr. Kramer and his research. This information came from an unlikely source—from Taylor himself. He blurted it out the other day when he came by my office to harass me."

Lisa raised an eyebrow. "It's bizarre that Johnson's grandson would have the same disease as the one Dr. Kramer needs our frogs for." She paused and twisted a strand of hair. "Hmm . . . I wonder if this is a 'God thing,' if you know what I mean?"

Stephen's eyes lit up. "I hadn't thought about it before, but if God can get to me after all these years, he can certainly create a divine 'coincidence' to get to a greedy jerk like Johnson."

"So, what do you propose to do?"

"Johnson will do anything to find a cure for his grandson. We'll use that against him. But we'll need help from the outside. As you've already guessed, the phones are bugged."

"Yes, I figured as much. We need to tell our mutual friend, Carl."

Stephen frowned. "I would hate to tell him. He'll be very disappointed in me. So will my family. They'll be disgraced." His lowered his head and looked away.

"Well, since we're making confessions, you should probably know that I've been dating Tom Moeller." She turned red as she remembered her recent date with Carl. "Tom knows what's going on, and he's helping us."

"I know. He and his associate came to talk to me a few weeks ago. I'm afraid I wasn't very nice to them."

"Tom talked to Joe Anders recently."

Stephen paused and cleared his throat. "So, Tom went to see Joe? That's good."

"What about the police, Stephen? Even though they threatened to harm my family, I can't see continuing on without notifying the authorities. Maybe I can send my sister away someplace safe, and then we can get the police involved." Lisa stopped, unsure of whether to tell Stephen anything more. "You know, a detective named Vande-geer was very helpful after the burglary in my home."

Stephen's eyes grew wide. "Burglary? What are you talking about?"

"Someone broke into my apartment and ransacked the place. I didn't tell Detective Vandegeer my suspicions at the time. Do you think—"

Stephen raised his hand. "I'm very sorry that happened to you, Lisa, but Johnson's too well connected. He's good friends with the police commissioner and may have bought off the entire department. No, we need to figure out how to take him down ourselves. But we can't do anything at the office. Let's see if we can all meet together at a safe location." He paused. "Hmm . . . I think I know just the place. Get hold of Mr. Moeller right away."

Stephen stood up and turned to the door. Just before he walked out, he turned and winked. "Don't worry, Lisa. God is on our side."

58

Eltout Forest

"There's not much water in that creek," Tom said to the tattooed field biologist from the Fish Division who had accompanied them earlier. He gestured toward the meager stream flowing down the creek bed. A gray mist shrouded the tall conifers that lined the channel, which was noisy with toads and crickets. The pair looked like bumblebees in their bright yellow rain slickers with black stripes.

They walked closer to the rocky bank to observe the silvery fish that darted back and forth across the narrow stream. Tom slipped on the wet undergrowth as he stepped over a fallen trunk near the stream's edge. "Be careful!" he said. He knew the field biologist was brilliant but not exactly the most careful, as he had seen the man slip and fall a number of times.

Tom saw two figures approaching on the opposite side of the bank. They were wearing shiny green slickers with the Environ-Logging logo emblazoned on the front. Stephen and Lisa waved at the pair through the mist and stepped on small stones to cross the creek. He looked at her as she approached, curious at why she had called him to schedule the hydraulic permit inspection right away. She looked beautiful as ever as she flicked away the wet strands of hair from her face.

The group made their introductions and shook hands all around. Stephen pointed at an area upstream. "That's where we plan to build the first bridge. Few salmon have been seen spawning in this area."

"But if they are," said the biologist, "in order to ensure their safety, you have to build the bridge so the fish can pass through, based on the applicable specifications and regulations."

"Yes, we know what to do," said Lisa. "We have a copy of the guidelines on fish passages." Stephen motioned for her to be quiet. She didn't understand why, but she nodded and said nothing further.

The four trudged through the wet forest canopy, their boots dripping in mud, and visited each stream-crossing site. At each spot, Stephen again lamely explained that few salmon were ever seen spawning.

At the final crossing, the biologist walked knee-deep into the flowing stream and examined the bottom. "This bridge definitely needs a correction to allow the fish to pass through," he announced.

"How can you be so sure?" asked Stephen.

"I just know," he responded matter-of-factly. "There are specified times listed in the rules when spawning or incubating salmonoids are least likely to be present." He opened his folder and squinted at the paperwork while trying to shield it from the rain. "The chart indicates that for the Eltout River, that time period is July 15 to August 16. That would be the preferred time to construct the bridge in order to avoid impact to incubating salmon."

"But that's months from now," said Stephen. "We want to build within the next two weeks."

"We'll have to do further study of this area, review your plans, and observe the spawning," said the biologist. "Have you considered mitigation measures?"

"We'd like to discuss that option further," said Stephen.

They shook hands all around, and the biologist walked away from the site. After he was out of earshot, Tom eyed Stephen and Lisa. "Are we ready to talk now?"

The three walked to a clearing surrounded by pine trees. The rain had stopped, and the sun was trying to peek out from behind the dark clouds. Tom's boots were clogged with mud, and he was sweating inside his thick rain gear.

Stephen opened his bag and pulled out several green file folders. "These are some of the original files before I . . . uh . . . altered them."

"So now you're willing to testify against Environ-Logging?" Tom asked. He wiped his brow and zipped open his rain slicker.

"Yes, I am," said Stephen.

Tom took out the folders, cast a glance at Lisa, and then thumbed through them. He paused and looked at Stephen. "Why the sudden change of heart? I'm sorry, but I can hardly believe you."

"It happened when I was on my boat. I was tired of all the lies and truly at the end of my rope. I believe that God stopped me from doing something incredibly rash. I now know that He has something else for me to do here on earth."

Tom took a step toward Stephen. "If you're setting us up, you'll live to regret it."

Stephen said nothing. Lisa stepped between them, put her hands on Tom's shoulders, and looked him in the eye. "Tom, I believe him. Let's move past this."

Tom moved away and looked at the folders. "These will provide good evidence to back you up in court when you testify, but we need more. We need to get Johnson on tape. I think that is the only way to convince the police that we're telling the truth about his violent tendencies."

"You think so?" asked Lisa. "Is that legal?"

"I'm not sure," said Tom. "I will need to find that out. In any case, I brought you a listening device." He reached into his pocket, pulled out a small metal object, and explained to Stephen how the bug worked.

"I'm not so sure about this, Tom," said Stephen, fingering the object. "Where do I put it? I mean . . . exactly where and how? And who'll be listening?"

"Johnson's office would be best. We need to catch him saying something that would incriminate him. It's not hard to place it—you just need to do it when he's not looking. We'll be listening at a remote location. Just be careful."

"I need to ask you guys something," said Lisa. She looked at Tom, and then turned to Stephen. "I know you said that Johnson might have the police in his pocket, but the detective I told you about—Richard Vandegeer—seemed genuine to me. I guess I'm asking you both . . .

or, maybe, suggesting that we bring him in on this sooner rather than later." She paused and cast a glance at Tom. "But—I'm scared."

Tom looked at her. At times she seemed so strong, but now she was so fragile. He resisted the urge to take her in his arms and hold her. "I agree with Stephen on this," he said. "It's too risky. Johnson could know this guy, and you said yourself that Taylor threatened your family. Based on their recent actions, it seems they're getting desperate. Who knows what they'll do once the police get involved? For now, let's just use the bug and try to get Johnson to confess to his crime." He stopped and turned to Stephen. "What about it, Mr. Hall?"

"Okay, I'll do it." Stephen shook hands with Tom and Lisa and walked to the car. Tom grabbed Lisa's hand and pulled her away behind a tree. He encircled her waist with his arms. "You look great today," he whispered.

She laughed. "You're kidding, right? I look like a drenched rat."

He cupped her face in his hand and gave her a soft kiss on the mouth. He could feel her lean into him and kiss him back. He felt a warm shiver as he cuddled her in his arms for a few moments.

"Tom," she said, drawing back, "I need to tell you something. I—"

"Lisa!" Stephen suddenly called from a distance.

Lisa flushed. "I need to go. Stephen's waiting for me."

Tom caressed her arm. "You can tell me later. Now, you don't need to worry any more. We'll nail these guys." He kept his tone optimistic, but inside he felt far from certain. What he did know was that he had come to care for this adorable young woman and would do anything to protect her. He just didn't know how.

59

Near Tract 128, Eltout Forest

Lisa weaved to avoid a pothole. The deserted forest road was draped in eerie shadows. Despite the turmoil of the past few weeks, she always felt a calmness and sense of peace when she was under the tall pines and majestic fir trees. The cool stillness and beauty of the evergreen forest revitalized her soul. She marveled at the Lord's amazing creation that created such a sense of worship and wonder in her.

When she spied the Environ-Logging logo on the fence by the side of the road, she knew she was close. Her heart skipped a beat as she passed the burned clearing near Tract 119, where she and Carl had brought Dr. Miyake. She opened the window and caught a whiff of burnt grass blended with fresh pine. She glanced at her GPS unit and logging map and continued driving. Finally, she pulled off the road, stopped the car, and slowly opened the car door.

She grabbed her Smith & Wesson from her backpack. She clicked off the safety, placed it in the holster on her right leg, and folded her pants leg back down. Her hand was trembling as she texted Tom to inform him of her arrival.

Lisa sat down on a nearby rock and pulled out the logging map. The area they were to visit was about a mile away. She relaxed for a moment and listened to the familiar forest sounds. The trees above her seemed to be pointing straight up toward heaven. *Lord, I sure love this place.*

A car sputtered in the distance. She rushed back to where she had parked her car and saw Tom's familiar SUV coming around the corner. He parked next to her car, got out, and stretched.

"I'm glad you finally made it, Tom. I was nervous that you wouldn't be able to find the place." She hugged him and then blushed.

Tom returned the hug. "Thanks for asking me to come."

She drew back and remembered their last meeting and his kiss in the forest. The guilt of her having gone on a date with Carl was lying heavily on her heart. She vowed to tell him about her renewed relationship with Carl before the end of their excursion.

Tom opened the back of the SUV and pulled out a black wooden box. "Your instructions and GPS readings were meticulous as usual. I'm glad you figured out what tract number we needed from Joe's notes, as he wasn't able to remember the exact location."

"Yeah, he had scribbled down some identifying landmarks. Did he know anything about the cave that Carl and I found?"

"Yes, he mentioned a cave. But I know we'd better get started on this little endeavor before we get discovered." He gestured to her while holding the box in both hands.

Lisa nodded. "I'm glad Dr. Miyake agreed to let us borrow his recorder."

"I guess you turned on the charm again."

She ignored him. "From his description of the frog and my Internet research, I should be able to spot it." She pulled a colored drawing of the frog from her backpack and showed it to Tom.

"It's beautiful. Let's get started."

Lisa tucked the picture in her back pocket, put the GPS unit in one hand, and held the map in the other. For more than an hour they scrambled over rocks and stumps and through the dense canopy of firs, pines, and thick underbrush. Lisa was sweaty but determined to find the endangered frog as she stepped gingerly over brambles and fallen logs, sloshed through muddy puddles, and slid over slimy leaf patches. This part of the forest had remained untouched, and there was no sign of human activity. Birds, crickets, and toads produced a cacophony of sounds.

Lisa stopped and held up her arm. "Here's the start of Tract 128, where they may have discovered the frog. Let's see Joe's notes again."

Tom pulled the papers out of his sack. "There's a crude map here and a description."

Lisa followed the notes and stopped at the location Anders had described. They set up the sound recorder, hunched behind a fallen log some distance away, and listened to the annoying racket. Lisa pulled out a pair of earplugs and handed another pair to Tom. After another two hours of being in the same hunched position, Lisa began to feel restless. She pulled out an earplug. "I wonder how much longer it will be. We can't stay here all night. Besides, I'm starving."

Tom reached into his backpack and pulled out two granola bars. An hour later, dusk approached and Lisa found herself having trouble staying awake. Out of half-closed eyes she saw Tom intently searching the area with binoculars. Suddenly, she felt a nudge and saw him pointing. In the dim light she saw a flash of green and yellow, and then a few seconds later a bright yellow and green blur. Even through the earplugs she could hear a high-pitched croaking noise. She rubbed her eyes and took the binoculars offered by Tom.

"Is that what I think it is?" she whispered. She quietly pulled out the drawing and held it in front of her. The frog in the viewfinder was an exact match. She looked at Tom, who smiled and shrugged.

"Now what do we do?" he asked.

"Try to capture it, of course." She reached inside her bag and pulled out a hand net.

"You come prepared, don't you?"

"I promised someone I would find another source of that elusive frog, and I always live up to my promises."

Tom reached for her shoulders and planted a tender kiss on her lips. "You're incredible," he whispered into her ear.

She giggled at the tingling sensation going down to her toes. The idea of telling him about Carl evaporated with the last rays of the sun.

60

Bellaire, Seattle suburbs

Dr. Kramer set the phone down. He shouted and felt like dancing a jig. He couldn't wait to tell Dr. Dougherty that another *Litoria latolevata* had been found. He raced home and found his colleague sitting in a large rocking chair on the porch admiring the garden. His wife's green thumb had resulted in a rich mixture of flowering plants, shrubs, and fruit trees. She had placed them in such a manner as to create an aesthetically pleasing and sweet-smelling landscape.

Dr. Kramer gently pulled the old man up by the shoulders. "Praise God!" he shouted. "You won't believe what just happened."

"Sounds like terribly good news," said Dr. Dougherty.

Dr. Kramer filled him in on the new discovery that Lisa had phoned him about. "I'm sorry I startled you, Ted. I'm just so thankful to God for giving us this miracle. I've been praying every day that a source would be found."

"We must inform Dr. Chan at the FDA," said Dr. Dougherty, slapping his colleague on the shoulder. "She'll be exceedingly glad, I imagine."

"Yes, I agree. We should call her right away. The FDA should have no trouble approving phase two now."

Dr. Kramer held the patio door open for the older man, and they sauntered into the living room. His wife was there reading the newspaper. She looked up and saw their broad smiles. "Good news, sweetheart?"

"I should say so," said Dr. Kramer. "My endangered frog's been found right here in Washington State."

"That's great news, dear. Dinner's almost ready, by the way." She put down the paper, stood up, stretched, and walked into the kitchen. They caught a whiff of savory aromas as the door swung open.

Dr. Kramer clapped his hands. "Let's have a celebratory toast. I'll be right back." He gestured for Dr. Dougherty to sit on the sofa and followed his wife into the kitchen. When he returned, he had two glasses of iced tea. He handed one to his guest. "To phase two," he said. They clinked glasses together.

Dr. Dougherty put his glass down. "You really believe this was God's doing?"

Dr. Kramer grinned. "Of course."

"Tell me more." Dr. Dougherty adjusted his glasses and shifted in his seat.

"So now you're interested in my faith?"

"I've been curious for some time about faith. I've met some people who had deep faith in God, including my wife. But I'm afraid I don't share the belief. It just seems impossible to reconcile science with faith."

"I can understand that. I have had to face that same issue as a Christian and a scientist. But I can assure you that you can. I can give you some books to read about it if you would like."

Dr. Dougherty nodded. "So, how can you prove that God exists? Does he speak to you?"

"I believe that God speaks to humans through nature and through Scripture. There are mysteries all around us that we can't explain. I see no conflict between being a scientist and having faith in God."

"It doesn't seem reasonable to believe in something you can't see or feel."

"That's the very definition of faith. You exhibit faith every day when you get in a taxi or on a bus. You have faith that the driver knows how to get you where you need to go." Dr. Kramer's eyes filled with passion as he spoke. "You give control of your life over to that driver. In a way, it's the same with God."

"I hadn't thought of it that way before."

"The Bible says in the book of Hebrews that without faith, it is impossible to please God, because anyone who comes to Him must believe that He exists and that He rewards those who earnestly seek Him." Dr. Kramer got up and sat next to his friend. "You once told me that you believe in God. That's the first step of faith."

Dr. Dougherty's eyes narrowed. "You sure know your Bible, Ray."

Dr. Kramer nodded. "God changed my life forever when I accepted His son, Jesus Christ, as my Savior and Lord. I'll be glad to talk more with you. Perhaps you could attend church with me this Sunday."

"I don't know if I'm ready for that yet, Ray. But I would like to discuss this later. Right now, however, I'd like to discuss the progress of the patients."

Dr. Kramer blushed. "Of course." He was beginning to care deeply for the older man, and by now he knew when to back off in discussing religious topics. He whispered a silent prayer that one day his colleague would come to understand the faith that he was so curious about.

61

Eagles Prairie, Olympia suburbs

Stephen leaned back in his favorite recliner in the den. He stared out the picture window at two late afternoon golfers who were getting ready to tee off. When they had first moved into the exclusive neighborhood, he had gotten up early at least three times a week for a quick round. He hadn't picked up a club in six months, and his golfing buddies had stopped calling.

He sipped his mug of ice-cold beer and contemplated what he would say to his family. It was confession time. He drummed his fingers on the table and recited the speech in his head. Since the events of a week ago, his world had turned upside-down. His job would soon be gone, and he would be facing state and federal charges—and possibly jail time. He would have to put the house and his sailboat up for sale.

He leaned back, closed his eyes, and pressed his temples with his thumbs. He had to relax and stop worrying. "Dear Lord," he prayed, "give me strength to say the right words—and please allow my family to forgive me."

He heard a knock on the door and jumped at the sound. His wife, Amanda, opened it. She was dressed in a bright blue T-shirt and a long flowered skirt. "Dear," she said, "they're here."

Stephen swallowed hard and sat up. He looked at her. She had put up with him for so long and with so little complaint. "You look quite nice tonight, dear."

She smiled and closed the door. He staggered to his feet and found that his knees were shaking. How do I tell my family that all of this is going away? he asked himself. *How do I bare my soul—perhaps for the first time ever?*

He grabbed his mug and opened the door to the living room, where he saw his two sons sitting on the bar stools, sipping beers and laughing. Roger's wife was sitting next to Amanda. As soon as he walked into the room, she nodded at him, excused herself, and left. He was relieved she did, because he wanted to disclose what he had to say with just his wife and sons present.

His youngest son, Ben, grinned, stood up, and walked toward him. He looked lean, tan, and muscular. Stephen grabbed his shoulder and gave him a bear hug. Ben's eyes widened, but he hugged his father back as if it happened all the time—though in fact it had been many months since they had last seen each other. Roger walked over to the pair and held out both arms for a group hug. Stephen embraced both sons, and Roger patted him affectionately on the back.

Stephen wiped his eyes with a tissue and gestured for his sons to take the couch opposite him. Amanda sat down and folded both hands as if in prayer. He remained standing as he spoke.

"Boys, thanks for coming. I know we could small talk for hours, but I want to get right down to business." He glanced sideways at his wife, who gave him an encouraging look. "I need to tell you something that I should have told you a long time ago."

"Dad," said, Roger, "you don't have to—"

"Please, Roger," said Stephen, "I must do this." He looked at his oldest son lovingly, cleared his throat, and continued. "Boys, you never knew my mother—your grandmother Clara. She died of pancreatic cancer before you were born, but I wish you could have met her. She was a remarkable woman—a hard-working single mom, uneducated, who slaved at two menial jobs to support my younger brother and me. She took her suffering with such strong faith. I could never understand how she did it." He stopped and took a sip of beer.

"When she was diagnosed," he continued, "I was eighteen and had just been accepted into college. But those hopes were soon dashed. My mother couldn't afford health insurance, so I had to give up my dream of going to college and take a series of jobs to pay for her treatments." He looked away from his sons.

"Dad, I'm so sorry," said Ben.

"It's okay, son." Stephen cleared his throat. "Anyway, after she died, I continued to provide for my younger brother. After working for five years, I was finally able to save up enough money to pay for college on my own. But then my brother got sick, and I had to quit college and start working again." He stopped and sat down.

Amanda patted his leg. "It's okay, honey. Take your time."

Stephen put his hand on hers and continued. "The types of jobs I held were back-breaking, sweaty jobs without much pay. I could see that I was going nowhere. I could never make enough money to be successful without a college degree. So I made a bad decision." He stopped and took a deep breath. "I faked my college diploma."

Ben gasped and stared at Stephen as if he couldn't believe what his father had just said. Roger looked away. Amanda simply shook her head.

"That's only the start. Somehow, Environ-Logging found out and threatened to fire me if I didn't do what they asked. I didn't want to lose the good pay, so I did." He stopped and looked down. "I wound up faking data and erasing information that would damage the company. I know it was terribly wrong.

"A week ago when I was out on the sailboat, I realized I couldn't hide this any longer. The weight was so heavy on me that I almost took my own life." Amanda gasped, and Stephen walked over and sat down next to her. "But . . . you see, my mother never gave up on me, and your mother has never stopped praying for me." He gazed at his wife, brushed the tears from her eyes, and squeezed her hand. "I found God again, and I've decided to do the right thing and turn myself in. I've written a confession and listed all the altered files." He reached into his pocket and held up a thumb drive. "I need to cooperate with the authorities to take Johnson down. The bad news is that I may wind up going to prison. We'll probably have to sell this house and my boat."

Roger jumped up and hugged his father. "You're doing the right thing, Dad. We'll hire the best lawyers to defend you."

Stephen's eyes filled with tears, and he gripped his son. He saw that Ben was glaring at the two of them.

"Roger," he said, "did you know about this?"

Roger turned and sat back down, but avoided his brother's gaze.

Stephen put a hand on Ben's shoulder. "Your brother knew part of the truth, but not all of it. This is the first time I have confessed to everyone. I'm sorry for hurting you." He put both hands on his son's shoulders and looked him in the eyes. "Can you ever forgive me?"

Ben's angry gaze softened, and he embraced his father.

Stephen sighed and wiped his tears. "Now the hard part begins. Let's ask God to guide us and show us what to do." He bowed his head, and the others followed suit.

62

University of Washington, Seattle

"We told you during our last meeting that the emphasis of phase one was on safety. So now, the emphasis of phase two is on effectiveness."

Dr. Kramer adjusted the Skype image of the petite Asian lady and turned up the computer speaker on his desk. "Go on, Dr. Chan." He cast a sidewise glance at the red-haired representative from Asclep who was seated next to him at the desk.

"The purpose of the phase two trials is to learn more about the dosages required and how well the drug works at each dose. How many volunteers do you plan to use?"

"We don't know at this time."

"We would like to see at least one hundred. Of course, we realize that with a rare disease like NPC, there are fewer patients available."

"We'll do the best we can. We have Asclep Pharmaceutical to help." Dr. Kramer gestured to the man sitting next to him. The young man had turned out to be of immense help on the project and was becoming a good friend.

"We are going to use a clinical trial data management system to help plan and manage the trial's operational aspects," said his red-haired colleague. "This will include electronic data capture that is capable of statistical analysis."

Dr. Chan nodded. "That's good. Many companies are using web-based electronic systems these days. It makes it easier for us to receive and review the data."

"We'll even have an interactive voice response system to register the enrollment of patients and allocate them to a particular treatment," added Dr. Kramer.

"Will you be comparing the drug to an inactive substance or placebo?" Dr. Chan asked, looking down at a clipboard.

The image of Dr. Dougherty suddenly flashed beside that of Dr. Chan. "We haven't decided yet," he said. "We're still working on the protocol." Dr. Dougherty had flown back to New York for an emergency and was scheduled to return in a week.

Dr. Chan smiled, looked at her notes, and adjusted her wire reading glasses. "Very well. We are going to approve phase two based on the fact that you were able to locate one of the frogs you need. However—"

"Uh oh, here it comes," Dr. Kramer whispered under his breath.

"As you are aware, there must be a greater supply to continue your work."

Dr. Kramer pursed his lips. "We're working on that."

"Kathy, no worries," said Dr. Dougherty. "We've got all the bases covered. We'll send you a detailed plan." Dr. Kramer breathed a sigh of relief.

"Well, then, I look forward to seeing that report soon," said Dr. Chan. "I can't think of anything else to discuss at the moment, but don't hesitate to call me if you have any questions. Congratulations once again on the approval to go to phase two." Her Skype icon clicked off.

Dr. Dougherty remained on the screen. "So, what do you think, Ted?" he asked.

"I think we've got a long way to go," said Dr. Kramer. "We'll have to start recruiting volunteer subjects right away. Then we'll have to hire more nurses and research assistants to help conduct the trials." Dr. Kramer looked at his colleague. "At least the electronic data system will help."

"Yes, it's quite sophisticated," said the Asclep representative. "It will help a great deal, so don't worry. We'll use patient databases, newspaper and radio advertisements, flyers, posters in doctor's offices, and personal recruitment of patients."

"We may have to use enticements to recruit folks," said Dr. Dougherty.

Dr. Kramer winked. "No problem. I think I have a few students who would be more than willing to get extra credit in my class. And by the way, old chap, good bluff when she asked about the frogs."

Dr. Dougherty returned the wink. "Just thinking fast, ole boy. I know it's a hot-button issue."

"We're hoping more frogs will be found, but there are complications, as you know."

Dr. Dougherty snickered. "I seem to recall someone telling me recently that God rewards those who earnestly seek Him. Are we losing faith now?"

"No, I haven't lost faith, Ted." Dr. Kramer smiled. "I believe God answers prayers three ways—yes, no, and wait, it's not time yet. The problem is that I just hate that third one."

63

Lisa's apartment, Olympia

"Lisa, meet me at the cave. I think I know what's going on." The strange words from Carl played over and over in Lisa's head. She retrieved her backpack and absentmindedly began stuffing in items she would need. She phoned Tom on a friend's cell phone to let him know where she was going.

"You must be kidding," Tom said. "I can't believe they're doing this. No way should you go there. It could be a trap." Lisa could hear him swearing under his breath.

"It was Carl, and I believe him, Tom. I'll be all right." She tried not to sound scared, even though her palms were sweating and her knees were shaking.

"I don't like it, Lisa." Tom's tone was calm but firm.

"Please, Tom. I need to do this on my own. I'll contact you the moment I arrive at the designated site."

Tom said nothing for a moment. She could tell he wasn't happy with the situation. "Things are getting out of control. You know I have feelings for you, and I don't want you getting hurt."

Lisa sighed. She had feelings for him as well, but ever since her date with Carl she had been thinking more and more about all the good times the two of them had shared. She was also concerned that she didn't know anything about Tom's faith.

"I know, Tom," she said at length. "But remember what we talked about? If this helps us take down Environ-Logging, it will be worth it." She stood up and swung the backpack on her shoulder. "Somehow this must fit into God's plan, and I know that He will protect me."

Tom gave a low whistle. "All right, you've convinced me. But just in case, I'm going to call that detective in three hours and get a search party organized. Take that GPS tracking unit I gave you the other day." She reached into her pocket and took out the small black box with a clip. "Turn it on when you get there, and clip it on the inside of your boot. That way, I'll be able to find you if I don't hear back from you."

"Yes, Tom, I will. Don't worry."

Rain began pelting against the windshield as she drove along the route. Soon the high, dense forest canopy blocked out the daylight, and fog and mist began to shroud the area. She slowed and drove at a cautious but steady pace toward the logging camp. The familiar roads flew by in a blur as she gripped the wheel and concentrated on staying on the slick road.

She thought for a brief moment about calling Stephen, but she didn't want to involve him at this point. She continued saying prayers with her eyes open, asking God to protect both her and Carl and to get her out of this continual nightmare.

She took the turnoff toward Tract 119 and the cave area, stopped the car, and got out. The forest was eerily quiet except for the wind whistling through the trees. She shivered in the cold and pulled her green sweatshirt out of the backpack. She put it on and then put on a hooded windbreaker and heavy hiking boots. Finally, she retrieved the GPS tracking device, turned it on, and clipped it to the side of her boot. The rain had lightened, but the temperature had dropped. She could smell the dampness of the leaves.

In the ensuing silence, she imagined a dozen different scenarios that could enfold. She closed her eyes and bowed her head. *God, I know you are here. Please stay with me and protect me. Be with Carl, and help him to trust you in this situation.*

She looked up and began walking toward Tract 119 and the cave area at the top of the hill beyond it. A gust of wind came up, and she pulled her windbreaker more tightly around her. Suddenly, she heard a dog barking in the distance. Her heart leapt to her throat and she froze. No, it couldn't be, she thought. Not again. The noise grew louder.

It was Oso. She looked around in a panic. Just then, a voice came out of nowhere.

"Ms. Stone. We meet again." Lisa whirled around to see Taylor pointing a gun at her. Johansen was close behind, holding onto Oso with a leash. Fear clamped her throat. It was a trap after all, she thought. She quickly reached down and pulled her cell phone out of her jeans. She turned her back to Taylor and began to text Tom.

"I'll take that," said Taylor. He approached her, grabbed the phone from her hand, threw it to the ground, and stomped on it. Lisa was shocked at the violent act. The phone was now dashed into pieces, and so were her hopes of Tom coming quickly. She fixed her eyes on the dog that was still barking and growling.

"You don't like dogs, do you, Ms. Stone?" said Taylor.

Lisa felt her heart racing. She was too petrified to answer.

"Johansen, let Oso loose." Johansen reached for the leash.

Lisa's felt the blood drain from her face. Her hand flew to the holster on her leg. In a flash she pulled out the gun and fired. The dog yelped and stopped in its tracks. "I don't want to hurt that dog," she said, waving the gun at Johansen. "But I will if you don't control it." Oso bared his teeth but did not back off.

Taylor sneered. "You shoot that dog, and I shoot you."

Oso slowly crept toward her. Lisa waved the gun again, but she knew it was no use. She could imagine the dog's teeth chomping into her flesh. The hand holding the gun was visibly shaking.

She quickly said a prayer. God, please don't let this happen again. *Help me!* Suddenly the dog lunged at her, knocked her down, and chomped into her arm. The gun went flying out of her hand as she fought to push off Oso. Taylor yelled and rushed to pull the dog off her. He stooped and grabbed the gun off the ground. Lisa clamped her forearm with her hand to stop the bleeding.

Taylor grabbed her by the elbow and yanked. "Now you know we mean business. Follow me."

Lisa smiled. "You won't get away with this, you know."

Taylor laughed and shoved her forward.

As she walked, she bowed her head and thanked God for giving her the courage to face Oso. The old, gnawing fear of dogs was gone, but it had been replaced by a crushing sense of dread of what was about to happen to her.

64

Environ-Logging Offices, Olympia

Stephen knocked on the door and heard a muffled, "Come in." He had only been in Johnson's office a few times, and each time to be reprimanded, so it held bad memories. He gritted his teeth and stepped inside.

Johnson gestured with one hand for him to enter while barking into a cell phone. He sat back in his leather office chair and propped his Italian leather shoes on the desk. Stephen felt like he should tiptoe as he crossed over the elegant Oriental rug. He sat in the leather armchair in front of Johnson and looked at the spacious office, lush décor, and ornate furniture. What a waste of the company's money, he thought.

Johnson put the phone down and looked at Stephen. "What do you want, Hall? I'm pretty busy."

Stephen swallowed. Ever since Taylor had revealed that Johnson's grandson had NPC, he had been looking for a way to use it as leverage. It was now or never. He reached into his pocket, took out a small object, and clenched it in his fist. "Mr. Johnson," he said, "I believe you are aware of new developments regarding the hydraulic permit."

Johnson was looking at his computer screen and appeared to be only half listening. "Yes, I know all about that. So what?" Stephen slipped the bug underneath the desk and secured it. Johnson was still looking at his monitor and didn't notice.

"It's important that we take this very carefully," said Stephen in a low tone. "One of the bridges is impacting a salmon spawning area. That means we will have major delays when we try to build the bridge. We'll have to build a fish passage—"

"Don't bother me with inconsequential details. I'm sure you can deal with these minor problems. We've had plenty of salmon issues before." He waved his hand as if to dismiss Stephen, but then placed it on his chin. Stephen rose to leave.

"Wait a minute," said Johnson. "I just thought of something I need you to do." Stephen sat back down. "There's a certain doctor in Seattle that I want you to contact, named Kramer. He works at the university. I want you to invite him to my home next week and drive him there personally. I want to donate some money to his cause, but I have to do it away from the office."

Stephen stood up and looked Johnson straight in the eye. "Of course, sir. No problem. I'll do it this afternoon."

"Good. Just tell him I'm a wealthy foreign investor who is interested in medical research. Once we secure the commitment from Dr. Kramer, I'll wire the funds and we'll make the transaction." He rubbed his hands. The look on his face almost made Stephen ill. This guy didn't care a bit about anyone else who had the disease, only his precious grandson.

"Is there anything else, sir?" Stephen asked, trying to maintain his composure.

"No, just keep me informed of your progress. I expect there to be no problems." He turned backed to his computer screen. "You can go now."

Stephen left the office. This was working out better than he expected. He entered his office, locked the door, and put on the earphones. He opened his desk drawer, turned on a listening device, and began to record the conversation.

Johnson was speaking to someone whose voice was low and crackled. Evidently Taylor was talking over a speakerphone.

"He doesn't know what he's about to get involved with," Johnson said. "I need to make sure that Dr. Kramer takes the bait. My grandson must get that medicine, no matter what."

"Of course, boss," said Taylor. "But why pick that little weasel to deliver the message? He's so spineless."

"That's precisely the reason. Dr. Kramer will never suspect him of anything but the purest motives." There was a slight pause. "By the way, Taylor, have you gotten rid of the girl and that pest, Ward?"

"It's in the works, boss. Just like we talked about."

Stephen gasped.

"Good," said Johnson. "It's too bad, though. I kind of liked that young lady. Quite a doll. But she was getting too close to the truth. We must tie up loose ends."

Stephen heard footfalls and a door slamming. He hid the earphones and grabbed his phone. He listened to Lisa's recorded message, dropped the phone down, and bowed his head. The hair on the back of his neck was tingling, and he couldn't help feeling that something bad was happening at that very moment.

He picked up the phone again to call the police, but then remembered that the phones were bugged. He quickly grabbed his coat, sped out the door, and ran down the street to a pay phone. All the while he prayed that Lisa and Carl would be safe and that God would protect them from harm.

He arrived at the pay phone and hesitated for a moment. What did Lisa say was that police detective's name?

65

Near the cave, Eltout Forest

Taylor grabbed Lisa by the shoulders, spun her around, and pushed her in the back toward the cave opening. She winced and clenched her fists. She wanted to belt him, but she felt a gun shoved into her back and decided to move along. She heard Oso growling and straining at the leash that Johansen was holding.

Lisa's face went hot and she gritted her teeth. She heard a deep-toned whooshing noise and looked up. A black helicopter with green Environ-Logging markings approached from a distance, flew overhead, and landed in the blackened clearing. Her heart leaped when she saw Carl, bound and gagged, being pushed out of the chopper. He looked as if he had been drugged—his head loped to one side, and two masked men had to hold him up. Just then, another man was shoved out the chopper and collapsed to the ground. Lisa nearly choked when she saw it was Tom. He was also bound, but not gagged. He looked at her with pleading eyes.

Taylor pulled Lisa's hands behind her back and bound them with a coarse rope. He pulled her up by the armpits and shoved her inside the cave, followed by Carl and Tom. All three were pushed down onto the floor. Lisa winced as the pain permeated the arm where Oso had bitten her. In the distance, she heard the helicopter taking off.

"You won't get away with this!" Tom yelled. "People know where we are." Taylor slapped him with the butt of the gun, snapping Tom's head back. Lisa screamed as Tom collapsed to the ground. Taylor glared at her, brought the pistol up, and yelled, "Your two boyfriends can share your misery now!" He made a gesture with his thumb as if he was firing the pistol at her head.

The ropes burned into her skin as she struggled to remove them. She thought about using the Swiss army knife, but then quickly realized that she had left it in her backpack. Seeing no other immediate options for escape, she silently prayed that God would deliver them and protect them from harm.

Carl's bloodshot eyes fluttered open and then closed again. Lisa shivered in the cold dampness and looked around at the eerily familiar area. She couldn't rub her arms to stave off the chill or wipe the sweat dripping into her mouth from her upper lip. Her mind raced as she tried to calculate a plan. She turned to Taylor. "I need to talk to you. Please. We know everything about—"

Taylor gave her a dismal laugh, grabbed a piece of cloth, and shoved a gag into her mouth. Her eyes blazed, and she kicked and squirmed. Carl sat still as a statue, his head resting on his chin. She wanted to scream that she knew Johnson's son had NPC and that they had someone who could find a cure. It was their ace in the hole.

She made grunting noises and tried to shove Carl to get him to react. Tom remained unmoving on the floor of the cave. She feared that he was seriously hurt—maybe even dead. Taylor's henchmen bound their legs with another thick rope. She was encouraged to see Tom move slightly when the men came to him.

"You see, little lady," said Taylor, "this is where it all ended for poor Mr. Grantham. He was getting a little too close to the truth, just like you. I followed him one day and found out about this cave." He leered at her. "Yeah, I shot him all right. I set the fire to burn his notes, and then dragged him up here in his own rug. I thought, why go to all the trouble to dig a grave when wolves would take care of the problem? I figured I'd come back and get the bones later."

Lisa winced and turned her head. Ed Grantham had been killed? She spied the rug in a corner and pictured Taylor dragging the bloody body all the way from the cabin. She felt sick and squirmed against the ropes. She searched for any sign of recognition from Tom or Carl but saw nothing but still forms. Taylor nodded at Johansen, who was still holding Oso by the leash.

"When I realized you guys were snooping around up here," continued Taylor, "I set a small fire to the clearing to get you out of there. I made sure there was a firebreak all around so it didn't do too much damage. After all, boss man doesn't like me to mess with fire. But I love it." He paused to snicker. "I ran up here and found the rug but no bones. Thought maybe you took 'em or something. I thought about closing the cave for good, but then I figured it might serve a purpose later. This time, there'll be no escape."

Lisa saw Taylor's men begin to place dark red sticks above the outside of the cave door. Other men soon brought in stacks of kindling and wood and set them just inside the entrance. Taylor's lip curled, and he stared at her with his cold, dark eyes. He held up a match, lit it, and threw it down on the kindling. Flames quickly shot up, and smoke began to filter into the cave. Oso snarled and pulled against his leash.

Taylor walked over to the entrance and turned to glance at her one last time. "You shoulda been a team player, Ms. Stone," he said, mimicking Johnson. He laughed and darted out of the cave between the rising flames.

Lisa stared at the place he had just left, which was rapidly filling with flames. She felt stunned and helpless, and her eyes started to smart from the smoke. Suddenly she heard a loud explosion, and rocks crashed down from the top of the cave entrance. When the dust cloud cleared, she saw that the entrance had been completely blocked.

Lisa's heart pounded and rising panic welled up inside her. She closed her eyes. Taylor's words echoed in her mind: This time, there'll be no escape.

66

Near Canyon Estates, outskirts of Olympia

Stephen kept his eyes glued to the road. His sports car handled the turns well, but he was not familiar with the route. Dr. Kramer sat next to him in the front seat. After calling Detective Vandegeer and informing him of the murder threat, he had turned his attention back to the matter at hand—getting Dr. Kramer to Johnson.

"I must admit, Dr. Kramer, that I have never been to my benefactor's home," he said. "But I appreciate you taking the time to come with me. I know how busy you are."

"Please call me Ray," said Dr. Kramer with a smile. "Yes, I was a little annoyed by having to travel down from Seattle, but I am intrigued to find out the amount of the donation. When you said your benefactor was interested in medical research and was quite wealthy, I couldn't resist."

Stephen tried not to smirk. "I don't blame you."

"I could certainly use all the funds I can get to continue my research." Dr. Kramer adjusted the collar of his tan button-down shirt. He looked comfortable in his brown khakis and dark blue blazer.

Stephen gripped the wheel more tightly. He hated deceiving the man, but it was for a good reason. Dr. Kramer didn't need to know all the details of the plan to ensnare Johnson. But he was scared. *Lord, I need you right now. Give me the strength to pull this off.*

He continued on Highway 101 until the urban area of Olympia was well behind them and then exited onto Gold Lake Road. Half an hour later, he spied a sign that read Canyon Estates. He turned onto a country road dotted with soaring firs and drove past the security gate. He zigzagged down one road after another, occasionally spying luxurious mansions through the gates and concrete walls.

Dr. Kramer was suitably impressed. "I can see that this gentleman is quite wealthy."

Stephen nodded. "You could say that."

They stopped at an ornate black gate with gold markings that depicted an eagle and a lion. Beside the gate were two concrete pillars and a small intercom box.

"May I help you?" the mechanical voice said.

Stephen leaned out the window. "Yes, this is Stephen Hall and Dr. Raymond Kramer. We are here to see Mr. Johnson." A camera angled toward the car—it appeared that someone was viewing them remotely. A buzzer sounded, and the gate creaked open. Stephen drove up the winding road and went past a stable, riding ring, and small golf course surrounded by pine trees. He stopped in front of a two-story French-style brick mansion that looked more like a castle.

A thuggish-looking uniformed man came out to meet them. He escorted them through an entryway with an elegant chandelier and stained glass windows and guided them to a room where Johnson and Taylor were sitting. The two men were holding elegant crystal goblets. The room was filled with eighteenth-century furniture of carved dark oak set off by colorful Persian rugs and Tiffany lamps.

"Thank you for coming, Dr. Kramer," said Johnson. Uncharacteristically, he stood up and extended his hand to the guest. He looked more relaxed than Stephen had ever seen him in his dark purple cardigan and navy Dockers. Johnson gestured to an open chair. "Please, take a seat."

Dr. Kramer sat down on a satin blue French provincial sofa and admired the delicate hand-carved wood frame and satin cover. Taylor offered him a drink, which he refused.

"We'll be having lunch shortly, if that's all right with you," said Johnson. "But for now, I'd like to get down to business." Stephen winced at Johnson's fake smile.

"Please, go ahead," said Dr. Kramer.

"I understand you are nearing a cure for NPC. Is that correct?" Johnson arched an eyebrow and took a sip from the goblet.

"Well, 'nearing' might not be the word I would use, but our research is promising."

"I have a family member who is in desperate need." Johnson's voice was flat and unemotional.

Stephen moved to the back of the room as the two continued to talk. He slipped out without being noticed and tiptoed across the entryway. His heart beat wildly as he glanced over his shoulder to make sure no one was following him and searched for Johnson's office. He soon found a room that was unlocked, dashed in, and closed the door behind him. He felt for the listening device that he had put in his pocket.

Stephen saw a large writing desk in the center of the room that was strewn with papers. Behind it was a modern, high-backed leather desk chair. He was astounded that he had found the office so quickly and mumbled a quick prayer of thanks. He flew to the desk, grabbed the bug from his pocket, and stuck it under the desk. He turned around and started walking back to the door. Just then, it opened.

A thuggish-looking servant towered in the doorway. "What are you doing in here?" he said.

Stephen's heart stopped. "I'm sorry . . . I was looking for the bathroom."

The man eyed him suspiciously. "Well, you can see that this is not a bathroom. Come this way." He grabbed Stephen's arm and pulled him through the door. Stephen breathed a sigh of relief.

When he reached the living room, a maid announced that lunch was being served on the veranda. They all proceeded to the back of the house and sat down under a covered patio area. It was laced with tropical foliage and overlooked an Olympic-size swimming pool. Lunch was a seven-course meal, including filet mignon and stuffed shrimp.

"So, Dr. Kramer," said Johnson when the lunch was over, "what do you think of my proposal?" He leaned back in his chair and pushed away his empty dessert plate.

Dr. Kramer shrugged. "I'm in awe of your generous offer, sir. It is very much appreciated. But I cannot promise how quickly I can provide a cure."

Johnson glared at Dr. Kramer but said nothing.

"I know the doctor is on the right track," said Stephen, mustering his courage. "He will come up with something soon." He glanced at Johnson, who was still glowering. "Well, Dr. Kramer has a busy schedule, so I think we should be going now. Thank you for the meal."

Johnson stood up and glared at Dr. Kramer. "I'm counting on you. Don't disappoint me."

Stephen's face turned red at the remark. He stood up and clenched his fists. He wanted to utter a profanity and take a swing at Johnson, but instead he took a deep breath, pulled Dr. Kramer by the arm, and stared back at Johnson.

"He won't disappoint you, sir," he muttered under his breath.

67

Cave in Eltout Forest

Smoke filled the cave and the flames continued to flicker. Lisa tried to scream, but the gag made her mouth dry as straw, and she could barely breathe. The ropes seared into her wrists and legs as she struggled to free herself. Her back and shoulders were throbbing from the treatment she had received during the past couple of hours. Her muffled cries had made no effect on her dormant companions.

She had never felt so hopeless in her life. She laid her head back against the wall and closed her eyes. Fear and rage filled every fiber of her being. Memories of the smoke-filled cabin that she and Carl had discovered came searing back into her mind. How had things gone so terribly wrong? She had tried to be so careful and anticipate the company's moves. She had brought the gun with her. She had called Tom, and he was supposed to have the police ready. How had he managed to be caught? Despite all her precautions, the tables had turned once again.

She let out a strangled cry through the irritating dry cloth. *God, please help me! I won't give up, and I refuse to believe that you have abandoned us here to die. There must be a way out. Show me, God!* Several moments passed. A peaceful feeling began to flood her soul.

She opened her eyes and searched the cave walls through the dense smoke for anything that would help. Suddenly, she realized the fire wasn't going out. When Taylor had blocked the entrance, it should have cut off the air, but the flames were advancing and reaching up to the ceiling. Could there be an airshaft? She squirmed to look at the back of the cave and saw that one side of the wall disappeared at the far back. Perhaps that was a way out.

She turned and squinted at Carl through the smoky haze. He was still lying motionless on his side, facing away from her. She wriggled over to him and shoved his shoulder with her bound feet. After several more hard shoves, his eyes fluttered for a few seconds until they finally opened. She twisted over to Tom and pushed him hard with her shoulder. He moved and half-turned to her. She pushed him harder, and he also opened his eyes and looked around in surprise.

She put her back against the wall, bent her knees, wriggled to a standing position, and bunny-hopped away from the flames. When she reached the back of the cave, she stretched out her hands and felt the back of the wall. Her hand touched a short, sharp-spiked protrusion. After several tries, she managed to push down the gag onto her chin.

"Guys, get up!" she cried. "We have to get out of here!"

Carl and Tom turned and began to maneuver in her direction. She turned her back to the wall and began rubbing her hands up and down on the spike. Her shoulders and arms burned like fire as she worked, but finally she felt the ropes tearing loose. She got one hand loose, flung off the rest of the rope, and then untied her feet.

The adrenaline shot through her as she flew to Tom and removed his bonds and gag. He looked at her sheepishly. "Sorry, babe," he said. "Those goons nabbed me before I could even—"

Lisa placed a finger on his mouth. "No time to talk about it now. Go untie Carl while I try to put out this fire."

Tom began removing the ropes from Carl while Lisa picked up the heavy rug and swatted the fire with it. Her arms ached and the heat was unbearable, but slowly the flames began to go out. Tom raced over to Lisa and grabbed her hand just as she was about to smother the last flame.

"Wait a sec. We'll need a torch to see where we're going. It's awfully dark in here." Tom tore off a portion of the rug and looked for something to wrap it around. Lisa caught sight of a broken broom handle and handed it to Tom. He wrapped the rug around the end and set it on fire.

Lisa sighed and took the torch from Tom. She wanted to kiss

him for thinking ahead, but she thought it might upset Carl. "I think I saw another opening at the back of the cave," she said. She looked at Carl, who was still seated and coughing hard.

"Carl, come on, let's go!" she screamed. "Tom, help me get him up." They each took a shoulder and heaved Carl to his feet. He looked dazed, but he cooperated as they helped him up. The three stumbled toward the back of the cave.

"What on earth is going on?" said Carl, shaking them off.

Tom began to explain what had happened. Lisa held the make-shift torch high, plunged toward the back of the cave, and groped along the cool wall. She had no idea if the opening she had spotted led to an escape, but she moved forward with determination. The two men she cared about were depending on her. They moved down a short hallway and were soon out of sight of the fire and smoke.

Lisa stopped short. "Oh no!" she moaned. "I can't believe it."

The two men crowded up against her. In the dim torchlight, they could see that the cave walls surrounded them on all sides. It was a dead end. Lisa ran her hands along the walls, desperate to find a crack or crevice. The two men followed suit. She prayed fervently under her breath for God to show her the way once more.

After several minutes, she felt a squeeze on her shoulder. "Don't give up, Lisa," Tom said. "We're going to get out of here. God's not through with us yet." Shocked, she turned and looked into his eyes. She had never heard him talk about God before.

"Look down," Tom said. "There are tracks." He pointed to shoe-prints in the dirt that were mixed with pine needles. "They seem to be concentrated in this one area." He smiled and pointed straight up. A ledge was directly above them, and beyond was a large dark opening.

"Give me a boost, guys," Lisa cried. Tom and Carl lifted her up, and she scrambled onto the ledge. They handed her the torch, and she moved it around the area. She spied a rusted metal ladder propped against the wall.

"Hey, guys, you won't believe this. There's a ladder up here! This is definitely a way out of the cave." She lifted the ladder and pushed it down toward the men. Tom and Carl clamored up quickly. Encouraged, they all marched on, following the small circle of light created by the torch.

Carl caught up to her. "I'm sorry about all this," he whispered. "They had a gun to my head when I called you. They forced me to ask you to come here." He squeezed her free hand. She nodded, her jaw trembling.

Lisa turned and continued forward. They followed the twisting and turning trail for some time. She noticed that the cave was widening and the air was becoming fresher. Finally, a light appeared in the distance. The three staggered out of the cave and collapsed on the needle-covered ground.

Lisa hunched onto her knees and bowed her head. "Thank you, God. We give you praise and glory for delivering us from near death."

Carl turned and gazed back at the cave opening. "Though I walk in the midst of trouble, you preserve my life; you stretch out your hand against the anger of my foes, with your right hand you save me."

The three stood up and did a group hug. After this, Lisa pulled Tom aside, squeezed him, and planted a soft kiss on his cheek. Her brush with death and God's swift answer had brought clarity and peace of mind. She had made her choice.

68

GreenForests Office, Kirkland

"That doctor better come through, or he'll wind up like the others," said Johnson. Lisa hunched closer to the speaker and glanced at Tom.

"Here it comes," Carl said. "Make sure we're recording this."

Stephen double-checked the recording device. "It's on."

Lisa, Carl, Tom, Stephen, and Detective Vandegeer sat huddled around tiny speakers perched on Carl's flimsy table. The air was filled with the scent of Chinese takeout, and paper cups and plates were scattered around the room. They had been monitoring the listening device for the past two hours.

"Want me to rough him up, boss?" said Taylor. His loathsome voice was faint but distinct.

"Not yet," said Johnson. "Let's allow things to play out. I need to find out where he is in the research. This is all for my grandson. I'll do anything for that precious little tyke." There was a long pause. "Are you sure that Carl fellow and Lisa are gone?"

Tom turned up the speaker up and looked at Detective Vandegeer.

"They're gone," said Taylor. "Just like you asked, boss."

A door slammed, and the speaker went silent.

"It's strange that he didn't mention you being there, Tom," said Carl.

"He was probably afraid what Johnson would say about killing a government official," said Stephen. "I think Taylor does whatever he wants—not necessarily according to Johnson's wishes." He walked over to Lisa and squeezed her shoulder. "I can't tell you how glad I am that you all escaped. I was so worried."

"That means a lot, Stephen," said Carl. He stood up and shook hands. "We know that God provided the means of escape."

Stephen nodded. "Amen to that. But let's not celebrate just yet. We have a long way to go."

"I agree," said Carl. "Let's discuss strategy."

Detective Vandegeer stood to his feet. "You've been tape-recording incriminating conversations, but as I've told you before, Washington privacy laws require that all parties be made aware of any recording of conversations."

Lisa looked at the diminutive man. "Yes, we know that. We wanted to get a court order, but it was just too risky to bring in the authorities. As you can see, our lives were in danger."

"So how about now?" said Tom. His eyes flashed. "Are you telling me that scumbag can just keep kidnapping and attempting to murder people and get away with it?"

Detective Vandegeer put down his paper cup and looked at Tom. "Based on what I've heard, we have probable cause to prosecute, but we still need to be careful. We need evidence that will stick in court."

Carl looked at him. "You have my testimony, that's for sure. And Lisa's, too."

"Yes," said Lisa. "Taylor confessed to murdering Grantham . . ." Her voice trailed off as she again pictured the bloody rug.

"It's Johnson we really want," said the detective. "Carl, you never actually saw Johnson when you were kidnapped, correct? Only Taylor?"

Carl gazed at the floor and nodded.

"Let's face it, guys," said Stephen. "Johnson has political connections."

"That megalomaniac will hire the best lawyers in the country," said Tom. "If he doesn't bribe someone to get off, he'll keep us in court forever."

"Don't forget about Joe Anders," said Lisa.

"Yes," said Detective Vandegeer, "I understand that he'll testify about covering up the endangered species. But kidnapping and murder are something else altogether. There's still no solid proof that

Johnson is involved except for the tape recordings, which are inadmissible in court."

"Dr. Kramer must be brought into this," said Stephen. "He must convince Johnson that everything hinges on finding the frog at Tract 128."

"If he can convince Johnson to come in person," said Lisa, "we can track him there and maybe get him to confess."

Detective Vandegeer nodded. "We're on the right track. Ideally, we need Johnson to admit his crime in front of witnesses."

"The guy's too smart for that," said Tom.

"Somehow, we need to make Johnson think that Dr. Kramer is unwilling to cooperate," said Carl. "Dr. Kramer has to confront him and get him angry enough to confess."

A silence descended on the room, and five minutes passed with no one speaking. Lisa looked at her watch and paced nervously. Carl walked to his desk and began reading his Bible.

"Guys," said Tom suddenly, "I need to tell you something."

"What's that?" Carl asked. He put down his Bible and eyed him curiously.

Tom shrugged his shoulders. "Just yesterday, Joe Anders said that he had information that would help us. I don't know what it is, but it seems that he's now willing to tell us. I guess he was afraid when I met with him before."

"If this man has information that will assist this case, I need to know right now," said Detective Vandegeer.

Lisa looked at Stephen. "Did you know anything about this?"

Stephen shook his head. "I don't know what Joe Anders knows. I haven't seen or spoken to him since Grantham left."

Carl stamped his foot. "Let's get him on the phone ASAP!"

Tom stood up and walked over to the speakerphone. He dialed and then put Joe on the speaker. "Joe, this is Tom speaking. I am here with Lisa Stone and Stephen Hall of Environ-Logging, Carl Ward of GreenForests, and Richard Vandegeer of the Olympia Police Department. We need to know the information you have right now."

Anders cleared his throat and paused before speaking. "Well . . . when I found out that Taylor had locked you guys in the cave and tried to kill you, I realized I should have been candid all along. I knew about that other entrance, because Ed and I often used to go in and out that way."

"Is that all you wanted to tell us?" said Tom. He sounded exasperated.

"No . . . there's more." Anders paused, and then raised his voice. "You see . . . Ed Grantham is not dead."

Everyone froze and stared at the speaker. Tom's eyes grew huge, Carl's jaw dropped, and Lisa appeared to be in shock.

"What?" said Stephen. "You've got to be kidding!"

"Nobody knows but me," said Anders. "You see, Ed and I had a secret pact to contact each other every night. We both knew we were in danger after that meeting where we told the company about the endangered frog and they did nothing about it." He stopped abruptly, and his voice dropped. "We had a two-way radio. That night, when Grantham didn't answer my call, I drove to his cabin. I saw blood on the floor and the remains of a fire, and I knew something had happened to him. I followed the trail of blood up the hill toward the cave. That's where I found him, in the bloody rug. He was bleeding but still alive."

Detective Vandegeer whistled. "Where is Grantham now?"

"I managed to get him to my car and then to a hospital. I made up a story about him being in a hunting accident and registered him under a false name. He's recovering but still weak. He is staying with a relative in Keno. We both agreed that it wasn't safe for him to surface—at least, not until now. When I told him yesterday what happened to you guys, he wanted to make sure Johnson wouldn't hurt anyone else again."

"Thanks, Joe," said Carl. "This will definitely help our cause."

"Watch out for Taylor," said Anders. "He's a loose cannon. I caught him following me a few times. I don't know what he knows or even how loyal he is. He might even turn on Johnson."

"The plot thickens," said Detective Vandegeer with a smile.

"So what's next?" asked Lisa.

"We set a trap for Johnson," said Carl. "A quintessential backcut, so to speak. We'll set him up to fall—hard and fast."

69

Bellaire, Seattle suburbs

Dr. Kramer gripped the phone and felt the panic rise in his throat. He fidgeted on the living room sofa, his forehead dripping with sweat. Less than a month before he had been a simple scientist looking for a cure to a horrible disease—a scientist blissfully unaware of dishonest industries like Environ-Logging. Now it seemed that everyone was counting on him to clean up an age-old mess and make everything right.

He took a deep breath and cleared his throat. "I've been thinking about your offer, sir. I, um, know how much your family member means to you, and—"

"What do you want?" Johnson shouted. "More money?"

Dr. Kramer glanced at Detective Vandegeer, who was listening on an extension on the other side of his living room. Stephen stood nearby, intently monitoring the conversation. The detective nodded and gestured for Dr. Kramer to continue.

"Let me explain," said Dr. Kramer. He steadied himself and found his voice. "As I told you the other day, I cannot proceed with my research until more of the frog species are found. I've been told they are in a certain forest area on your company's property, so I need your assistance to capture and contain them."

"That's it?" asked Johnson.

"No, not exactly." Dr. Kramer steeled himself. "I want you to double your offer."

An explosion of cursing followed. Dr. Kramer held the phone away from his ear and winced.

"So, that's how it is?" said Johnson. "You're giving me an ultimatum?"

"If you want your . . . family member to have the cure . . . yes." A long pause followed. Dr. Kramer had never done anything like this in his life. His heart was pounding and he couldn't stop shaking.

He hated lying. In spite of his promising research, he knew that a solid cure for NPC was years away. Fortunately, this Johnson fellow didn't know that—all he knew was that his grandson was dying. Just like Patrick. Dr. Kramer uttered a silent prayer for God to give him strength and the right words.

"All right," Johnson muttered. "What do you want me to do?"

Dr. Kramer swallowed hard and explained the plan. He could hear Johnson sighing and cursing, but he said nothing more. Detective Vandegeer wrote on a sketchpad and held it up. The words said, "Make sure Johnson himself agrees to come. But stall him." Dr. Kramer nodded.

Some time later, Dr. Kramer hung up the phone and looked at Stephen and Detective Vandegeer. "We're set. I don't know how I convinced Johnson to be there. Stephen, you must come as well. But as you both heard, I didn't tell him when or where that will be yet. Will Grantham show up?"

"Yes," said the detective. "We have him in a safe place. He's cooperating fully. Great job, by the way."

Detective Vandegeer and Stephen said their goodbyes and left through the front door. After they left, Dr. Kramer dropped to his knees, closed his eyes, and rested his forehead on the seat of the couch. He poured his heart out to God, thanking the Lord for getting him through the ordeal. He asked God to protect him and everyone involved in the plot. He continued praying until he heard a sound in the room.

Dr. Dougherty was standing in the doorway and watching him with a curious expression. He walked over and sat across from the kneeling man. "Is there anything I can do, Ray?" he asked.

"Ted, if there was ever a time I needed you to talk to God, now would be that time." He stayed on his knees and looked up at Dr. Dougherty. "Would you pray with me?"

Dr. Dougherty nodded and painfully bent on one knee. "It would be a privilege."

"Dear God," said Dr. Kramer, "my friend Ted is here praying with me. He doesn't know you well, but I know he has heard about you and wants to know more. Please speak to him through your Spirit and show him who you are and what you are capable of doing. We leave everything in your hands. In the name of your son, Jesus Christ, I pray. Amen."

Dr. Kramer helped his friend rise to his feet. He did not know if the older man understood the words he had just said, but he thanked God that Dr. Dougherty was there and that he was showing compassion and concern.

70

Eltout Forest, Tract 128

Lisa shifted and rubbed her sore leg. She was once again in a cramped position behind a giant hollow log. She looked down and felt awkward in her bulky camouflaged clothing. Carl sat next to her, also in camouflage, and peered through a set of binoculars. The forest was semi-dark and eerily quiet. Rain had just swept through, making the air smell clean and fresh.

"Do you see Tom and Vandegeer?" she asked, nervously tugging on her jacket. The jungle-like undergrowth made it difficult to see.

Carl scrunched his eyes and pointed at the walkie-talkie in his lap. "No, I don't see them, but I've contacted them once already. I'm sure they're there."

Lisa remembered what had happened at this very spot just a few weeks before. Under different circumstances, she would have been exhilarated and light-hearted. She was near the spot where she and Tom had looked for the frog together—and where he had tenderly kissed her for the second time.

Now her nerves were shot and her body was bone-tired. Only the thought of the nightmare finally coming to an end gave her the courage and stamina to continue waiting. Dr. Kramer, Stephen, Johnson, and Taylor were supposed to show up soon. The plan was coming to fruition.

Carl broke her reverie. "There's a car coming." He pulled out the walkie-talkie and relayed the information to Detective Vandegeer. As soon as they heard a confession from Johnson, they were to report to the detective and Tom, who were stationed nearby with state troopers in tow.

A jeep appeared and stopped at the site. "I can't believe they were able to drive through this brush," Lisa whispered as the occupants got out of the vehicle.

The men stepped gingerly as they followed Dr. Kramer, who was holding a notebook. "Over here, sir," he said, motioning toward an open area. "According to the log notes, the species *Litoria latolevata* was found here. I think this area is called Tract 128."

Johnson snickered. "So, how do we get this . . . er . . . frog to come to us?"

Lisa noticed that Taylor was backing away toward the jeep.

"It's not easy, but it can be done," said Dr. Kramer.

From Lisa's position, she could see a lone figure move out from behind a tree and walk toward the group. She suddenly heard a gasp.

"Grantham!" Johnson yelled. "How in the world—"

"Hello, Mr. Johnson." The grey-haired figure bowed slightly, looking amused.

Johnson backed away and turned toward the car. "Taylor, where are you?"

Lisa saw Taylor inside the jeep, frantically trying to start the engine. "He's trying to escape!" she whispered to Carl.

Johnson raced to the car and jerked open the door. "Get out of there, you weasel!" He grabbed Taylor by the collar and yanked him to the ground. "Explain to me how this . . . gentleman . . . is here?" His eyes appeared to be bulging.

"I can explain, sir," cried Taylor. "You see, I really thought he was dead. It wasn't until later that I found out—"

"How long have you known?" Johnson roared. He grabbed Taylor by the throat.

"A little while," Taylor choked out.

Grantham stepped forward. "Mr. Johnson, you ordered Taylor to kill me, didn't you? Why? I wasn't going to say anything."

"Shut up," yelled Johnson. "I'll deal with you later." He let go of

Taylor and pulled a cell phone from his pocket. Taylor massaged his throat. "Johansen," Johnson shouted into the phone, "Come to Tract 128 immediately. We have a problem."

"What are we going to do?" said Lisa. "He's not confessing."

"Shh!" said Carl. "Be patient."

Stephen stepped forward and faced Johnson. "Mr. Johnson, Taylor has double-crossed you. He told me that your grandson has NPC. So it's no secret why you want Dr. Kramer's help." He paused and then motioned for Dr. Kramer and Grantham to back away.

Taylor glared at Johnson. "I've been doing your dirty work for fifteen years, and I'm fed up. When you ordered me to kill Grantham, I should have realized how low you would stoop to hide the truth."

Lisa saw Johnson's face turn red, and he started cursing.

"I should have had the courage a long time ago to stop being your lackey," said Stephen. "Ed Grantham was my friend and colleague. I can't believe you would have him killed. And now I find out you ordered Lisa killed as well—an innocent young girl." He paused to keep his voice from choking. "You're a monster!"

"I'll kill you right now, you traitor!" yelled Johnson, lunging at Stephen.

"Here it comes," Carl whispered.

"It's true, isn't it, Johnson?" Stephen shrieked as he grabbed for Johnson's arms.

"Stop right there." All eyes turned to Taylor, who was pointing his Smith & Wesson at Johnson. "I'm also tired of your condescending and pompous attitude. I'm in charge now." He gestured with the gun for everyone to move closer together.

Johnson let go of Stephen and faced Taylor. "I guess I should have expected this from you."

Taylor sneered. "You've treated me like scum all these years. Now it's payback time. I'm not the idiot you think I am. Yes, I had an idea that Grantham might not be dead when I realized his remains were gone from the cave. I've been following Anders, and I figured out that Grantham was still alive."

Lisa saw the blood drain from Johnson's face. He straightened up.

"So," continued Taylor, "besides knowing all your dirty little secrets—bribing congressmen, offshore accounts, trysts with that floosy secretary—this tidbit of news was the icing on the cake. It was the little extra leverage I needed." He leered and waved the gun in his hand. "Now you know who's really in charge."

Johnson suddenly laughed. "You needn't point that gun at me, you sleazebag. You'd never use that information against me. You're too afraid of losing that huge pot of money I give you every month." He turned to Stephen. "And you, Mr. Hall. Suddenly getting a dose of courage? I hardly think so. Don't you remember our little secret? You want to lose that expensive house of yours? That yacht? Your fat retirement fund?" He paused for effect, and then turned to Grantham. "Yes, I ordered Taylor to kill you. And that's what you'll soon be—dead—along with everyone else here. I've just called my associate to fly here and clean up this mess."

"Now!" Carl yelled into the walkie-talkie. Just then, a shot rang out and echoed through the forest. Lisa jumped up and saw Stephen and Dr. Kramer rush toward Taylor, tackle him, and yank the smoldering gun away. They held him down as he howled in fury and tried to free himself. Grantham rushed toward Johnson, who was holding his arm and screaming in pain. Detective Vandegeer, Tom, and five uniformed police sprang out of nowhere and surrounded the group.

Johnson swore and shrieked when he saw the police approach. Blood was pouring from his wound. He glared at Stephen as they handcuffed him and Taylor and marched them toward waiting patrol cars. Lisa and Carl slowly approached. Johnson's eyes grew wide with recognition.

"It's over, Johnson," said Carl.

Johnson cursed and spit. "You've got nothing on me. I've got good lawyers."

"We've been building evidence against you for some time now." Carl's eyes pierced through Johnson and his voice rose. "You'll never hurt anyone again."

Lisa saw Tom standing next to Detective Vandegeer. She sprinted over, gave him a bear hug, and kissed him on the cheek. He took her in his arms and kissed her full on the mouth.

71

Children's Hospital, Seattle

Dr. Kramer beamed as Patrick scurried around the room. He was packing his Spiderman suitcase while downing a chocolate milkshake that had splattered on his chin. "Boy, I can't wait to get home!" he squealed in between slurps.

After several months of experimental treatments, the boy had responded so well to Dr. Kramer's new drug that he was being discharged. The doctors had been amazed at his turn for the better.

Dr. Kramer patted the boy on the head and turned to his mother. "Take good care of this guy, mom. I'll see him next Saturday." He had promised to take Patrick to a Seattle Mariners game. He waved goodbye and went on his rounds to check on the other patients who had been given the new drug. Many had responded so well that they were also being sent home.

Dr. Kramer finally returned to his office. He was eager to call Dr. Dougherty and give him the latest update on Patrick. He glanced at his watch and started up his computer, hoping it wouldn't be too late for his friend in New York City. He clicked on the Skype icon and waited for the call to pick up. The image of the older man soon appeared on the screen. He was balancing a teacup in one hand and adjusting his robe with the other.

"Greetings, my good fellow," he said. "What's up?"

"I'm sorry for disturbing you so late, Ted, but I wanted to let you know that Patrick went home for good today. He's been in and out of the hospital for more than six months. The kid was practically bouncing off the walls."

"I can certainly picture it. Good job, Ray. So, what about that CEO's grandson—what's his name—Danny? "

"Danny is also doing great. What a blessing that both of those young men, along with countless others, now have a chance at a longer life. I can never thank you enough for helping."

"Finding those endangered frogs was the key. Phase two went quickly after we were able to get so much serum, and now phase three is well underway. By the way, I keep getting calls about that journal article we wrote."

"Me, too. That's what I had hoped would happen when I decided to write it—that doctors with NPC patients from all over the world would find out about the new drug." Dr. Kramer paused. "So, what about you, my friend?" He hoped the older man would share more intimately about his own personal experiences. He had come to love the man like a father, and he treasured the time spent with him.

"Things are quite well, thank you. You'll be happy to know that I attended church with Doris and my wife the other day. You remember Doris—the mother of the boy who died?"

"Of course," Dr. Kramer said. "I remember you talking about her." He recalled his friend's initial reluctance to talk about his faith and marveled at how much the man's attitude had softened during the weeks they had spent together. He had first noticed the change when he took Dr. Dougherty to visit his church. The older man had seemed visibly moved during the altar call.

"So," said Dr. Kramer, "how was the service?"

"Well, as you know, I am not a religious man." Dr. Dougherty paused. "But, I must say that was the first time in years I had felt comfortable inside a church. It was quite an experience, I must admit. I plan to return next week."

Dr. Kramer smiled and again thanked God for the change he had made in the older man's attitude. The two talked for another half hour and then said goodnight. Dr. Kramer shut down the computer, and then, on impulse, got down on his knees and bowed beside the desk.

"Lord, thank you for saving Patrick and all the other children who will benefit from the drug you helped us create. Thank you for what you're doing in the life of my friend, Ted Dougherty. May he see your presence more clearly every day, until he realizes his need for you in his life."

72

Portland, Oregon

Tom and Lisa sat on the deck of a waterfront restaurant overlooking the Columbia River. The gold and red sunset provided a magnificent backdrop to the scene, with sailboats and fishing boats drifting back into the harbor for the evening.

"It's magnificent," said Lisa as she pushed away the dessert plate.

Tom nodded, put his fork down, and draped his arm around her chair.

Lisa shivered. "I can't believe Johnson got off with such a light sentence."

"Seven years in prison is not shabby. The fines were hefty—and remember, he lost his business." He reached for Lisa's sweater behind the seat and draped it around her shoulders.

"It's too bad, because Environ-Logging could have done so much good for the logging industry. I feel sorry for Stephen, even though he said he would just retire early." Lisa turned toward the sunset again.

"I understand he sold his house and yacht. At least his testimony prevented him from getting a prison sentence—he only had to pay a hefty fine. Evidently, he will live more simply from now on." Tom squeezed her hand.

"He said that would give him more time with his wife and family—and to try to make amends for what he did. He has a new reason to live." She returned Tom's squeeze. "You know, it's Taylor that I pity most of all."

"Why's that?"

"He started out just following orders, not thinking about what was right or wrong. Then he let pride and greed get the better of him, and he went out of control. He fell apart during the trial."

"Yes, it was hard seeing that. I hope his years in prison will make him a better man."

They fell silent for a moment as they soaked in the quiet beauty of their surroundings. "So how's the new job?" Tom said, breaking the reverie.

"Are you kidding? Environmental Supervisor at the Department of Timber Resources? How could I not love it?" Lisa grinned.

"I owe Kevin twice over now. First he hired my old college girl-friend, and now you. What a guy!"

Lisa twisted her body and gave a wry smile. "So, does that mean I'll wind up like her—an ex-girlfriend?"

Tom interlocked his fingers in hers. "No, that's not going to happen."

"Thanks for that! One thing's for sure—living closer to Portland has its advantages. There are so many things to do and see. I just love it!" She clutched the sweater and snuggled closer to Tom. "You haven't forgotten your promise to go to that new church with me next weekend?"

"Of course not. How could I forget? I'm looking forward to see-ing you in your element." He paused to sip his beer. "Carl will be pleased as well."

Lisa's cheeks reddened. "Carl will always be a great friend. And you know that he gave his blessing to us."

"Yes, I know."

She let go of his hand, stood up, and squinted to check a wooden pier post a short distance away. Her German Shepherd was sitting there obediently. He wagged his tail when he saw her stand. She sat down again and turned her head to Tom.

"What's the matter, Lisa?"

"Oh, I'm just checking on Oso."

Tom snickered and grabbed her hand again.

Lisa lifted her glass. "I'd like to propose a toast. To overcoming my fears and ending a nightmarish first job."

Tom rose, lifted his beer mug, and clicked it to her glass. "To a new beginning."

— THE END —

Cynthia Soule Levesque (MCM, Wayland Baptist University, San Antonio, TX; MS, environmental management, University of Texas at San Antonio, TX; BS, biology, Texas A&M University) has always loved science, writing, and foreign missions. After serving as a missionary teacher in Central America right after college, she combined her scientific curiosity and her passion for trying to keep the planet clean in a career in environmental management. She retired early, as God called her back to the mission field; she and her husband lived in China for four years, where she taught English at a college and at the registered Protestant Chinese church. Cynthia and her husband live in San Antonio, Texas, and enjoy their ten grandchildren.

Author web site:
cslevesque.com